TC

Author DAVID ANTHONY

This is a work of fiction. Names, characters, organisations, places, events, and incidents are either products of the author's imagination or are used fictitiously. Any resemblance to actual persons, living or dead, or actual events is purely coincidental.

For Luke & Katherine.

Chapter 1

Towards the setting sun Tonmawr, an adult female Panther, surveyed her territory which stretched from beyond a distant high green line, ambled through wet ground and ended at flowing water. She absorbed the scent of last light scouring the air before leaving her cubs asleep in their den. This ritual was repeated night after night. The low sun cast shadows across the dense, bracken covered rocks at the entrance and the vegetation provided covered trails which twisted away from the sanctuary. She followed the hidden tracks until she had to break cover. Tonmawr cantered with a low tail towards the burrows of a dense woodland across open ground which left her exposed to predators. She eyed left and right searching the high ground for dark figures. Her shoulder twitched as she relived the searing pain triggered last summer by a screeching bullet.

Tonmawr, a female in her seventh year had commanded her territory for at least four seasons without a challenge. Her mother raised her in similar ground further west in Carmarthenshire. She and her siblings branched out in their second year and

Tonmawr settled in the Afan Forest. The deep narrow valleys and forested peaks provided a variety of prey in a secluded environment by night. Daylight hours were more treacherous for Tonmawr and her cubs, walkers, sporting activities and hunters riddled the area seeking pleasure and restricting Tonmawrs movements.

A solitary male and two females made up her second litter. Her first litter of three did not survive their first winter. The cubs were only six weeks old when they were eaten by foxes whilst Tonmawr was hunting away from the den. That devastating lesson taught her to survive on less and take fewer risks. Her custom was to navigate the extremes of her territory each night, which she could achieve with ease. Tonight though the journey, twelve miles to the north reaching the Brecon National Park and eight miles to the west to the banks of the River Towy would be cut short.

Now under cover of the woodland, Tonmawr began to circle in wide arcs, marking with spray and clawing the thicker trunks. The ingrained scent of humans sparked her senses where a meandering track crossed her path. Dog walkers and ramblers passed through the woodland by day seduced by the calm seclusion and heady essence of natural vegetation. Tonmawr picked up their scent at dusk but it was rare to encounter them after dark. Only the occasional hardy walker would venture out to this rural location at night. They were not a threat, more of a nuisance as the dogs would track her aura until human call or whistle broke the pursuit. She headed through the heart of the woodland to a fallen tree which provided cover to stalk her nightly prey of rabbit.

The scent of her mate hung heavy to the underside of the fallen trunk giving rise to a sustained focus, taking in the air with a high nose, snorting to clear and sniffing again. The tang was deep-seated. She had not encountered her mate since last spring, over nine months had passed and now the scent had returned. Her mate was larger in stature but younger by two full seasons and his territory covered twice or three times hers. Tonmawr shifted her elbows into position lying prone ready to pounce, she waited, composed ready for her prey to hop within striking distance.

It wasn't her prey which caused her to move but her mate stalking the same woodland. As he approached she was overwhelmed by the scent, stronger than usual. Her mate would not kill her cubs, she knew also that her mate would not help her hunt nor share a kill. She rose to greet him, with a deep growl he grew in stature, trying to circle her. Tonmawrs instinct turned her to protect her hind as she growled back. The sudden realization that this was not her mate but a new male on her patch startled Tonmawr. She viewed an unfamiliar grey patch above his shoulder, confirming that this was a new male stalking her territory, but why was the scent so familiar? The male did not move closer but dug in his claws to the soft earth, his pounce would reach her with ease. The confusion and fear induced a twist away as Tonmawr launched herself towards the dense fern which patched the woodland.

Fleeing now she was clear of the woodland and heading south, the opposite direction to her den. Her focus had snapped back to her cubs, she had to protect them and not lead the male back to her sanctuary. Confused and agitated by the new male she covered mile after mile on a long loop heading back to the cubs. As she reached a stream, which bordered Lower Field on the southern fringes of her territory, a small flock of sheep were startled and escaped through a gap in the hedge line. This southern extent of her territory bordered a working farm. Out of breath she slowed to change course and cover her scent in the water. Just as she turned, bright headlights from a Subaru pick up framed her form, she looked back for a split second then continued. No sign of the large male, no scent trails left, she headed back to the den. She took most of the night to arrive back on the outskirts of her den. One final check for the male before she entered the twisting trails .Exhausted and without food to share she slumped under the overgrown rock-strewn outcrop where her three cubs were sleeping. Only twelve weeks old but already their appetite was overwhelming, she needed to increase her consumption.

Grey, the male Panther, dismissed his encounter with Tonmawr and adopted the prone position in wait for the rabbits who would emerge after dusk from their countless warrens within the woods, making easy prey. The food although plentiful did not placate his appetite. For three nights he had prowled the same area of woodland and enjoyed the bounty, but the bitter after-taste was now too much and he wanted change. As shadows darkened he crept through the woodland towards the managed fields below, where larger prey fed in open grassland. This was an uncertain venture for the young male but his inexperience of hunting in this his first fully grown year pushed him to a greater prize. Following no particular path for three hours, although the animal trails were easy to find, he crossed the land in a more direct line regardless of the obstacles, using up valuable energy. Deer in herds of six or seven followed more natural paths to the lowlands at night for the thicker grassland devoid of the harsh bracken of the high ground. Too risky in daylight, the herds would move at dusk, grazing along the way to review their course and check for predators, which were few.

Grey was too leaden and made wanton noise whilst he clambered and jumped. His deep Sienna coat appeared black in the night sky. The Deer herd were aroused early on their journey, knowing they could outrun the cat as long as they knew where he was, their strength being their ability to anticipate the predator. They changed from slow grazing to gallop and could clear undergrowth in leaps of ten feet or more at the slightest change in atmosphere. Many pairs of eyes, many pairs of ears with one collective responsibility.

His direct route was unwittingly his good fortune as he arrived at the edge of the prize ground. The field was empty except for a lone horse grazing. The large male predator moved into position inside the boundary fence on the crest of an overgrown ditch as the Deer arrived.

Chapter 2

Martin Quinn was ten feet from the Subaru as the door opened-then it appeared, dropping from the seat, pushing Alan Price aside with ease, slipping at first before all four pads gripped. With a shifting momentum it launched at Quinn who was stranded in the middle of the yard. Human instinct drew Quinn's body a half turn to the right, both arms closed in, bent at the elbow, hands not clasped but protecting the jugular, pupils set focused, on his toes ready to fend off the loose dog.

The dog stopped short of attacking, but stood with front legs outstretched and taught, voicing its anger through a ferocious spittle covered muzzle. Alan Prices' commanding expletives quelled the moment as the Doberman drew back to his side.

'Gooo-oood boy, go on your daddy's calling.' Quinn stuttered. As his shoulders relaxed the comment raised a condescending smile from Alan Price. 'Round one to you, I can't believe I just called him Daddy!' Quinn mused.

The gloss of the Dobermans coat disappeared into the pick-up-mission accomplished. Quinn edged his six foot frame to the passenger side keeping one eye on the panting dog, he felt uneasy being close to Alan Price. The sheep farmers arrogant bellowing voice grated on Martin as he fought for space in the sour odor saturated cabin. The pick-up, at an uncomfortable angle, gripped to the track with ease as it bumped down Lower Field towards the site of Quinn's team who were laying cables in a trench. The construction site snaked up towards the heights of Cimla Mountain where a dozen wind turbines were being installed.

'Mr. Price, how are you this fine day, is everything ok?'

'Don't push your luck, it's not a fine day, and I wouldn't be wasting my time with you if everything was ok.'

'Good to hear, I'm fine as well.' Quinn muttered.

'If it's about the re-instatement of the bottom field we should be finished laying cable by the end of the week, I thought Miss. De Mota had explained…'Quinn was cut short by a raised hand, sideward glance and brash snort.

'Don't mention that woman again she has already accused me of false claims, her arrogance knows no-limits.' Quinn hesitated for a moment thinking of a defence but knowing Claire's manner he kept quiet.

For the second time this month Martin Quinn, Construction Manager for Western Wind Turbines PLC had been summoned to the farmhouse by Alan Price. Quinn had enough to deal with; the installation was behind schedule and over budget. Landowner disputes were common, normally dealt with by the

WWT land liaison agent Claire Da Mota. Where was she when Quinn needed her?

Conversation rarely flowed between the two but Alan Price was quieter than normal, he always had negative comments about something or other but not today. Quinn decided to break the ice, 'Some dog you have back there, what happened to the sheep dog?' Alan Price did not respond but continued to squint and bob his head side to side in an effort to see through the film of dirt on the windscreen. Quinn wanted to switch on the wipers and was about to break the silence again as Alan Price flicked the wash wipe, slowed the Subaru and pointed to the trench.

'Do you see that?' Pointing across Quinn's vision to the open five bar gate wedged to the incline of the field. 'How am I expected to keep my stock safe when your men continue to abuse my land?'

Quinn was embarrassed at the lack of care shown. The lads should know better he thought. 'Im sure it's an isolated incident, I'll sort it out with them'. He replied.

As the pair approached the trench the foreman Pete acting as a look-out rallied the team. 'Heads up boys the boss is walking over with Alan Price.'

Within the confines of the shored trench the clay and rainwater mixture slopped over the men's boots. Mick, a towering laborer sowed the cable being fed from a large drum into the furrow with cradling arms. The action from his thick set shoulders and wide arms constrained by the sodden folds of fluorescent nylon binding him produced flowing sweat which poured into his eyes. He dropped the weight and arched up to glare at Pete. 'What the fuck do they want now?'

'If its Alan Price you're talking about he probably wants to know why you left the gate open!' Pete retorted.

'I'm a cable layer not a fucking sheep farmer Pete so go fuck yourself'.

'You'll be an unemployed cable layer pretty soon Mick with a dentist bill if you carry on like that!'

As Quinn grew closer he sensed the camaraderie and banter rising from the trench. Following Quinn's nods and half hellos Pete took the lead and met him on the crest of the excavation with a welcoming smile and handshake. 'Well the jobs moving slow today Martin, the weather you know, it's a real struggle in this rain what with the drainage...'Quinn cut Pete short.

'Mr. Price here is again finding himself closing gates behind you and counting stock, when are you going to learn?' Quinn's forced rebuke fell on deaf ears, Alan Price was no mug, he knew the score, these are not country folk, they try but it's just not in them. As Alan Price tied the blue cord around the now closed gate, out of earshot Pete started.

'What the fuck is up with him now? he's been a pain in the arse all fucking week, if you want us out of this field tell him to leave us alone, every time he stops us it takes me an hour to get these fuckers working again in this weather.'

'I wish I knew Pete, just keep him sweet and tell the lads to play the game, it's not much to ask to keep the gates shut.'

The journey back to Alan Prices farm across Lower Field proved to be far more treacherous. The back end of the pick-up was slipping as the tyres fought to keep traction on the sodden track. The extent of land owned by Alan Price was laid out before them in a panoramic view. To the east some five miles was the rise of Cimla Mountain up to fifteen hundred feet, starting with wide bands of deep green fields lined with high hedges. Dark ribbons of stone walling in the mid distance defined the levels until the incline raised with a sharpness to reveal bare stone and heather. Outcrops of coniferous forest swathed the summit except for the ridge running south which was now home to the wind turbines. Across to the west dense forest patched the view in varying shades from lime to black. Fire breaks, bare patches and access roads riddled the upper layers rising higher to open moorland and the Brecon Beacons beyond.

At the high hedge line of Lower Field, livestock sheltered from the westerly lashings of winter rains. The fading light of late-afternoon prompted Alan Price to flick on the headlights which failed to make a difference to the track ahead. The lights at once sparked movement to Quinn's left at the lee of the hedge line. As Quinn's eyes focused on the point, the last of the uprooted flock scampered through a gap in the hedge to the field beyond. Alan Price brought the Subaru to a sliding stop causing Quinn to turn his gaze forward focusing on a pair of orange eyes reflecting in the dusk. As the mirrored orbs disappeared a dark feline profile loped down the hedge line.

'Mr. Price...look at the size of that, what the?. Can you see it?' Quinn shouted.

Alan Price broke his silence, 'I've never seen one so close to the farm before, it must be really hungry, it looks tired, see its mouth is open and its tongue falling.'

Quinn repeated his question in disbelief 'What is it? It looks like a Panther or something.'

Alan Price nodded and continued, 'That's exactly what it is Martin, they've been around these parts for years, everyone knows about them, we see or hear them once or twice a year and pick up the odd sheep's carcass from the mountain. Reckon they were let loose in the seventies by idiots who bought them as pets and didn't know what to do with them, since then they've survived around here.'

The animal continued along the hedge line and moved out of site, in the opposite direction to which the sheep were heading. Alan Price crunched into first gear and continued onto the farm buildings. Quinn was surprised at the nonchalant reaction from Alan Price; it's not every day you see something like that, yet why was he so unmoved? I'll never understand these farmers Quinn thought. The Doberman was now agitated beyond control. Constrained to the seat less back she was whimpering whilst padding in half circles. Alan Price soothed the animal with a comforting ruffle to the nape of its thick neck and uncharacteristic words of calm.

'I see now why you have a Doberman Mr. Price, you need her on your side with that beast on the loose, I might get one for myself!' Quinn tried to lighten the mood. 'Then again I don't think she'd be much help.'

As he watched the forlorn animal drop with reluctance from the safety of the Subaru, Alan Price strode out in the direction of his farmhouse calling over his shoulder to Quinn.

'Join me in the kitchen Martin so we can discuss my compensation claim, I like to keep on top of these matters.'

'Robbing bastard, what's he after now? We've already paid him thousands for the lease of the land and now he's trying it on with another claim.' Quinn thought.

'I'll be with you in a minute Mr. Price, I need my notes from the truck.' Quinn pulled off his fluorescent coat and placed it inside out onto the back seat. He thought about changing into his shoes but was distracted by images of the forlorn Panther. Shaking his head he closed the door and flipped open his mobile. Seven missed calls, two messages and over twenty email notifications. Quinn decided to call Claire De Mota, he needed the latest information about Alan Price' claims and to keep her informed about today's events. The call went to answerphone after five rings, 'Come on Claire answer your phone for once.' Quinn sounded whilst his subconscious scanned the yard.

'Hello your through to the voicemail of Claire De Mota, I am not able to take your call at the moment, please leave a message and I will call you back within the hour'. Quinn didn't leave a message, nor did he believe the curt tones of Claire. He imagined her sat at her desk browsing the internet shopping sites or maybe chatting to her friends on Messenger.

This was the first time Quinn had been invited into the farmhouse, although he remembered the direction that Alan Price approached the rear of the building, he wasn't sure of the layout. He came across the half open kitchen door and waited to be invited over the threshold. Quinn kicked his boots at the cast iron scraper which was set in dressed stone, weathered and scored by years of use. Alan Price was on the phone to somebody, his paused monologue drifted through to Quinn outside.

'Yes that's right, in the open, in daylight …No, no-one, look, when did you last see him?.....just sort him out Tom, I thought we'd agreed, ok, ok.'

With that Quinn sensed the call had ended and heard the shuffle of wellingtons on flag stones as Alan Price walked over to the kitchen door. Quinn receded to give the impression he had just arrived and had not been eavesdropping. Resuming his boot cleaning Quinn looked up to greet Alan Price.

'Ah here you are, come on in Martin, don't worry about the mud, it's a farm not a hotel.'

Chapter 3

Quinn pulled into the pub car park just after six o'clock for his usual hour of relaxation and catch up with the team. The afternoon had been eventful but also painful in the company of Alan Price. The Crown car park brimmed with farm vehicles and transit vans, men at the end of a working day with a thirst. Through double doors the pub opened up into one large room, no dividing walls or booths just a bar which ran the width of the far wall. Distinctive areas did exist, to the left six or seven small round tables each with two or three wooden chairs, empty except one which was occupied by a small group, deep in conversation next to an open fire. To the right below a large screen, which showed Sky Sports, sat the regulars, retired men side by side on a long bench seat with perfect viewing of the comings and goings in the pub. Quinn had been a regular for a couple of years and knew most by sight and some by name, he greeted them all with a nod and headed to the bar.

'Alright Martin be with you in a minute.' Gemma was serving four fresh pints to the group by the fire and also managed to start pouring a Guinness for Martin. As he leaned back to see who was in, Pete and the rest of the team walked in and greeted Martin with smiles and laughter.

'Well that was perfect timing Boss, four pints it is! '

'Bet you twats were waiting in the car park for me to get in first weren't you?'

'Martin how very dare you.' Said Pete with a knowing laugh.

Shaking his head and turning to Gemma, Martin said with a resigned smile. ' So I've copped for it again Gem…'

' I'll bring them over here's your Guinness, so how was your day?'

'All good Gemma usual shite to deal with, oh I almost forgot, I was over at Alan Prices Farm this afternoon and saw a big cat, probably a Panther in Lower Field, couldn't believe it! Alan Price reckons they've been around here for years.' Gemma bowed and stretched side to side with expert balance as she continued to pour pints of beer, she didn't look up but replied.

'Really… wow that's mad, yeah I've heard of sightings but never took it too serious, you know these lot they talk bollocks most of the time.' Saying it loud enough for the regulars to hear, Gemma looked over at the bench as to a man they shouted back 'hey I heard that'.

Martin sat with his foreman Pete and the rest of the team opposite the regulars who wrestled for shoulder room and the opportunity to be heard. The drying clay from sodden boots sprinkled the tiled floor as they caught up on the day's events but Martin could not stop thinking about his sighting of the big cat. It looked so natural in its habitat, such a beautiful creature, the strong shoulders, confident walk and silk like sheen to its coat. As he returned to the bar one of the group from near the fire came over and leaning in close whispered.

'Heard you saw a big cat today in Lower Field.' As he turned to the woman in her early forties Gemma butted in.

'Martin, this is Louise, sorry I told her about the big cat as she's into all that stuff, innit Lou?' Louise was chuckling and Martin smiled as he could sense a set up. Louise's deep tones were in sharp contrast to Gemma's high pitched wailing.

'Ok you lot have a good laugh I'm just saying what I saw was real, and Gemma, I can't believe you told everyone, well actually yes I can!!' Louise let out another chuckle and turned to Martin.

'Hi, sorry about that, just having a laugh with Gemma, I was wondering if I could have a chat about your sighting?'

'Yeah sure not much to say really, why the interest? ' Martin asked whilst eying her form which was tall and athletic, his eyes rose to meet her gaze before it became too obvious that he was checking her out.

'As Gemma quite eloquently explained I'm into that stuff apparently! Well actually I've been studying the big cats for some years now and we are trying to log the sightings to build up a picture of how many are in the area…'

'We ?'Martin interrupted

'Oh sorry, yes my friends over there, well we're part of the Wildlife Trust a sort of countryside alliance, so we actively monitor wildlife in our area, kind of a study to understand natural habitats'.

'Ah like animal activists you mean?'

'Absolutely not Martin, we are conservationists, we don't get involved with that group. It's all about finding a co-existence in the countryside, so when a predator enters the eco-system then naturally we are interested'. Martin realized he had touched a nerve, held up his hands in an apologetic gesture and continued.

'Ok I was being a bit unfair, just we've had run ins with protesters before on the wind farm installations and well I don't really want anything to do with them.'

Louise picked up the conversation after a brief silence. 'So where exactly was the sighting Martin?'

'The Panther was just casually walking along the hedgline at Lower Field, opposite the forest track road up to Cimla, you know it?'

'Yes I think so, just before the cross roads up from Alan Prices' farm?'

'Yeh that's it, Alan Price was driving so I got a good look, I was shocked Louise to see such a beautiful animal, I just never knew they lived here, Mr. Price explained to me that he'd seen them around here for years and they weren't any trouble really.'

Louise leaned in closer and asked. 'Can you remember how big it was, any distinctive markings?'

'Like a large dog really, but its tail was very long, and the way it moved so smooth, if you know what I mean, so I knew it wasn't a dog.'

'And colour was it dark brown?'

'Yeh I'd say so, the light was fading so it's difficult to be accurate but it wasn't jet black, nor spotty, sorry Im not much use really, just I've never seen anything like it before and I'm not exactly a wildlife expert.'

'No, no that's ok I get it Martin, well it sounds similar to what other people have reported so don't think you're going mad or anything.'

Martin felt at ease and opened up his wide shoulders to face her warm tones. Shoulder length straight brown hair framed her smiling round features, she was very attractive in his eyes and the kind of woman he would normally go for. There seemed something else which aroused a sense of mischief which he couldn't digest but he found it appealing. Martin recalled that he had noticed her in the pub a couple of times over the past year, always with a group as he asked. 'So Louise, what's your interest then, in the big cat I mean?'

Louise looked into his eyes and smiled whilst pushing her hair back, warming too to Martin. 'Im a country girl Martin always have been, my father was a vet, my ex-husband is a vet, I've always worked around animals. I did some wildlife rescue work for a while, and I guess over the years when the sightings were reported I just got more and more involved and before you know it I seem to be treated like the expert around here. Im just trying to understand them more and raise awareness really.' Louise paused with a brief sip of her real ale before asking. 'You've been working down this way for a while haven't you? I've seen you in here before?'

'Feels like I've been here forever but actually it's just under two years, we started up on Cimla Mountain with a twelve turbine contract and its grown to forty-eight. I think we'll be here for another year or so.'

'How do you find working with Alan Price?'

Martin sensed Louise knew what he was like and was cautious with his reply.

'He's a farmer Louise, they are all the same to me, passionate about their land and stock, hardworking but also out for every penny. How do you know him?'

Louise leant back on the bar looking around the room and replied. 'Yep, that's him alright, apart from the passion. My father was his vet so I've known him for years. Never liked the man, he has no compassion for his animals.'

Martin sensed the bitterness in her tenor, and added. 'Don't get me wrong he's a pain in the arse to work with, he's constantly on our backs complaining. We're trying to complete the sub-station which backs on to his farm buildings, he's meant to give us free access through his yard as we've bought the land but he blocks the gate with trailers all the time. Plus thefts have increased, we lose a lot of diesel and now the cables have started to arrive which cost thousands to replace. We've had to employ a security guard which costs us a fortune. Unfortunately we won't be out of his backyard for another six months or so.'

Louise folded back her denim collar and flicked out trapped hair at the back and added. 'You think he's bad just wait till you meet his brothers they're worse. His old man died about five years ago and his will carved up the land between the three of them. Tom is the worst he's sold acres to housing development near to the village, ok fair enough we need houses but what is left is just scrubland now and he rents out every acre he can to anyone who will pay for whatever reason. Then there's Jim who owns the upper reaches to Tonna Mountain, it's all for sheep grazing just like Alans land, but the Deer roam that land and they both carry out illegal hunting. Alan Price also rents out his yards too and they are into all sorts with Davies Transport, a bunch of fat old men all in it together for their own gain. My ex used to be the vet for them, when they had horses, dairy and sheep but that's just dwindled over the years to next to nothing. Sorry im just rattling on, it's just he's a bad example of a farmer and he's letting this area down.'

'Well Louise money does that to people, I just try and keep out of his way and let our land agent deal with him.' Martin looked over to the lads whilst finishing his sentence. 'Sorry we'll have to finish this another time, thirsty lot they are.'

'That's ok, Im sure we can catch up again, nice to meet you Martin, if you see any more just let me know that's all. Here's my number.' As Louise took out her phone Martin did the same, typing it in as she read it out, then pressing call. 'Oh its ringing, of course it is Dumbo that's you right ?' Louise looked embarrassed but detracted the moment with pursed lips.

'See you again Louise, hopefully soon.' Martin replied with a boyish grin as he watched her swagger back to her group who were deep in conversation. As Louise approached the table her friend Gill looked up.

'Who's that Lou? You two looked pretty close.' Asked Gill.

'That, Gill, is Martin Quinn he works up at the windfarm installation, he sighted a Panther this afternoon close to Alan Prices farm.'

Louise slid back into her seat with a smug expression waiting for her friends to ask for more. She looked forward to the weekly meeting with Gill and her sons Rhys and Lewis. The group had been actively tracking and researching Panther sightings in south and mid Wales for a number of years. Their group had alliances with other 'big cat' groups all over the UK. Their weekly meet in the pub was an opportunity to update their web page and catch up on any new sightings. So to have an actual sighting on pub night filled Louise with excitement.

'Tell me more Louise, do you believe him?' Gill asked with a quizzical expression.

'Of course, but we will have to follow up the sighting with a survey of the area, check for prints and markings.'

Rhys leaned forward on the round table and tilted the glasses with his weight. 'Wow that was close, nearly spilt the lot, so Lou we could go tomorrow afternoon and have a look, ill set up a wildlife camera as well. It could be Tonmawr but there's also a male in the area, we took some prints and had a capture on the camera up by the waterfalls last weekend. There seems to be an increase in the sightings, maybe its due to winter coming to an end and more people are about.'

Louise loved the buzz of excitement in the group, it gave her focus in an otherwise dull, solitary existence. Since her marriage break up and job change the Panther research had been the steadying influence, focusing her energy.

Martin sat down next to Pete and leaned back taking in what Louise had said about Alan Price. There was something niggling but he just couldn't work it out. Then something sparked. ' Pete, when did Alan Price give us access to the yard?'

'Oh fuck me your back then, thought you and Lou were gonna slip away together, you want to watch that one Martin.'

'Alright Pete we were just talking about Alan Price, when did we set the sub-station site up, can you remember?'

'About six weeks now Martin, we finished the fenceline just before Christmas so yeah about six weeks, why?'

'Well the thefts haven't stopped even though we've had security on site for two weeks now. I reckon its Alan Price taking the diesel right from under our noses.'

Pete nodded his head with a knowing smile. 'I've been saying that to the lads, every time we lock up at night he appears, has a quick chat and disappears into that long barn, Im sure he's letting someone in to his yard then slinging a hose over to the diesel tank.'

'Well he's not getting away with it any more, come on Pete, drink up were going over there now. He knows we all end up in The Crown about six and security don't start till eight, so I bet now is when he's doing it.'

Chapter 4

'Annie….Annie….come on girl…Annie….'

Calling her horse in the early morning, Jo expected the thump, thump of a steady trot towards the gate which she struggled to lift open. No response so she dragged the feed from the boot of her car and threw it to the ground to disturb the small bale. With the aid of her cars headlights the crest of the field was visible, but Annie did not come. Jos' shadow skewed and stretched up the slope of the field to the wooded area beyond the crown where Annie sheltered on cold nights. She strode out towards the wood calling again.

'Annie….Annie….come on girl…Annie….'

Still nothing, Jo knew something was wrong, she thought Annie may have escaped the field. 'Did I leave the gate open last night? Was it the broken fence behind the wood?' Annie had escaped before but was found across the lane in the next field grazing as if nothing was wrong. Another tentative step forward and she called again into the darkness. Jo struggled with wet hands to press the torch icon on her mobile, when it lit she held the phone high to spread the beam through the trees. She again stepped further to the edge of the wood but stopped when she sensed her left foot was now in wet ground. She aimed the beam lower to see what she had stepped in. Jos' scream echoed out as the torch illuminated the empty carcass, the animals head at an unnatural angle. Bright red blood glowing in the white light Jo viewed the still warm remains of a female adult Deer. Annie was motionless at the fenceline deep in the wood. Jos' shock turned to relief as Annie finally came to her, bobbing and nuzzling in close with wide eyes.

'It's ok girl come on.' Jo lead Annie back down the slope to the gate to feed, glancing back and wondering what or who had killed the Deer. Poachers or gamekeepers they were much the same in Jo's eyes. One has a license to kill these beautiful animals the other has not, but with the same result. Jo recalled with a smile the first time the Deer appeared in Annie's field, they shared the thick grass, feeding together without cause for concern. Annie was calm and eating as Jo raked the hey out and mixed in a bag of feed. Her thoughts were what to do about the dead Deer, she couldn't just leave it there, nor could she move it. Foxes would eat the soft tissue and at light the crows would pick the rest. She wondered about calling the owner of the field a local farmer Guy Davies, but apart from taking her rent each month he rebuffed her complaints about the poor state of the fence or lack of water supply. There was a much safer option. 'Of course she'll help.' Jo said in a calm voice to herself.

'Hi Louise, really sorry to bother you so early, are you busy?'

'Oh hi Jo what's up, you don't sound right?'

'I'm ok, well I'm not really, I'm over at Annie's field and there's a dead Deer, I can't move it and I don't know what to do.'

'Give me ten minutes, don't touch it, or let Annie near it'.

With that Jo looked over towards the dead animal but stayed close to Annie ruffling her main as her horse nuzzled her feed.

Jo began to think about how good a friend Louise was, despite their previous differences. Jo and Louise had known each other since primary school and had remained friends through many changing times, children, failed marriages, deaths and friendships. They had a brief falling out three years ago when Louise was mixed up with the local hunt. It was against both of their beliefs, yet Louise who assisted her then husband Paul at his veterinary practice was seen at a hunt meet. Jo and Louise had a public argument at The Crown and didn't speak for nearly a year. Louise and Paul went their separate ways about the same time, Jo didn't know exactly why but it was messy. Her kids had moved away after university and Louise was a loose cannon. But as true friends do they picked up and dusted down their differences.

Louise no longer gets involved with the hunt but stops short of joining the protests with Jo. In this male dominated environment they had learned to look out for each other along with their other close friends and help each other whenever needed.

As Louise arrived first light was blossoming into a bright clear morning. 'Hi Jo you ok?'

'Sorry Lou, didn't know what to do, I was gonna go up to the farm building, you know Guy he owns the field, but he's a miserable old bastard and...'

'Jo its ok, let's have a look, the main thing is their blood could be toxic if they were spooked before the attack so we'll have to keep Annie out of the area.' Leaving Annie to feed they strode out together and soon saw the full horror of the dead animal. Jos' hand covered her mouth as she cried out in disbelief.

'Lou I thought a poacher had shot her but look at that.'

'I know Jo, it might well have been at first but then the foxes get to work and the crows, listen, you go back and look after Annie, oh and call Guy, he's gonna have to remove the carcass and burn it.'

Louise now had the peace to examine the remains in more detail. Latex gloves and a paper mask were taken from her coat pocket and as she put them on she paced around observing the animal from all angles.

Starting at the head she studied the pool of blood staining the grass from the underside of its neck. Through the mottled fur she could not see a wound so she looked around for a stick to move the head not wanting to touch the animal. A vertical stem was snapped from the base of a Beech tree on the hedge line, stripping twigs and bending its length to test its strength Louise returned to the animal. She prised the head and neck to reveal a hole at the larynx, the throat completely torn and flesh hanging. The eyes of the Deer were open and black. Moving down the claw scarred neck to its shoulders revealed torn and missing skin down to its hind quarters. The Deer's underbelly was largely missing with the cavity open. Its back and front legs were intact although Louise did notice its back left foot was badly broken, twisted forward at an unnatural angle. Its hind quarters were scared on both sides in a symmetrical pattern. Louise knelt down closer to the back of the Deer's head and focused between the ears at the crown of the skull. There were four distinctive puncture wounds, splitting the skull between the ears as if a heavy blow had cracked the bone.

Louise's first impression led her to believe it was a Panther attack. She needed to record a more in-depth examination so took her mobile phone out. She noticed three missed calls from an unknown mobile number and two voicemails. She walked around the Deer's mutilated corpse zooming in and talking through her observations. Panning around she sensed movement in her peripheral and froze. The movement came from the edge of the wood close to a large fern outcrop. Keeping the recording going Louise skulked toward the fern, her phone pointing at the ground. Whatever was there had gone when she reached the spot. She disturbed the ferns with her Beech stick to reveal more blood and Deer fur.

As she returned to the carcass Louise bobbed down and took a closer look at the neck wound. She teased off a piece of hanging flesh at the point of incision with a pair of extended tweezers and dropped it in a sample bag. She then laid a pen between the puncture wounds on the Deer's head and took a close up image and dropped the pen into her sample bag. Jo returned at the same time, Annie remained tied up at the gate enjoying her feed.

'Hey Lou so I called Guy he actually was alright about it and he's on his way down, what happened then Lou?'

Louise strained to stand up and removed her mask, wet now with condensed breath, as she replied. 'Definitely a big cat Jo, massive neck wound, claw marks everywhere and most of the organs gone. I just can't work out this back leg, probably done whilst trying to escape but its broken above the knee joint, almost clean off, and worse than that there's puncture wounds on the scalp, very strange, I'm gonna have to speak to someone about that, I've never seen anything like it. There's some more blood and fur over by that fern, probably where a fox dragged off some of the scraps. She's a big female Jo, I've never seen a Deer this big taken down by one of our Panthers though.' Looking at Jo for an answer Louise continued. 'How's Annie now?'

'Well she's feeding ok and calm now, thanks ever so much Lou for coming out, I knew you'd want to anyway but at such short notice that's really kind.'

'Hey that's ok Jo we're all here to help each other you know that. I just can't work out what's happening with the cats, it's really strange behavior. I was in the pub last night and bumped into one of the wind turbine contractors, he saw one down at Lower Field late in the afternoon and they've never been reported that close to the farm, and now this right on our doorstep.'

Jo could see the concern and asked Louise. 'What's that Panther called Lou, the one we first saw together, is she still around?'

'Tonmawr, yes she's still around, I think that is who was spotted last night, but she couldn't have done this, she's just not big enough Jo.'

'So we have another big cat in the area then?'

'Looks like it Jo, there are males roaming further up in the Brecon's, we've seen evidence when tracking Tonmawr. We have a recent image of one of the large males he's a beauty, he has a small grey patch behind his left shoulder so we called him Grey. I think Tonmawr has had a litter recently but I haven't found her den yet. Im hoping to spend the weekend tracking with Gill and her boys if you fancy joining us? We're staying up at my forest lodge, bring some wine and stay over it'd be good to have a proper catch up.'

'Sounds good Lou ill see if my busy social life will allow me to fit you in.' Jo let out a laugh and hugged Louise.

With Annie settled next to the gate the two friends sat in Louise's car waiting for Guy Davies. Out of the blue Jo asked. 'So what exactly happened with you and Paul then? I couldn't work you out at the time and didn't want to ask.'

'It's a long painful story Jo, and it all got too much, we'll talk more at the weekend if you can make it up to the lodge. I just had to get away from him, he was getting into all sorts and we just never had time for each other, and Im sorry I was a real cow at the time. That hunt stuff wasn't for me Jo it was all about Paul, his image, trying to impress the fucking farmers.'

'I guessed that Lou but just couldn't work you out, cos you hated that lot.'

'I know, I know, and Paul just kept pushing all the time, he would arrange dinner parties with his university colleagues and expect me to just get on with it, not my kind of evening I can assure you pampering those wankers. Then to top it all he arranged an exchange with a Korean university lecturing in animal genetics, I'd had enough by then so asked him to leave.'

'Such a shame Lou, you two seemed the perfect couple, what with the vet practice doing so well.'

'That was the trouble Jo, it was all show, Paul loved the idea of his own practice and it was doing really well but I could tell his heart wasn't in it, he was always distracted with the hunt and his uni pals. Now it's his in name only, I haven't seen him properly since he came back from Seoul over two years ago, that's when I broke links with the practice, it was always his, never ours as it should have been. My Dad built that place up and when he died and left it to me and Paul I thought wow! That's us set for life but within a year it all started to fall apart. Paul was trying to stop the domestic work and concentrate on the farms, but that's the part I loved, real people with animals that were wanted. Anyway, glad Im out of it Jo, im happy doing a couple of days a week over at Oaktree practice, they're a good bunch of vets and it's a happy place.'

'Good for you Louise, I don't blame you, just wished you talked to me back then that's all....Oh look here's Guy Davies, oh God not looking forward to this.'

'It'll be alright Jo c'mon I'll stay with you.'

Guy Davies dropped down from his tractor with ease, his tall wiry body was both agile and strong despite his rugged appearance. 'Hi Jo, got a dead Deer in the field have we?' Guys deep tones with a friendly accent comforted Jo, she was expecting the opposite.

'Thanks ever so much Guy for coming down I just didn't know how to sort it out, this is my friend Louise.'

Guy looked over at Louise and changed his stature to a more defensive position.

'Hello Louise how are you? Haven't seen you for years…..and so sorry about your dad, I know it's been a while but I still remember him with fondness such a great man.'

Louise was taken aback, her dad was such a force in this area and a massive part of her life. 'Thank you Guy that's very kind.'

'Are you still up at the practice with Paul?'

'No Guy I'm at Oaktree helping out a couple of days a week that's all, Paul & I are divorced now.'

'I did hear rumors but you know what people are like so I'd rather here it from the horse's mouth, Im sorry to hear that, life goes on though Louise, you're looking well so somethings working?'

Louise was again taken aback, she had known Guy since she was a little girl on visits with her dad to the farms and his brash nature was a breath of fresh air.

'Guy your flattery will get you everywhere.'

All three were at ease as they headed up the incline of the field to view the carcass, which by now was covered in bluebottles, they stopped a few yards from the Deer.

'Looks like a big cat attack Guy, I've taken all the photos and measurements I need.'

Guy folded his arms and looked across at the neck wound and said.

'It's been the first attack in over a year Jo, don't worry about your horse, they wouldn't attack her anyway, too big. Unless there's anything more Louise, have you all the information you need? I'll pick her up on the forks and take her up to the yard, I've got a fire going behind the milking shed and some old sleepers to burn, that'll return her to dust.

'Guy can I show you the fence at the back it needs repairing?' Said Jo as she turned to Louise. 'Right I'll let you know about the weekend Lou, thanks again.'

' Bye Jo, hope you can make it, send me a text when it's all sorted.'

Back at her car Louise flipped the indicator and pulled out onto the road then remembered the missed calls, she checked the rear view mirror and pulled in straight away. The road was clear and she could see in the distance Guy Davies and Jo walking back smiling and chatting. Jo listened intently in a state of shock to the answer phone message, it was from Martin Quinn, she put two and two together and matched the number from last night at the pub. She pressed call return and waited-no answer.

'Shit, shit, shit.' Louise shouted to herself, she rammed the car into first speeding off towards the wind farm installation.

Chapter 5

Grey, the large male predator rocked to ease the discomfort on his elbows whilst keeping his head low and eyes fixed on the Fallow Deer herd. One large female in her third season and seven smaller males and females were scattered in the field, no more than a bodies length apart from each other.

He had been in this field before stalking and each time had failed to get close enough to his prey. Each time he got within striking distance the lead Doe or Stag spotted him and alerted the herd with a bark or cry. He had given chase but was outrun by the Deer, their ability to clear hedges and land without losing pace had left Grey floundering behind until he gave up the chase. This night his position was more favorable. He had cover to his right which would lead him to within striking distance. To his left however, was enough open ground for the Deer to escape without fear of being trapped, he needed to push them into the wooded area at the top of the field where confusion would scatter the herd. His eyes were fixed on the large female Deer, an awkward stance and graceless gait revealed a weak hind leg.

As the herd grazed on the edge of the wood Annie trotted towards them, slowing as she came close and grazing herself, at ease with her guests.

Annie unnerved the predator, she was far too large and unpredictable for him. Annie was of working cob stock, thick set legs, a thumping gallop and heavy in the neck and shoulder.

The male worked out his plan, move under cover to the right, follow the hedgline then dart to the centre of the field, cutting off their route to freedom and push the herd towards the wood, then pick off the slowest before they reached the fenceline. The wood was small, it could be covered in three to four skips by the Deer, but there was no direct route out, the Deer would have to change direction to avoid the trees. The key for Grey was to remain undetected until he reached the centre of the field, an almost impossible task, but a straight out frontal assault from where he lay would give them enough space to escape.

The herd had been grazing on fresh grass for an hour and in a slow advance were heading closer to the wild garlic fringed wood line. Soon they would move to the neighboring field or settle down in the wood. Their grazing pattern could not be predicted by the predator, the herd did not remain stationary for more time than necessary. Whilst some rested others remained alert. The main herd of fifty Deer were rarely all together but roamed in groups of six or seven, interchanging daily. If one became separated they would soon find a fragment of the main herd. Tonight though the group were satisfied and the eight began to settle in the wood, Annie too graduated to the covered ground.

Grey felt that now was the time to strike, he tested his movement, wooden at first, then more flexible. He squatted low whilst his legs rotated forward in a slow deliberate motion, not a sound was created. The ground was wet and rain fell as a mist laden drizzle as he continued along the hedgline, gradually closing in on the herd which had not been alerted to his presence. Scent at this point was the usual alarm, close enough that the slightest whiff of the pungent essence from the feline would scatter the Deer. The rain charged atmosphere smothered the Panthers scent, conditions were perfect. Now was the right time. Sight at this proximity was the Deer's last line of defence. The Deer bobbed down and up twitching, looking, listening, inhaling through wide nostrils in a continual rhythm.

Annie shook her rain soaked mane which smacked against her neck before trotting deep into the wood for shelter. The noise from this immaterial random act translated to the herd causing the ones resting to jump up. Now the eight were all on foot and as randomly as they arrived they instinctively agreed it was time to move on.

The male knew it was now or never, a night wasted or rewarded hung on the next few moments. Eying the large female he darted from his cover transitioning with ease from a low bodied stride to shoulder high sprint. Once in full stride he was surprised how quickly the Deer as one moved. The alarmed Fallow pronked at first but this stiff legged high gait changed to full flight in an instant. To his right the large female bounded into the wood along with three of the herd, the others made for open ground and disappeared into the mist. The predator was now in control closing in as each change in route slowed the Deer.

Annie, alerted by the commotion was frantic and bolted towards the open field almost colliding with the throng. The large female Deer dug in and changed direction again towards the open ground, a deafening crack echoed as her weakened left leg finally gave way. Grey changed direction without losing ground as dense muscle powered his pursuit. Exposed and weakened the Deer's speed diminished, unable to bound away. Not realizing his good fortune the cat launched himself and centered on the hind quarters of the Deer, causing her to collapse on the rain soaked grass. The Deer barked in vain as teeth and claws battered her strained body. The weight kept her hind down but she managed to free both front legs and straightened in an attempt to break away. The jaws were moving closer to her head, claws digging in to her back and with no purchase from her hind leg she collapsed again. The jaws like a hammer blow sunk into the crown of her skull, a wide bite unable to clamp against the tough bone, but in the same movement he released and swung around to her throat. The cats agility and strength allowed its bite to crush any remaining fight left in the shattered frame. The stranglehold asphyxiated the Deer and as the twitching stopped the cat tore away the throat and spat it out with a victorious growl.

Holding his prey was the satisfaction the large male predator lusted after. The instant gratification of adrenalin pumping through his body as he gulped in oxygen. His heavy breathing through an open mouth decelerated, the cooling mist merged with the heat rising from both animals in billowing clouds which engulfed their bodies.

Moving the carcass was his next instinctive act but this proved too much as flesh and bone tore from the body. The Deer was twice the weight of Grey. He circled his quarry and settled on the warm underbelly. With teeth gripped on the soft hairless skin and his weight transferred through front feet planted on the Deer's rump he tore the skin, spilling the steaming organs. Feeding for at least an hour on the soft nutrition satisfied the predator. He struggled to rise and tugged to move the body of the Deer but again failed.

Annie had remained in the open field trotting left and right, glancing at the scene. As the predator rose from his feast the cob bolted along the hedgline to the perceived safety of the wood. The cat cantered in the opposite direction wary of the horse.

From one instinctive act to the next- his quest was to find the female Panther, Tonmawr, who he encountered earlier that evening.

Chapter 6

Martin Quinn paced the site office waiting for the arrival of Clair Da Mota, she had promised to be there at nine thirty and it was now after ten. He had a site meeting at eleven and needed to leave in the next ten minutes. As he gathered his coat and hard hat he heard a car pull up outside on the loose gravel, so he sat back down and waited for her to breeze in.

The door flung open and Martin without looking up sighed and said. ' At last, Id given up on you! Im due on site at eleven so you've got ten minutes or you'll have to wait till this afternoon!'

'Sorry to barge in Martin, only just picked up your message.'

'Louise! I was expecting someone else... sorry that wasn't meant for you, just our land agent who is always late, you didn't have to come up here I'd have met you at the pub later.' Louise looked flustered, she was out of breath, the rain had soaked her dark hair matting it to her face. She pulled the strands of hair from her mouth before replying.

'Thought it best if we looked into this straight away, but that's ok I should have realized you had things on, work I mean.'

'No, no that's fine, but I have a site meeting which won't take long if you don't mind waiting?'

'No that's ok Martin, I should have called you first, it's just that Im shocked by what you said and I just want to make sure I've got my facts right before I go in guns blazing.'

'Like I said on the phone Louise I'm not one hundred percent sure, I was going to ring the RSPCA but remembered what you said last night in the pub so…anyway please wait, look, help yourself to coffee, milks in the fridge, I'll be twenty minutes max, promise.'

With that Martin stepped out into the car park and headed towards the site entrance. Louise watched him disappear through the gate, he looked bigger than last night in the pub she thought. She followed her gaze up to the distant cluster of fully built wind turbines, not yet turning but so imposing, dominating the skyline. She thought about the effect they would have on the big cats, their territory was gradually being swallowed up by the advancing needs of people. The deep drone of turning blades must put the Panthers off guard, drowning the senses. She turned to study the plans covering the walls of Martins office. Swathes of land divided up into compounds, gates, fences, small buildings, concrete bases and power lines.

These once barren and open lands provided the vast swathes which predators needed to define their territories.

Following the line of the Cimla mountain road she traced the route back to Alan Prices farmyard. His large Georgian house held a commanding viewpoint over the farm buildings and land below. The buildings were dominated by a long low barn to which the new sub-station backed onto, outlined in red on Martins Map.

What is that man up to in there? Why would Alan Price keep a Panther locked up in his barn? Louise asked herself. Curiosity was eating away at Louise as she moved around the office, feeling her way, not knowing what she was looking for. Three desks covered in paperwork dominated the centre, coffee cups and dust covering their surfaces. A planner on the wall outlined the timeline for construction, potted with post-its and numbers which meant nothing to Louise. What she needed must be in the desk draws she thought. She tried the draw where Martin had been sitting, it was open. She searched through the usual draw rubbish looking for keys to the substation compound, but to no avail. Then she noticed a key cabinet on the wall near the exit, it was locked. So where does he keep the key? Probably on his key ring. Louise resigned herself to not finding the it, and did it really matter? If she could persuade Martin to help, he has the keys anyway.

She returned to Martins desk for another look in the draw as Claire Da Mota's car pulled up outside. Louise heard the car and moved away from Martins desk, she watched as Claire stepped out of her Range Rover Evoque onto the gravel car park.

Louise went into panic saying to herself. 'Fuck, what's she doing here?' She had to get out before Claire saw her, but what about Martin? She moved to the office door then stopped as she realized it opened directly onto the car park, and there was no way she could get out of the back window in time. She resigned herself to facing up to Claire, but what would she say? Claire would recognize her instantly. 'Deep breaths girl come on, it'll be ok.' Louise eyed Claire with dread as she moved towards Martins office door. As always she looked amazing, dressed as if attending a country fair, confident with beautiful skin and hair. Another voice was heard, although Louise couldn't make out what was being said to Claire, the man walked back to Claire's car and the conversation continued, it looked like one of Martins colleagues from the pub last night but she couldn't be sure. Claire took out a fluorescent jacket and hard hat from the boot, wrestled them on and followed the man towards the site gate.

Louise breathed a sigh of relief and realized she had to get out now. She watched Claire disappear through the site gate and left the office, running to her car she pulled out her mobile and called Martin.

'Hi Louise, really sorry I'll be ten more minutes…'Louise cut him short.

'Listen Martin, I've got to go, your visitor has arrived, the one you were waiting for, well she's on her way up to you I think. Look do me a favour don't mention to her that Im here, or don't talk to her about the sightings, I'll explain later, you ok with that?'

'I can see her now, walking up, er yes ok are you alright? I didn't know you knew each other.'

'I'll explain later, see you in the pub about six, gotta go, bye.' Louise didn't wait for a reply.

Martin put his phone away as Claire approached, ' Well at long last Claire, Id given up on you coming.' They shook hands, hers being cold to the touch, soft and slender. Martin took in the perfumed scent and clear complexion, despite heavy eye make-up which accentuated deep brown eyes. Claire was a natural beauty, tall and with a slim figure shaped by horse riding, clothed in tweed which oozed wealth despite being covered with an oversized fluorescent coat.

Claire tried to explain her lateness to Martin who half listened and continued walking down the pathway. ' Seen as you're here Claire we might as well have a look around site, get you up to speed.'

Claire composed herself and followed in his steps. 'So what is the problem with Alan Price, is he not co-operating Martin?'

'He'll be putting in a claim for lost sheep because we left a gate open, I've detailed it all on the email, dates times and what he said.' Martin felt he would get no help from Claire. His company were paying her a fortune to deal with the landowners but so far he seemed to be doing all the work.

'I've seen the email thanks Martin. I've made an appointment with Alan Price for this afternoon. Hopefully I can nip this one in the bud before it gets out of hand.'

'That would be great Claire he's starting to get under our feet on site. There's something else but leave it with me for a couple of days and if it's an issue I'll give you a call.'

'Martin, Im intrigued, what is it?'

Martin was familiar with Claire's character and nonchalant disinterest in anything that was day to day. He was teasing her with a snippet to ensure she answered his call the next time. 'It may be nothing Claire, like I said give me a couple of days that's all. Are you staying over this way tonight?'

' I'd love to Martin but unfortunately I have to be back in the Cheltenham office first thing for a meeting. I do need to spend more time down here as the project expansion is kicking in and I must to get up to speed with all the new landowners, I'll clear some space in the diary for next week.'

Claire's smile was seductive and she used it to her advantage but Martin had seen it all before and knew her self-interest would never wain. As they reached Martins site office he offered Claire a coffee and was relieved by her refusal as she put her coat and hat in the boot of her car. Martin struggled with small talk, especially with Claire Da Mota who's world seemed a million miles from his, Cheltenham, hunting, horse racing, landowners, all the traits he detested in privileged upbringings. Martin had started with nothing and worked his way up a long hard road from laboring to being a site manager, he loved his job, the outdoors and the real people he met along the way.

Martin watched Claire's crisp white Range Rover Evoque speed off down the site road towards Alan Prices farm, as he did his thoughts again turned to Louise. What had happened with her and Claire? Why did she run? And most important of all to Martin could Louise explain his latest sighting in Alan Prices barn last night?

Throughout the afternoon of phone calls, site meetings and planning, Martins thoughts were not his own. Six o'clock could not have arrived sooner. As he pulled into The Crown car park Louise was waiting in her car and jumped out into the drizzle to greet Martin before he went into the pub. She tapped on the passenger window and as Martin lowered it she shouted. 'Are you gonna let me in or watch me getting soaked ?'

'Jump in its open, thought we were meeting inside, my thirst may get the better of me, I was hoping for a pint…'

'Do you mind if we go somewhere else, have you tried The Sawyers Arms on the Ferry road?' Martin knew the place, one of those chain pubs that sold more food than it did beer but was only a few hundred yards down the main road on the roundabout.

'I don't mind, we could have walked down if it wasn't for this shitty weather.' Martin swung his truck around and turned left onto the main road towards the Sawyers Arms whilst he listened to Louise talk about her encounter with Jo and Annie that morning. He knew she was building up to asking him about last night's sighting at Alan Prices barn and avoiding the issue with Claire Da Mota. Martin couldn't get a word in as they were shown into a booth at the pub and handed two menus, shown the specials board and asked what drinks they wanted by, what seemed to Martin, to be a twelve year old boy.

Louise looked agitated, she tapped the edge of the card menu on the table as she ordered her drink, Martin asked for his usual Guinness, anticipating a pint which had been stripped of life. She then blurted out. 'So Martin, what exactly happened at the barn, you think you saw another Panther?'

'Yes Im sure of it, after we spoke in The Crown last night I was talking with Pete our foreman about the thefts from the sub-station site, so we decided to go and have a look because we were both convinced Alan Price was behind it. Anyway we got there before our security guy turned up and we were looking along the back wall of the barn which backs onto our compound for hoses and diesel spillages, that's how the thieves normally do it. So we got near the far end, nothing. Pete went back up to the gate to look and I carried on looking along the barn. The wall was damp in the corner and there was an old oil drum under the gutter downpipe, so I climbed up and with the torch I had a look into the barn through a small gap in the steel cladding. I swear to you Louise there was a Panther in there similar to what I saw in Lower Field, it was in a wire mesh enclosure inside the barn lying down, it was the same orange glow reflecting and the coat so smooth. It didn't move, just looked up and yawned, its teeth were huge Louise, I fuckin shit myself and jumped down.'

Louise sat back and shook her head in disbelief. ' Did you see anyone in there Martin, was Alan Price around at all?'

'No, the yard was empty, no lights on anywhere. Our security man turned up when I got back up to see Pete in the compound. We asked him to log when anyone came into the farmyard and to move the CCTV around to cover the diesel tank. I thought we would find out because we are convinced Alan Price has something to do with it, but I guess you're more interested in the Panther?'

'I need to see it Martin, not that I don't believe you, of course I do. I should be able to see if it's one we have previously sighted by its size and colouring. Trouble is I won't get an invite from Alan Price, we have a bit of history.'

Martin was glad to get the encounter off his chest as he had said nothing to Pete, not for fear of ridicule, he was used to that, more that he felt a certain obligation towards Louise, although he could not work out why. Now was the time to get all the cards on the table, he leaned in to Louise over the table, looking her directly in the eyes and asked. 'What's the deal with Claire Da Mota?'

Louise's embarrassment was clear to see as the drinks were served. Martin declined the request to order a meal, instead asking for the same drinks again. Louise opened up.

' Ok so this goes no further please Martin. She used to come to our house when I was with my ex-husband Paul for dinner and hunt parties. Paul was the hunt vet and the practice used to look after all the local farmers stock. She turned up with Alan Price to a pre-hunt dinner party we had organized. Look I'm ashamed to have been involved with the hunt and that crowd, I just got swept along in it all, Paul on the other hand couldn't get enough of it. I took an instant dislike to Claire, she was so full of herself, bragging about her stables in Cheltenham, the people she knew and she used to flirt like hell with Paul. I never rode with the hunt but helped out with all the bullshit tradition and all that.' Louise took a large gulp from her pint glass and continued.

'I had a bust up with Claire after the hunt, we'd both had a lot to drink and she was all over Paul, and he was lapping it up of course. I let her know in no uncertain terms how I felt and told her to back off. I haven't seen her since and Im sorry for running out on you but when I saw her pull up I just couldn't bear the thought of having to see her again.'

Martin was taking it all in and was trying to work out why Claire hadn't told him about his involvement with Alan Price. 'Ok so when was this Louise?'

' Must have been about three years ago, shortly before me and Paul went our separate ways, so what's her involvement with the wind turbines?'

'I guess that was about the time when we were buying the land and drawing up the lease agreements with Alan Price so she would have been our representative. Claire still deals with any land issues on our behalf, but from what your telling me she's a bit too close to Alan Price for my liking, although it doesn't surprise me in the slightest'.

Louise was more relaxed now and added. ' I knew she would have recognized me today Martin and I just didn't want you getting involved in another slanging match, plus she's up to something with Alan Price, I don't know what it is, and after what you saw in the barn, well Im just lost as to what's going on. I need to find out Martin and need your help. You see Alan Price has an injunction against me to stay away from his farm and land. I was going through a bad time after the split with Paul, I blamed Alan Price and his brothers for changing Paul and one drunken night, well I crashed through his gate and smashed up his outbuildings, I was arrested and the court served an injunction as he accused me of harassing him. It wasn't pretty Martin and I guess I deserved it as I was out of control.'

Martin felt he was getting involved in something way above his pay scale and shook his head before answering.' Sorry Louise, this is way out of my league and I can't see what I can do to help, I don't know the first thing about these animals and its more than my jobs worth to get involved.'

'Im not asking you to do anything, I wouldn't dare jeopardize your job, Martin I trust you, don't ask me why because we've only just met, but, well, I don't know how to say this, I'll get to the bottom of what's going on but I need you to maybe turn a blind eye if I happen to take a look in the barn.'

Louise's smile pleased Martin, he felt at ease in her company, despite what she had just told him he didn't feel threatened, if anything he was a little excited. 'Well the feelings mutual Louise, I trust you and quite like you as well, let me have a think about it'

Louise leaned in close to Martin. 'Martin we don't have time for that we need to act, and act now!'

They both looked at their drinks, picked them up in unison and necked the contents as if by way of confirmation. 'We'll go in my truck Louise we can pick your car up later if that's ok?'

'Thank you Martin, look I'll be as quick as possible, what time does the security guard start?'

'Normally he's there for 7.30, so we've got half an hour tops. Just one thing Louise I can't quite work out, why would there be a captive wild animal like a Panther locked up in a shed at a Welsh farm? What the fuck goes on around here?'

'Neither can I work it out Martin, it's not normal behavior, but you're dealing with people who think they are above the law and are a rule to themselves. The Prices think they own the right to shoot anything around here and keep whatever they want, the Police are not interested as they are from out of this area, we don't even have a station anymore just a call box on the wall where the copshop used to be.'

As they arrived at Alan Prices yard there were no lights or cars to greet them, even the distant farmhouse was in darkness. Martin stopped in the yard opposite the gates to the substation compound. ' Ok Ill open the gates and we'll go round the back of the barn and I'll show you where I saw it'.

He left the engine running and lights on and opened the gates. As he jumped back into the truck he caught Louise's' shadow fall across the bonnet then watched her disappear into the darkness along the front of the barn.' Louise wait, for fucks sake , where you going?'

Not wanting to alert anyone he decided to sit in the truck with the gate open and lights on pointing away from the barn, it seemed perfectly natural as if he was waiting for the security to turn up. Alan Price was used to the traffic and would recognize Martin's truck.

Louise was prepared for her task, black boots, dark jeans and a dark green parka. With her hood up she could have been anybody. The barn was in total darkness and as Louise sneaked along its length she kept close to the wall. She remembered that the end of the barn had a large wooden full height door with a smaller access door inset. When she reached it a roller steel door had replaced the old wooden panels, galvanized and new, and locked tight. Louise kicked the bottom rail in frustration and sent a ripple of unwanted noise to the top. She attempted to dampen the blow by placing her palms on the cold steel then rushed back towards where Martin was sitting in his truck, interior light on and headlights on full beam illuminating the entrance to his compound. The top end of the barn had an open bay in which was parked a flat back trailer. Louise slipped into the barn and climbed under the trailer to a dividing wall, she followed the blockwork to the corner which had an opening. She squeezed her body around drums, boxes and farm machinery covered in dust there was little or no light in the second bay.

Louise was confused by the new layout and dividing walls, the barn as she remembered was large and open with stalls for milking running the length of the back wall. She paced her way back to the trailer and measured that the barn had been divided into three bays, the furthest being where she needed to be. Her eyes were adjusting well to the low light as she moved to the final dividing wall which was full height. In the corner adjoining the yard was a small doorway recessed into the blockwork. The steel framed door was closed and could only be opened by pulling it towards herself. Louise took out her phone and illuminated the door handle which was covered by a thick brass padlock, no key hole, but four numbers in a line showing 7239. Louise knew she needed more time and was thinking, 'Do I leave now and come back tomorrow, or ask Martin to break the lock?' She turned resigned to the failure and started walking back through the barn, dejected. She checked her stride in a moment of realisation, span round and made her way back to the steel framed door. She took the lock in her hand and rolled the first number from 7 round to 1, 2 round to 9, 3 round to 6 and 9 remained. Louise pushed the button and watched the lock spring open.

As she let out a triumphant 'Yes!' Louise pulled the door open and crept into the third bay. In the far corner of the room, in the old milking pens was a caged area just as Martin had described. Her view of the cage floor was obscured by the pen wall, Louise stepped towards the cage and bent double as it came into view. At the same time an incoming message vibrated in her hand quelling her elation, 'You got 5 mins hurry up pls'. It was Martin.

'Fuck off.' Louise said to herself. The cage was empty but as she touched the wire on its door she could sense the hint of a feline. The concrete floor was stained a deep yellow and the cast drain clogged with feces. Louise took out her gloves and clear bag then picked up a dried sample. She also pulled matted fur from the frame of the cage where it joined the gulley which fell through the wall of the barn. Putting it into her coat pocket she crept through the door and eased it closed behind her. She snapped the lock back on and rolled the numbers, 'Shit what were the numbers?' She thought in panic, remembered the 7 but forgot the rest so left a random selection and made her way back to Martin.

'Martin, working late again?' Alan Price stood still directly against the driver's door of Martins truck.

'Jeez Mr. Price you scared the living shit out of me! Yes you know me Im a slave to it, waiting for our security to turn up that's all.'

'Security? Alan Price leaned on Martins door with an inquisitive look.

'Yes we've had some diesel stolen last week so watch your vehicles Mr. Price, I don't know if it's an isolated incident or what, plus we have a lot of cables delivered which are expensive to replace'. Martin was shaking inside and his voice he knew was higher than normal, he wanted to warn Louise but was strangled by the farmers proximity.

'Thanks Martin, yes I'll let Davies Transport know as well. Oh by the way Claire dropped by this afternoon, surprisingly helpful she was, I've decided not to claim on the sheep this time but make sure those men shut the gates in future.'

'That's no problem Mr. Price it won't happen again, goodnight'. Martin was looking over the farmers shoulder for Louise as he tried to end the conversation his mind in disarray invoking thoughts of anguish. 'Where the fuck is she, please don't come out yet.'

'Goodnight Martin, right I need to find this dog of mine, he ran off towards the barn I think, you didn't see him did you?'

Martins throat closed up but managed to stutter. 'No not this time, I've learnt to stay In the truck when he's about!'

'Ah yes, he's harmless really, barks worse than the bite, ah here he comes, see you again.' Alan Price turned away and bent down to ruffle the Dobermans neck as they walked away together towards the darkened façade of his farmhouse.

Martin punched letters into his keypad to warn Louise as the passenger door opened and she slid in and sank low into the seat.

'That was fucking close! I thought he would come into the barn.' Louise started to giggle, her diaphragm billowing and recessing without control, and the infection spread to Martin.

'Jeez my heart Louise, don't do that to me again, did you see it?'

'Wasted journey after all that, the place is like Fort Knox Martin the end bay is locked up, looks like he's renting it out to someone.'

Martin looked confused as he held onto the steering wheel tightly. 'I definitely saw it Louise.'

'I believe you Martin, I doubt it would still be there, whoever has managed to catch one of these animals must know what they're doing.'

'I don't get it Lou, who would?'

Louise put her hand on Martins and said 'I'll ask around, someone is bound to know, leave it with me, now let's get out of here, Im starving, fancy dinner?'

Martin smiled and nodded his approval as headlights appeared in the rear view mirror then pulled alongside. The driver of the car leaned over and Martin recognized the security guard Rhys, waving him through. ' God knows I need a pint now.' Martin said as he put the truck into reverse and drove them out of the yard.

Chapter 7

Tonmawr awoke before daybreak, her cubs were restless and hungry. She stretched and yawned as the cubs licked her dry mouth searching for any scrap of food. She shook them off, pushed them further into the den with her nose and made off into the dark. Her mind was made up, time to leave her territory. The young male predator was too strong, she had to find a new home where her cubs could be raised in relative safety. Before the exploration she had to eat and feed her cubs, they had to be strong enough for the journey, it could be seven days before they ate again. Sufficient food was hard to come by unless she took a risk. In her first season away from her mother she was tempted by sheep and took advantage of the plentiful supply, until man hunted her down and drove her high into the desolate Beacons. Since then she associated the meat with threat. A greater peril was imminent though, the large male Panther with the grey mark would find her and kill her cubs if she didn't act soon.

Tonmawr cantered at a steady pace across the hillside towards the pastures at Lower Field through the ebbing tide of darkness. She slowed at a hedgline and trudged through boggy ground to a five bar gate. The sheep beyond the gate were disturbed from their slumber and stood up in unison. Tonmawr had no time to stalk and pick out the weakest. She raced into the herd scattering the slow animals and snared the first fleece within reach, felling the hapless yew with ease. With one suffocating bite she killed the animal and with strained neck and shoulder muscles dragged it out of the field through a small gap in the hedge.

The journey back to her den was laborious yet disciplined. On the flat ground she managed to hold the yew high enough to avoid tripping on its trailing hind legs and her pace was measured. The inclines proved more difficult as she resorted to clamping a back leg in her jaw and reversing with the mass in short stints. With some two miles left in her journey Tonmawr took rest in a small wood. Her breathing soon settled and she rose again to haul her catch back to the den whilst her senses were on high alert. No scent, no noise or change in atmosphere were detected. Her goal was to return before day break, time which was fast running out, but slowed by the dark clouds of winter rain.

The twisting trails through fern and rock proved treacherous for Tonmawr, a path normally covered with ease was snagging her every turn. The yews wool tangling with briar, she tripped on fallen branches, slipped on rock outcrops. As she approached close to her den instinct changed her tact. Tonmawr dragged the body into dense fern and briar and left it there covered with mud and foliage matted into the wool. The final approach to her den was covered in a methodical interweaving, checking scent trails, stopping to listen for predators, rising above on rock outcrops, searching, searching. Only when she was satisfied that she was alone did she dart to the den entrance to wake her cubs.

Of the three cubs the strongest was the solitary male, at twelve weeks he was ready to follow his mother and eager to do so. The two females were as eager but not as strong. Their hunger spilled out into desperate frustration as their mother had nothing again, or so they thought. Excited and teasing Tonmawr wrestled the male and pinned him playfully. They spilled out of the den and followed mothers gentle trot through the undergrowth to the feast that awaited.

Under the protective blanket of darkness and heavy rain Tonmawr tore the underside of the yew spilling its organs. The male cub pounced and was knocked back heavily by his mother, even in these desperate times there was order. She snarled as she ate, a paw raised and swiped as each cub tried to join the feast. The yews head became detached at an oozing neck providing the cubs with a manageable piece to tear at. Small sharp teeth tugged and battled tearing bitesize morsels of satisfying flesh and warm blood. As daybreak illuminated the scene the carcass was empty. The four mouths had practically stripped the yew leaving torn trails of fleece and exposed joints. Tonmawr raised her full satisfied body and led the cubs on another crisscross of deception back to the den.

Her plan was to rest during daylight and travel at dusk. The family groomed each other and settled down to contented sleep. Tonmawr was half awake and reacted to the slightest noise or scent whilst her cubs slept.

At dusk they awoke, the cubs rolling around playing and enticing their mother to join in. Their waking routine was about to change. Instead of being pushed back into the den when their mother left, this night they were encouraged out of the den and in a playful act their mother pounced then hid until they were on new ground.

Tonmawr stood and looked back at the den and the familiar land, second thoughts bought her this final moment before she re-focused on the journey, stretching and yawning, gulping in oxygen, preparing for the departure into the unknown. Her territory to the north was open moorland with little cover other than deep ravines bottomed with tributaries flowing west to the wide river. Progress was sluggish as the cubs first journey outside the comfort of the den and its surroundings was rich with unfamiliar scents. Tonmawr checked her progress and regrouped the family at every turn, scolding the cubs with a swipe of her paw.

Halfway through the night they reached a high ridge line where the wind changed direction bringing westerly's leaden with moisture. By now the cubs had learnt to keep up with their mother and follow her natural lead. When she stopped to scent the air they did the same, high noses taking in the bouquet. As she brushed past a growth of fern or heather they followed with over exaggerated movements against the foliage. Still relatively safe within her own territory, Tonmawr lead the group down a steep ravine to take water and rest away from the severe lashings of rain and wind which had accelerated. The cubs were not yet feeling the pace due to the excitement of their journey. They drank and looked up, they had learnt more in the last few hours than in their whole lives so far.

The male cub had a larger frame and thicker set legs than the females. Though equal in height the two females had their distinct differences in gait. One being more inquisitive had a shorter step and held her head higher. The other walked with a long loping stride keeping her head low. These small differences set them apart and presented weaknesses to her mother who could see the short stepped daughter being the most vulnerable of the litter. The male cub was learning quicker than the females. He was always the closest to Tonmawr. His hunting skills more pronounced, quick to follow his mother's lead as she changed pace or direction.

After a brief respite the family climbed the ravine to the ridge to face the lashing rain. The first wind turbine farm in her territory was now complete and the blades twirled with a steady thump in the distance. Tonmawr s family headed towards them along a natural trail which alone she had travelled many times. Her goal this night was to reach the waterfalls at the limit of her domain. The short stepping female cub was lagging behind. Tonmawr was aware and checked their advancement in a constant battle of progress against devotion.

Tonmawr stopped as they arrived under the first turbine. The network of tracks coiled to join each turbine in a neural pattern slicing through her natural trails. The deep drone created by the turning momentum confused the cubs and agitated their mother. It drowned out the natural sound of wildlife.

The subtle noises which layered her senses with information were lost, the natural scents carried along in the wind were gone. Her normal route was sliced by rounded tracks confusing her progresses as she retraced back on herself. Each turbine had a garden of tended grass and concrete hard standing for vehicles. Impulse drove her on a wide excursion along a sheep trail with a steep drop on one side to a valley towns lights. The path was narrow and rocky so she allowed time for the group to bunch up. She moved to the back pushing the male cub to take the lead. There was no direction required from her plus she wanted to test his resolve whilst keeping the cubs moving along. He relished the opportunity and paced along well, even stopping at any twist or turn to survey potential threats and check the group were intact. The natural order was shaping up well, in this short period of time they had gained a togetherness that would continue for two full seasons until they were fully grown and ready to strike out on their own.

Their first night was almost over as they turned the hillside, skirted a reservoir and headed on to the waterfalls. Tonmawr first found sanctuary in this area after leaving her mother some five years before. The waterfall network provided ample cover and rich pickings of wildlife. The cubs were exhausted as Tonmawr found a familiar den overlooking a pool under the cover of cascading water. She marked the scored bark of a large fir tree, her own scent still lingered within the knurled trunk. Together they settled to sleep as daybreak awakened the crows.

Grey picked up the family scent from their abandoned sheep's carcass and tracked the odor towards the wind farm covering ground at three times their rate. The high ridge line was traversed at pace and he soon arrived at the turbines skirting around the same sheep trail without the need for rest. He would soon arrive at the waterfalls.

Chapter 8

'Who was it Alan?'

Alan Price shook off the droplets from his waxed coat and replied to his brother Tom. 'Martin Quinn from the wind turbines waiting for his security guard to turn up that's all.'

Tom Price poured himself another whiskey, took a slow satisfying slurp and slammed his glass down on the kitchen table. 'I knew this would be trouble for us Alan but you wouldn't fucking listen! They are right under our feet now with this wind farm, even using your yard. I need access to that barn without those contractors nosing about.'

Alan Price looked down on his brother across the table with distain, curbing his temper and rocking the back of his chair with clenched fists. 'If you hadn't given all Dads' buildings away you wouldn't need my barn would you!'

Alan and Tom Price had been at loggerheads since the passing of their father. Old Harry Price had a stronghold on the area. He was a respected farmer who was not only a successful landowner but generous to his tenants. His business thrived despite the downturn in farming and the difficulties of the legislation and grant schemes. His secret was people, he nurtured and encouraged his tenants, provided good housing and equipment. His downfall was his will, a three way split between his sons, Alan the eldest, Jim the middle son and the youngest Tom.

Jim was from his fathers mold and was content to take on the family home on the edge of the Brecon's. A rambling mansion which he held onto, far too large for his needs but nostalgia and the memory of his father, and grandfather who built the place, tied him. Alan was the business man, shrewd and unforgiving. One of his first acts on receiving his vast ribbon of land was to sell a lease to Western Power for the development of windfarms. This cut a ribbon of roads and tracks through the uplands of the Afan Forest and rendered lower pastures redundant. He closed the dairy side of the business and put many locals out of work. The once thriving dairy provided the co-operative with a steady supply of locally produced milk. Tom was left with the scraps of land which were rented to smallholders and mixed arable fields. Tom had no interest in farming, he had spent his youth and now his middle age bumbling through life. His only interest being hunting game. His network of friends from similar background stumbled from hunt to hunt around south and mid Wales. He funded this lavish lifestyle through selling any scrap of land he could, mainly for housing development or business use.

'Ok, Ok, Ok, I've had enough of your bickering, we need to sort out this weekend's visitors and make arrangements for the week after. If we want more of this business we have to make this run smoothly, these people won't be messed about and want the best. I need updates gentlemen for my meeting tomorrow in Cheltenham, Alan you've sorted out the rifles and ammunition I presume? Tom I trust you have the entertainment and Jim, how is the accommodation and catering coming along? With arms spread wide palms facing up Claire De Mota glared at the trio and wanted answers.

Jim was the first to answer. 'Have these people of yours ever shot a Deer before Claire?'

Of course Jim, they are not amateurs, I've organised Highland trips for them and they know their hunting. That is why we have to be professional if this is to succeed. I've arranged for the hospitality company to arrive at your farm on Friday morning to set up the marquee and prep the food Jim, have you finished the fourth bedroom suite yet?'

'It's looking palatial Claire as requested, my house now resembles the Ritz I just hope all this investment is worth it.'

'Jim you rattle around in an eight bedroomed mansion of course it's worth it, I could rent out that space every weekend if you'd let me'.

Jim smiled at Claire. 'I suppose I could move into the barn conversion.'

Claire continued, 'Exactly Jim, now come on will it all be ready?'

'Yes Claire there are four suites and three double rooms, the dining area and hall are set up, reception room has the open fire as requested m'lady.'

'Very funny Jim.' Claire raised a smile then turned to Alan. 'They should all be bringing their own but just in case we need enough rifles and ammunition for say four people, is that ok?'

'Can't see that being a problem Claire unless they bring anything exotic but I'd expect if they do they'll have their own cartridges as well. There's a Ruger and three Browning's available plus my spare Sako 75, the .308 Winchesters should suit most but I've varied the weights, my only concern is keeping them pissed up toffs safe.'

The group continued their preparations and as Claire got up to leave she ushered the youngest brother Tom to one side. ' Don't let them wind you up Tom, I need you to be focused this weekend Im relying on you to introduce Paul and sell the Panther idea ok?'

'Don't worry Claire, they don't bother me, bit of an issue with the female Panther though, had to move it back to Pauls this afternoon as its not looking good. Hopefully he'll sort it out before Saturday. If not we should have the young male available but we'll have to sedate him, he's a bit lively.'

Claire's anger rose, her firm grip on Toms wrist twisted as she leant in to his face. 'So where is the young male Tom, I thought you had him caged at the practice?'

Toms confidence drained when talking to Claire, his discomfort was clear as he avoided her glare. 'The tracker isn't picking up his signal, not sure why but we have a good idea where he is, there was a doe killed yesterday over at Guys farm so he can't be far.'

'This is all getting messy Tom, I'll speak to Paul and sort him out, you concentrate on getting the Panther ready for Saturday.' Claire's grasp released and Tom lifted his arm to rub away the pain whilst looking over to his two elder brothers hoping they did not sense his fear.

Chapter 9

Martin found himself stood in Louise's kitchen as she unwrapped the card lids from the foil containers. 'Steaming hot takeaway Chinese food always smelt so good.' He thought.

Watching her expert movements around the narrow galley dishing out the hot food and cold wine Louise poured her life to date over Martin. His occasional questions did not interrupt her stride as she narrated her failed marriage, her two sons, her network of close friends and her Panther research.

The narrow kitchen opened at the far end to a granite breakfast bar with two stools where they ate and drank to satisfy their appetite before resting back, full and content.

'We needed that Martin, I was starving, so tell me about you, I've been boring you with my life so far.'

'It's not as exciting as yours Louise I can assure you of that. I've been moving around from contract to contract since I can remember, mainly in construction. I did my first wind turbine job ten years ago, although it's been good for the past couple of years being in the same place. I've got used to it I guess. Still single much to my mother's disdain, and she constantly reminds me about grandchildren. I really don't know where the years have gone!'

Louise smiled and interrupted. 'So how old are you Martin?'

He smiled a knowing smile and replied. 'Forty-two this year, and you?'

Louise looked up and ushered 'Too close to fifty I'm afraid, I'll be Forty-eight this summer.'

Martin was taken aback as he had reckoned she was younger than he was and with genuine shock replied. 'Really! Well Louise it must be the outside air or is it the risks you take which keep you looking so young?'

'Oh please, I'm an old hag and you know it!' They both laughed out loud and Martin reached out his hand touching Louise's hand across the cold granite surface. Their eyes locked together and the silent moment of knowing seeped into them both at the same time.

Louise bolted up and said. 'Wait there Martin I want to show you something.'

Martin drew a breath as he waited, wondering what she was going to do. Hoping for an invite to the sofa or even maybe the bedroom. Louise breezed back in with a laptop and set it down so they could both see the screen, she half sat on his lap and put her left arm around him for balance with the toes of her right foot on the stools foot rest. Martin felt the warmness of her body and curled his right arm around her waist as she asked. 'Is this ok?'

The screen revealed a Google map of the swathes of forest and moorland covering Tonmawr, the village where Louise lived. She zoomed in and placed the cursor over the wind turbine installation. Martin recognised the ground and pointed out Alan Prices farmhouse. Louise took a drink from her glass of wine and set it back down behind the screen before starting. ' Ok so you know the area, if you notice I've uploaded the map so I can annotate it with sightings and territories. The red dots are sightings confirmed, the yellow are unconfirmed. The black boundary lines are where the territories have been charted. If you hover over the dots a link pops up to photos and documents about the sightings. For example, errrr, are here we go, this sighting was reported last summer by a man called Mal Harris whilst he was out walking his dog north of the waterfalls. We visited the site and found tracks, and if I open the other link, there, photo and cast of the footprint with measurements.'

'Wow Im impressed Louise, so where is my sighting from yesterday?'

'Give me a chance Martin Jeeez, I've been busy if you recall! So this map is for sightings of a Panther I call Tonmawr, named after where she was first spotted about five years ago. If you notice she's been sighted about a dozen times and we've manged to track her boundary which is marked by the black line.'

Martin moved the curser around the map and was in awe at the number of sightings and the distances travelled. He hovered over the northern part of the territory line which was some twenty miles from the turbines and asked. 'How do you track the Panthers over such distances?'

'Well it's not just me Martin, the people I was with in the pub last night, Gill, her two boys and a couple of other friends all contribute. Rhys and Lewis, Gills boys, regularly go out tracking up to Brecon. They have found other Panther tracks as well on their travels. We all update the forum on our website with information and sightings. Some of the more detailed information we don't publish such as territories and dens we have come across.'

Martin was trying to piece together the recent events and looked puzzled as he listened because the incidents didn't add up, so he asked. ' Ok so I get the female Panthers sightings because I've seen it for myself but the kill you mentioned in the horses field, that doesn't seem to fit?'

Louise shifted off Martins lap and stood whilst still leaning on the worktop on her elbows, Martins gaze fell to her curvaceous behind which as she leaned forward revealed a slither of skin above the waist band of her black jeans. She looked over her shoulder and answered Martin, noticing his gaze. 'Your right, it doesn't fit with Tonmaws' pattern of behaviour. However if you look at this other map'.

Louise opened a different file marked 'males'. 'Here we go, this map plots the other sightings and tracks for the males we know about. We are almost certain there are three fully grown males in the south and west Wales area although their territory is limited to the rural parts.' Louise zoomed in to the Carmarthenshire region west of Tonmawr territory. 'Out west is where the males originated as did Tonmawr and her mother, we haven't seen her mother for a couple of years. Gill has a theory that she moved further west when Tonmawr settled here and has probably died naturally. So the Panther you saw in the barn I think is one of the males, probably one we call Grey, he has a distinctive grey mark above his shoulder, here we've got a grainy image from a wildlife camera the boys set up. They have vast territories and rarely visit this area, which makes me wonder how he was caught and by whom. He most certainly wasn't the male that attacked the Deer in Annie's field last night because you saw this one in the barn earlier in the evening. I've taken some samples and have photos which I'll try to match up with the other information we have.'

Martin was beginning to see how it all fitted together, he smiled as Louise turned to look at him after her explanation. 'So Louise who would want to capture the Panther and why?'

Louise stood up, arched her back with hands on her hips to stretch out and pulled another bottle of wine from the fridge. Pouring the wine Martin thanked her and she continued. ' As I said earlier Alan Price must know, he lives there and rents out the barn. My gut feel is that his younger brother Tom and his crowd came across the Panther whilst out poaching Deer and have somehow managed to capture it, its probably injured or been shot, but Im worried about what he's going to do next with it, unless it's already dead. What's bothering me the most is that someone is interfering with the natural order. These animals have learnt to survive amongst us and rarely attack stock or pets. I think these beautiful Panthers have the right to live here and be left alone.'

Martin took a sip of his wine and checked his watch. 'Im beginning to understand The Prices now

Louise, I agree they're a bad bunch with lots of land and money and it's just a big playground for them. Be careful, in my experience they won't think twice about hurting anyone who gets in their way. Look I'd love to finish this wine and maybe some more but I've got an early start so…'Louise put down her glass and moved close to Martin.

'Running out on me again Martin? That's two nights on the trot, Im beginning to think you don't like me.' Her smile belied the truth as Martin put down his glass moving in even closer to Louise.

Chapter 10

Tonmawr was woken not by noise but the scent of the large male predator. Any noise was smothered by the reaction of the cascading falls of water on rock. Scent was masked by fresh water and vegetation. No line of sight could arouse her, blinded by shadow and mist. Her cubs were unaware of the impending confrontation. Tonmawr could do nothing other than wait in still silence armed with the element of surprise.

Grey took in the scent of the mist laden cold air. He did not react nor quicken his search but merely drank from the swirling pool. He took rest and worked out his next direction as the fading afternoon light touched the pool surface. As his scent rose within the spray Tonmawr sat fast on the edge of a flat rock at the den entrance which provided a springboard to the route down to the pool. If the large male predator were to climb the moss laden rock steps from the pool up to the den she would pounce, having the upper ground and ability to strike first and shock him into withdrawal.

The cubs did not stir, exhausted from the journey they were in a deep sleep. Tonmawr groomed her large paws, individual claws were extended and the join at the pad cleaned using her barbed tongue. Her deep brown coat had a thick and healthy sheen, she was feeling strong and refreshed from the last feed which would provide the energy required for the next few days. Grey lumbered to the bottom of the damp, moss covered rock steps and inhaled the scent from the ferns which sprung from each crevice. He looked up into the falling water, splashes of cold fresh liquid brought about a sharp shake of his head as he skulked up to the next rock. The further up he climbed the more he came out of the saturated air. He felt exposed as his taught hind legs fought to purchase the rock, pushing his full weight in short jerks whilst clawing with extended front limbs. His slow scramble stopped briefly as he managed to shuffle his four pads close together on one step and embrace the rock face with his long slender tail. He reviewed his progress by looking down to the pool, this minute movement tipped his weight momentarily over the fulcrum of a precarious balance.

As he looked up towards the den Tonmawr struck hard on the males shoulder with a downwards swipe sending him headlong towards the pool. He struck the rocks and glided in heavy bumps whilst straining to claw leverage from anything he could reach. Tonmawr had a fierce growl which demonstrated her solid position and physical size. The male gulped air as his hind legs slipped in the bottom of the pool struggling to keep his head above water. He scrambled to dry land and he shook violently then looked up to see Tonmawr towering over him with an intimidating growl.

This display of power, tactic and confidence hit Grey hard, he had never experienced this level of pain and intimidation, no experience of play with older siblings, no memory of the strength in parents. Although larger in stature he was no match for Tonmawr. His next movement was one of subservience to Tonmawr, he acknowledged her higher standing and lowered his head whilst moving to the flat mud bank where he lay on his side in submission. Tonmawr with rounded high shoulders marched towards the male. His scent sparked memories of her mate. Now she had the upper hand and confidence to inspect the male with intimacy. His underside rose and fell quickened by his short breaths, his hind legs of highly defined muscle above the shin were different, as was the fur colouring, much darker than her mate apart from the small grey patch on his shoulder. His head shape and eyes were identical to her mate as Tonmawr leant in and inhaled. Grey attempted to groom her but she would not allow him and emitted a long deep growl with incisors on show. Tonmawr walked away and sprayed the tree stumps on the bank, she uncoiled back to the male and in a mock pounce shook Grey into standing. He looked her in the eye and then bounded away into the darkness.

Victory was hers but he would learn from this encounter and perhaps return. He also knew that Tonmawr was protecting her cubs, but his urge to kill them and mate with her was lost during the encounter. A more powerful urge returned, to hone his proven skills in killing Deer, the taste of succulent satisfying warm flesh and blood were a strong addiction.

Tonmawr was however not as sure, the unpredictable nature of this male and his ability to track her course was still a threat. She had won a tactical battle, had been in control and was confident he wouldn't attack, but for how long she didn't know. As she climbed up to the den, shafts of evening sunlight filtered through the waterfall projecting light spots which danced on the wet rocks.

The cubs awoke as mother entered the den, unsteady on their feet they greeted her wet fur and brushed against her warm body. She licked and nuzzled each cub in turn with love and patience. They were preparing to move again under the cover of darkness. Their second night on the move would be far more treacherous.

Tonmawr, like the night before, surveyed her surroundings and longed to remain in the comfort of familiar territory. The cubs sensed the next adventure was imminent. Their mother was still wary of the large male predator and edged down on to the rocks towards the pool. The cubs were able to negotiate the descent with ease seeing it as a game. The playground of waterfalls and pools distracted their progress as the cubs curiosity was kept alive at every turn. Birds were taking in water and bustling as dusk enveloped the network of streams, trees and rocks.

They rose high above the falls into a clear night lit by a full moon. The crisp darkness was welcome relief from the previous days downpours. Tonmawr plotted their course with a natural ability keeping their forms in shadow as much as possible. The opportunity to eat was limited to birds and rabbits and their need was not essential however any prospect that arose could not be discounted. Tonmawr stalked a hedgline which led to a densely wooded area and settled low amongst fern outcrops, the cubs followed their mothers lead. Silence was broken by the subtle sounds of rabbits bobbing and scuttling amongst grass and bushes, they were searching out the succulent bulbs of wild garlic and snowdrops. Tonmawr waited, motionless, until the rabbits were far enough from their burrows that she could strike. A chase was always required with rabbit and their turn of speed meant a kill was difficult unless they were in open ground and away from the burrows. The cubs were about to learn this tactic from their mother for the first time. As Tonmawr focused on a cluster of three rabbits all facing away from her the male cub broke their containment and sprung forward. The alerted rabbits looked, span around and bounded into the open field, disappearing behind grass tussocks and re-appearing. The male cub lead the charge and soon pounced on a struggling doe. Tonmawr was able to snare another as the two girls chased the remaining rabbit into the darkness. The male cub had claimed his first kill.

Tonmawr, with a dead rabbit in her mouth rounded on the male cub and encouraged him to follow away from the glare of the moon. The pair stepped high with their prizes and met with the heavy breathing and empty mouths of the two female cubs. The family trotted onwards to the next field to find more cover before tearing into their catch. The females eagerly pounced and teased in the hope of a morsel but nothing was left for them.

With no time to rest progress needed to be made. Tonmawr was driven to clear her territory and find a new home on unfamiliar ground well before daybreak.

Chapter 11

On the first chime of the alarm Martin dragged leaden legs from the warmth of an unfamiliar bed. He walked with a heavy head down the stairs wearing just his boxers and a T shirt to find the kettle. Louise was already fully dressed and laughed at Martin. ' I thought you had to be up early, I've been out to feed horses, walk dogs and milk cows already'.

Martin looked over to Louise as he filled the kettle,. 'You were doing ok, I believed you until you mentioned milking cows.'

'Ok so I may be exaggerating, but for someone who claims to work hard and long hours you're not exactly with it in the mornings are you?'

Martin leaned on the countertop of Louise's kitchen and replied. ' Ok you got me I'm rubbish in the mornings, it takes three coffees before I can function.' Louise washed her hands in the sink and dried them on a tea towel taken from the radiator. She held Martins waist from behind and kissed his neck.

'Thank you for staying last night'. Martin was aroused and spun around to hold her hips.

'No, thank you'. Martin hadn't felt this good for a long time and kissed Louise on the lips. Louise finished making the coffee as Martin went back upstairs to wash and dress. They returned to the same breakfast bar where they had shared their first meal and Martin drank his coffee.

'Right I need to get a move on Martin, could you drop me at the pub so I can pick up my car please? I've got a busy day at the practice'. Martin slugged the last of his strong black coffee and wiped his mouth with the back of his hand.

' Ready when you are Louise.'

The short journey to The Crown took ten minutes during which they yakked without pausing. Martin felt comfortable with Louise, they got on so well he thought. Her persona hadn't changed from the night before, friendly, open and without regret.

Before she jumped out of his truck Martin held her hand and asked. ' So what is your next move with Alan Price and the Panther?'

Louise stopped herself for a moment, she was fired up ready for whatever the day was going to reveal but took Martins calming tones as a check on her enthusiasm. 'Well the first thing is to analyse these samples.'

'Samples?' Martin asked her with a puzzled look.

'Oh, err, I took samples from the attack in Annie's field, thought I'd told you?'

'You probably did, so much has happened in the last two days.' Martin responded.

Louise leant in and kissed Martin full on the lips whilst holding his face with her left palm. 'I'll call you this evening and let you know how things are developing.'

'Have a good day, thanks again for last night, I really enjoyed your company Louise.'

With that Louise jumped out of the truck and unlocked her frost covered car. The VW Passat Estate fired into life at the first turn of the key as Louise clasped her hands and waited for the heater to warm her cold body.

The journey to work at Oaktree Veterinary Practice allowed Louise time to reflect on the previous twenty four hours. She was awake most of the previous night but to her own surprise fully awake and excited about this new day. As she turned into the practice car park the lights from the reception and the surgery illuminated the way through frosted glass. It was just before seven a.m. but Gill was already in work.

Gill Hughes one of the three partners at the practice was an experienced vet. She was as practical as a school mistress but full of fun and mischief which attracted Louise as they could talk about anything and always seemed to end up laughing. Gill was a natural hard worker. Even though she could afford to relax a little she was always the first in and last to leave. Her passion for the pets she treated inspired Louise who was content being an assistant at the practice. Often helping during emergency surgery but in the main Louise took care of the day to day ordering of medicines, scheduling the staff and managing the appointments. Gills eldest son Rhys worked on the reception and Lewis an undergraduate was studying Veterinary Science at Swansea University. He lived at home and was often found at the practice assisting Gill. Louise loved the family atmosphere as she missed her own sons who were both away working in London.

Louise picked up her samples and walked through reception and into the surgery suite. 'Good morning Gill, you piss the bed again?'

Gill span around on her high stool pulled down her reading glasses and replied. 'Well look who had a shag last night then, you don't waste much time do you?'

Louise giggled and replied. 'Gill don't, is it that obvious?'

'Err yes, your beaming Lou, and look like a weight has been lifted off your shoulders, I take it from your text last night that Martin ended up staying over? When I saw your car at The Crown we went in and no one had seen you, I was worried that's all, and that's why I messaged you.'

Louise hugged Gill and carried on. 'That's ok Gill, I know it looked a bit strange, a lot has happened and I need your help, I've got some samples to analyse if you don't mind.'

Gill viewed the clear plastic bags and laid them out on her worktop. 'So what do we have here Louise?'

Louise went on to explain the events of last night at the barn and the attack in Annie's field. 'So what were you thinking going into Alans barn? You could have been arrested Louise if he'd have seen you, what did Martin say about what you found?'

Louise felt she was being scolded and apologetically replied. 'I didn't tell him Gill, I don't know why, obviously he was there with me waiting in his truck but I told him the barn was locked up. I guess I don't want him to get into trouble and lose his job.'

Gill shook her head and turned to Louise. ' Ok I get it but when he does find out what then?' Gill turned back to the first sample and held it to the light. Louise took a pen from the worktop and pointed at the flesh samples taken from the Deer.

'This is from the Deer, see the claw marks, we need to measure and compare with the data we have, I think it's that male Rhys caught on camera, the one we named Grey.'

'Ok that'll take a while, I'll ask Lewis to look when he comes in later.' Gill picked up the second sample bag containing the fur and poo from the barn. Louise explained how the cage in the barn was mottled with fur and there was little in the way of wet samples. Gill squeezed the sample of poo through the bag. ' We might get something from this, at least what it had eaten, maybe enough moisture content to get a profile. I'll take a look under the scope and perhaps speak to my friend at the lab if we find anything interesting that's worth exploring more. The fur in this bag is definitely Panther, I've looked at so many I can tell straight away, this was from the wire mesh you said. So explain to me again how you got in there?'

Louise was changing into her work clothes as Gill continued to look at the samples and turn on the microscope. Louise buttoned up her dark blue cotton work top and adjusted her name badge then replied as she walked back to Gill.

'So the barn was divided into three bays, the farthest one has a new roller steel door at the front and a small door at the side you can only get in through the second bay. I couldn't believe it when I first saw it but the padlock was a combination lock and then it dawned on me, it was Pauls lock from the drugs cabinet at his practice. I tried the combination and bingo I was in!'

Gill held her hand on her mouth and in shock said. ' Jeeez Louise so Paul has been using the barn and he must know about the Panther!'

'Exactly Gill, but what do I do next? I want to confront him, but with this injunction, and he's still involved with the Prices.'

Gill emptied the contents onto the glass slide and turned to Louise. ' Well for starters you can't confront him, he's unstable Louise as you well know. I haven't seen him for a few weeks but I've heard he's not looking good. I can't work out how or why they would keep a Panther at the barn. All the research and tracking we have done over the past few years and we haven't even come close to one, ok we know their patterns, territories and numbers but they are so elusive Louise, I just don't get it.'

Louise looked puzzled and replied. ' Well here's my theory for what it's worth, Tom Price came across it by chance whilst poaching Deer, they must have shot it and taken it back to the barn. They use Paul maybe to carry out surgery or check it over. Then I guess they are going to release it back. It must be a male, but it can't be the same male that attacked the Deer in Annie's field, so we have two males in the area. Tonmawr must be on the move also, she wouldn't be comfortable here with two males roaming her territory.'

Gill nodded in agreement and added. 'Plus we haven't seen Tonmawrs mother for over three years,

Lewis and Rhys were tracking her well when they were staying in Carmarthenshire four summers ago. They even caught her with five cubs on the wildlife camera, so what has happened to them?' The two women looked at each other in silence trying to work out what had changed.

Gill tapped her spatula on the countertop. 'Ok here's what we do, so this weekend we are all up at your forest lodge planning to do some tracking updating the database and maps yes?' Louise excitedly agreed. 'Tonmawr is our priority, from the sightings at Christmas we are pretty sure she was pregnant, and Lewis has a good idea where her dens are, I'll ask the boys to pull in all the auto cameras, I think they have about a dozen running at the moment. We can review the footage, then start tracking from there.'

Louise was dismayed, as that was pretty much what they had planned to do she thought. 'But what about the barn and Paul? Gill rose to her feet and looked directly at Louise. ' Just forget it Louise, let them play their games, our priority is preservation and research, if what they are doing interferes with the natural order then we will act, but let's get the facts first.'

'Your such a bore Gill but your right! So we have a full appointment book and a long day in front of us'.

'Louise I'm sure we will work this one out we always do, and at the weekend we can have some fun as well, it's going to be a cold dry weekend up in the forest, we can get that fire going, good food and wine of course. Hey here's a thought why don't you invite Martin up on the Saturday, you could do with a good man in your life, he could meet the boys and help out with the tracking?'

Louise smiled and replied. ' What a good idea, not quite sure he'll be interested in tracking though, plus we've only just met I don't want to scare him off.'

'Well if you don't ask him I will.'

'Hey leave him he's mine!'

' Oh Im more than happy with Mike thank you, no worries there, It'll be company for Mike as well?'

'Well let me ask him first Gill. Now come on let's get on with it.'

Chapter 12

Paul Morris was feeling that life could not get any more complicated than it already was as he examined the heavily sedated animal lying on its side on the operating table. Tom Price had transported her twenty four hours ago and Paul had made no progress with a diagnosis. Tom had just arrived for an update, he was agitated and asked. ' So what's wrong with it?'

Paul looked at the vital signs on the monitors and shook his head. 'Everything looks normal except blood pressure. I'll have to do some more tests'.

Tom dragged the surgery door open with force causing it to bang against its stopper. 'Just sort it out Paul, we need it for Saturday. I'll be back in an hour.' An equally forceful slam of the door as Tom left sent a shudder through the ceiling tiles and light fittings. Paul looked up at the lights then turned his attention back to the forlorn animal before him.

Since his split with Louise, Paul struggled to sustain focus on the programme he had signed up to. The root cause of the break up was Pauls arrogance, and he knew it. Paul and Louise were both excited when they first encountered the Panther which now lay before him, dying. The female had been captured by the pair and their agreement was to analyse the species, take samples and catalogue, then release her back into the wild. Paul however had an ego which surpassed his bond with Louise. He had been working with a team of vets in South Korea and in his haste to impress promised a specimen for further research and manipulation. This betrayal of trust had been the final straw for Louise.

Paul administered the third sedative in twenty-four hours to the animals hind leg, he knew this had to be the last before it was moved back to the barn. He picked up his mobile and pressed to call Dr Kam Myung Dae.

'Hello Dr Paul my friend how can I help you?'

'Hello Dr Kam thank you for answering my call, it must be late in Seoul.'

'Yes Paul it is but I am still working at the University, actually working on our project. I should have some promising news soon.'

'Dr Kam I have a problem with Number One, we still have high blood pressure?'

'That is for two days now, I need to log on Dr Paul, let me take a look at the data and I call you, ok'.

'No problem it's all hooked up and we are on-line. Thank you speak soon.'

Paul turned to the array of six monitors on the wall behind the operating table and watched as Dr Kam logged in and viewed the live data from the animal. His mobile phone rang and he answered without looking at the number. 'Hi Paul its Louise, are you ok to talk?'

Paul walked away from his workstation and replied. ' Err just a moment let me go somewhere quiet.' As he reached the quiet of the reception area Louise asked.

'It's nothing urgent just wanted to talk to you about the boys that's all, maybe I could pop over later?'

Paul held the phone to his chest for a moment and looked around the room, his brain whirling as he searched for an excuse. ' Im a bit busy today sorry I'll be at the surgery till late, how about tomorrow?'

Louise sensed there was an issue, and she felt she knew why so she pressed further.

'What is more important than our kids Paul, and I won't disturb you whilst you work, just a quick chat face to face that's all?' Paul was cornered and didn't have a reason strong enough to counter Louise's argument.

'Ok, Ok, but not at the surgery, come round to the house, say seven thirty?'

Louise agreed and hung up, she looked over at Gill and said. 'Ok he's fallen for it Gill, hell be out of the surgery by seven.'

'Im not sure about this Lou, why should we get involved? And how do you propose to break into his surgery, find something and get back to his place in half an hour?' Louise put her arm around Gill and replied.

'We need to gather facts Gill like you said, it's obvious Paul is involved and we know they have a Panther in captivity, if that isn't interfering with the natural order then tell me what is?'

Dr Kam Myung Dae stood and looked at the array of monitors which covered his office wall. In the centre was the live feed to Paul Morris' surgery. The Panthers vital signs were refreshing automatically every three or four seconds. Dr Kams' demeaner was unassuming and softly spoken, he turned from the monitors to address the four students wearing white coats, all wearing glasses and carrying clipboards. 'So which of you can provide a diagnosis to this condition?' Quietness fell as the students studied the data before them. Dr Kam continued. ' Firstly you are aware of the age of the animal almost into its ninth year, its pedigree is unknown however we can assume there are no hereditary diseases. Births have all been healthy and numbered between three and five for each litter. We have been actively monitoring the animal for five years and this is the first occasion where high blood pressure is not being controlled. Dr Paul has administered thirty millilitres of sedatives in three doses over the past twenty four hours, I must add this is not due to the condition but for the purpose of safe transport.'

Dr Kam smiled as he looked at the students, he then left the office and walked with confidence along a brightly lit corridor to a set of double swinging doors. Pushing the left door open led Dr Kam into a large open ward lined on each side with cages. The first cage on the left was empty, the second housed a fully grown Panther, jet black in colour, the label on the cage stated ' Male 2 yrs. #27'. The third cage was empty and the fourth housed a similar animal, its label read the same except the number which read #28. Dr Kam knelt in front of the cage and beckoned the Panther who pounced forward and nuzzled Dr Kams hand. The room was brightly lit and as Dr Kam turned to survey his surroundings one of the four students approached him. The girl had a quizzical look and bowed before asking.

' Dr Kam, the animal has, in my opinion, a foetus dead and the body is trying to reject it.'

Dr Kam put his arm on the girls slender shoulder and replied. ' Well done, you are of course correct as you always are my girl. I suggest that you call Dr Paul and provide him with the information and your intended course of action. It will not be easy for him so arrange to visit Paul at your earliest convenience.'

The student smiled and replied. 'Yes father, thank you.'

Paul Morris slumped into his chair and tossed the mobile phone across his desk after hearing the news that he needed to perform a c-section on the animal within five days. He then opened his desk draw and removed a round plastic container, as he unscrewed the lid he looked over at the forlorn creature and said 'Ok girl it's gonna be a tough few days for you.' He removed another small bag from the container and spilled the contents onto the work surface. The white powder was chopped and caressed with care as his head bobbed down. He inhaled through one nostril, taking the full dose of cocaine deep inside.

Louise drove past the front entrance of Paul Morris' veterinary practice in second gear, slow enough to observe without suspicion. There was only one car in the car park, a silver Range Rover which she presumed to be Pauls. She continued along the road to a large industrial estate and turned up the hill and parked up with a clear view of rear car park of Paul Morris's surgery.

It was a building she knew well. Her time there had shifted from childhood bliss working with her father to the grind of coping with Pauls mood swings. The single storey square red brick building was purpose built by her father in the early seventies. The architect he employed was forward thinking for the time and incorporated the needs of a veterinary practice that would not be out of place in today's designs. Parking for farm vehicles, horse boxes was comfortable with the functionality to drive all the way around the building without reversing. Large double doors at the back of the building with a covered walkway to adjoining stables catered for the larger animals. She first met Paul when he joined the practice directly from university in 1989, he was a bright open and friendly man who was passionate about his profession. Louise gradually got to know him and within two years they were an item, her father gave them his blessing and they were married within the year. Paul was an asset to the practice and was soon offered a partnership with Louise's father. Paul had no shortage of money, his family were Gloucestershire farmers and had, as it appeared, unlimited wealth. Paul invested heavily in the practice procuring the latest equipment to assist with treatments and surgery. His surgery techniques developed alongside Louise's fathers knowledge and skill. It was his research contacts and teamwork with universities which brought the practice a high standing in the profession. They partnered clinical trials and were the favoured practice for the introduction of new techniques. An internship at the practice was considered an honour by any student worldwide.

Louise looked down on the building without remorse, to her now it was just an empty shell. Her father's intimate legacy had been replaced by a functional, cold business, devoid of compassion. The painful split was stripped of reason by Pauls money and his ability to force Louise into accepting a buy out through a bullish solicitor. Louise was able to start afresh without the need to work or worry financially. This freedom afforded Louise the opportunity to renew her passion, her love of the countryside and its natural wildlife. The Panthers raised this to a new level as her compulsion to protect, enhance and nurture their natural development and survival filled her waking hours. Her plan was to wait to see Paul leave before trying the key that she had kept for the rear door. Gill would wait outside Pauls house to confirm his presence.

As Louise sat waiting Tom Price pulled up at the front of the building and barged his way into Pauls surgery. 'Right, is she ready?'

'She cant go anywhere Tom, I need to operate so you'll have to cancel.'

Tom Price punched the metal cabinet above Pauls desk and shouted. 'Fuck, we can't cancel Paul, what about one of the males?'

'No I can't do it Tom they are part of the project and they're not ready and in any case Dr Kam is sending....' Paul stopped mid-sentence as Toms fist again crashed into the cabinet.

'Just remember Paul you owe me a lot of money and this is how you suggested I'd get it back, Claire will not cancel at this late stage, there's more at stake than you know.'

Paul started to shake and looked around the room for inspiration, but he was sinking. As well as the money that Tom Price had loaned him, Claire also invested in his surgery building. Paul had overstretched his borrowing with the bank, he had re-mortgaged twice and was running out of capital when he approached Claire. She agreed to provide forty thousand pounds but in exchange for a fifty percent share of the business. It was an outlandish and cruel exchange, Claire's half was worth at least a million pounds. Paul did not see it, he only saw the cash he needed to buy the equipment he needed to keep the programme going.

'You released number seven again last week, and the tracker stopped signalling yesterday, so he can't be far from here, plus we know he was at Guys farm last night so why ...'

Tom for the third time smashed his fist and shouted. 'Forget it Paul, get me a Panther to the back door now, Im taking it to the barn in your Range Rover, mines full of stuff, meet me at the barn later.' Tom grabbed Pauls keys from the desk and made his way to the front of the building.

Tom Price left through the front door of the practice at six-forty-five, he got into Pauls Range Rover and drove around to the back door, obscuring Louise's view of the double doors, he dropped down the boot hatch and went inside. A male adult Panther had been moved to a transport cage and with the use of an extendable trolley he raised it to the level of the boot and pushed the cage with ease and closed the hatch.

Louise did not see the animal being loaded nor did she suspect anything. As she waited for Paul to leave the surgery her mobile rang, it was Martin.

'Hi how are you?'

'Im good thanks Lou, just wondering if you're going to the pub that's all, maybe we could meet up?' Louise knew this was coming, she enjoyed Martins company but needed to focus on gathering information and keeping in touch with Gill. She tried to sound excited and replied.

' I'd love to Martin but Im working late with Gill at the practice and could do with an early night sorry.'

'Hey that's ok, just didn't want you thinking it was a one night stand, not a problem we can catch up at the weekend'.

Louise was relieved and replied. 'Sure I'd love to, oh by the way, and you don't have to give me an answer straight away but I've got a lodge up in the forest and I'm up there this weekend, Gill is coming up with her husband and boys to do some tracking, but it would be nice to see you and you'd get on great with everyone.'

Martin went silent for a few seconds and was caught off guard. 'Yeah sure, sounds good, I'll let you know for definite tomorrow if that's ok? I just need to check the work schedule for this weekend.'

Louise was distracted by movement at the practice and didn't really catch all of what Martin said, she replied 'Ok give me a call then, gotta go.'

Martin felt a little confused and thought, maybe I've upset her by not saying yes? Maybe she didn't really want me to come? His schedule was crammed at the moment so he wasn't lying. He mused. It was Friday tomorrow so I can call her and confirm, I would like to spend more time getting to know her and the lodge sounds like the perfect place, even with her friends there. Martin walked from the kitchen into the living room of the house he had been renting for close on two years. The two bedroomed terrace was easy to look after, its furnishings were simple and comfortable. Music was always on in the background, he enjoyed the quiet company of his favourite bands, mostly heavy rock from the seventies and eighties mixed with the latest Metal and Punk. The small flat screen TV was rarely on except for the occasional rugby game or late evening drama when the need to switch off from the day was required. Tonight he also needed rest and he slumped onto the low sofa, put his head back and drifted away thinking of Louise.

As Louise ended her call with Martin she saw the Range Rover speed away from the building. She sent a text to Gill ' Paul just left in silver Range Rover x'. Louise left her car parked in the industrial estate and made her way on foot across a vacant plot of land earmarked for future development. A small drop down a bank led her to the low wire mesh fenceline of the practice car park. She presumed CCTV in the car park was still active as she pulled up the hood on her coat. The fire door of the practice was in darkness as Louise plied the keys and selected a Yale key with a red tab attached. The key opened the lock and Louise opened the door, stepped inside and pulled the exit bar behind her until the light click confirmed it was closed. The rear lobby was dimly lit by a fire exit sign above her head allowing her just enough light to navigate.

Louise moved with confident steps along the corridor but checked her stride as her training shoes squeaked on the polished vinyl floor. A more heal toe stepped gait quelled the irritating noise. She knew the place was empty but still felt the need to be as quiet as possible. Pauls surgery door was open but in darkness as she bobbed her head inside to look before entering. She took out her phone and illuminated the room with its backlight, just enough to prevent her bumping into obstacles. Since her last visit the room layout had changed. The examination table used for pets had gone, the cabinets holding drugs which covered the length of one wall had also been removed. In their place were monitors covering the wall and a large stainless steel operating table with a winch set above. The room resembled a control centre, for what, Louise did not know. Louise opened a blue file on Pauls desk and thumbed through its documents one by one. Gills message vibrated Louise's phone and she flipped it over to read the message. 'No sign of him yet you ok x'

Tom Price arrived at his brothers farm and drove straight to the roller shutter doors of the furthest bay and reversed Paul Morris' Range Rover until its tailgate nudged the slats. By seven o'clock in the evening Tom Price was way over the legal drink driving limit as he was almost every day since his father's death. He let his foot off the brake and allowed the Range Rover to roll a safe distance from the door and waited. His only real passion in life was hunting Deer but this too was suffering under his reliance on alcohol. Tonight however his preparations with Paul Morris were the start of an activity to raise the hunting stakes to a level where he needed to be in control.

Louise could find nothing other than routine information in her search and left Pauls surgery room. She pondered as to where Paul might keep a Panther and walked to the reception area. There was no appointment book, calendar, or the normal leaflets and magazines associated with a working practice. Realising that he worked alone without assistants or staff Louise decided to check her father's old surgery room and the other three ward rooms. As she walked through the reception area she noticed a dark red Land Rover parked directly outside the front entrance. Louise couldn't work out who's it was, maybe broken down, she viewed the registration TP50, it dawned on her, 'Tom Price that arrogant prick, that's his Land Rover.' She panicked. 'Could he be in the building?' Louise decided it was too risky to carry on her search and made her way back to the fire exit. She raced up the banking to the sanctuary of her car, breathless.

She called Gill. 'Hi Lou he's still not here, are you sure he left its been half an hour?'

'He's definitely gone Gill, but I had to leave I think Tom Price is in the building his Land Rovers outside. Maybe Pauls gone to the barn, I'll head up there and call you.'

'Louise no! Just leave it, Louise! Lou! For fucks sake.' Gill tried to reconnect but the call went straight to answerphone.

On the opposite side of the building to where Louise had been snooping around the surgery, Paul Morris was in the stables preparing a tranquilizer shot before loading it into his pistol. A fully grown male

Panther was housed in a steel transport cages before him, to its left in a second cage was the sedated pregnant female the sign on her cage stated #1.

Chapter 13

Tonmawr felt the moist ground penetrating her soft underbelly fur. Sleep had been snatched in small bursts throughout the mist laden day. The bare branches of a Hawthorn hedge provided the family little protection from above yet hid their makeshift den from passing humans. The previous night's travel had been restricted to less than one hour due to the unfamiliar barrier that lay before them. A steep embankment led the way up to a trunk road which thundered above them and would only fall quiet long after dusk. This landmark of hard grey tarmac was the gateway to unknown territory, its constant rumbling disguised the natural sounds which Tonmawr craved. Her cubs were not disturbed as they could sense their mothers warmth but she was restless now, hungry for information from this unfamiliar environment. The grey noise muddied the picture she tried to create of her surroundings, essential to provide her with the information to make an informed decision. She needed to see the way so she crawled up the litter ridden bank and peered into the unknown. The camber of the Heads of the Valleys Road restricted her view and her field of vision was blocked by a central reservation crash barrier. Headlights appeared to her right towards which she focused her attention, cowering as they approached but noting the time available to reach safety. Her frustrations pushed her back to the makeshift den where she sat again and waited. One full night and one full day of waiting at Rhigos had to be broken and she knew it had to be tonight. The male cub awoke first and teased the females until they too rose, stretched and branched out toying the paper cups and plastic straws which lay around them. Tonmawr paced along the terrace keeping the cubs from crossing an imaginary threshold towards the road above. No vehicles had passed for over an hour, and the cubs were beyond control, they too wanted out of this soulless verge. Tonmawr crawled up the embankment beckoning her cubs with a growl, they copied her movement which was low and deliberate. At the crest she took one look and bounded to the central reservation, they bunched against the cold galvanised steel together, exposed and vulnerable. Tonmawr arched her neck over the barrier and leapt into the road, the cubs were able to scamper underneath in pursuit, clearing the road with ease in two bounds they huddled on the side of safety, except the high stepping female cub who remained frozen at the central reservation as headlights approached. The car zipped past at high speed, Tonmawr willed the cub to cross but she remained glued to the spot. Another car sped by at high speed, then a truck sending a buffer of wind and noise forcing Tonmawr to cower, as she looked up again towards the central reservation her cub was not there. She called out in vain and paced up and down the kerb, still nothing. The other two cubs stood with their mother glaring at the road. The distant rumble of a large truck attracted Tonmawrs attention and as its lights swung around illuminating the road she disappeared down the embankment with two cubs in tow.

The high stepping female cub had returned to the temporary den and sat calling for her mother, hoping she would return. Alone and lost in an unfamiliar world the female cub lay amongst the litter and waited.

The family of four was now three, they groomed each other under the protection of tightly packed firs in the Brecon National Park over a mile from where the high stepping female cub lay. Tonmawr scouted the immediate area, checking for traces of her kind. Confident that she was not under threat she marked the treeline with her scent. This was the start of her boundary marking, next she had to find a natural barrier or landmark to the north, the direction inbuilt would drive her for six or seven hours and a distance she could easily cover during darkness even with her cubs. As they travelled Tonmawr soaked in the surroundings looking for safe routes and natural cover. The landscape was a varied but not difficult terrain, it undulated gently providing deciduous tree cover, fresh narrow streams and fern outcrops. The ground was becoming increasingly barren and turning to bog as they approached yet another wind farm installation. Beyond the windfarm the land fell from the heights to a horshoe crest with a view of distant lights, the town of Sennybridge. The trio followed the rim down to an open flat valley bottom dissected by a tributary, looking back

Tonmawr eyed the North facing steep rise before her which provided ideal terrain to search out a den. The cliff faces were inaccessible to humans but made for Panthers, their muscle mass provided the spring required to leap and secure a foothold. The rock formations were terraced with vertical cracks which in places opened a deep crevice into the hillside. This would be Tonmawrs northern most point of reference and ideal first den.

The cubs wanted to rest but Tonmaws motive was to mark and move. She would now head south again on a wide western arc until she found her first marked tree. As she set out from the crag the first squawks of morning crows forced her to re-think her options. Daylight would open the cover within the hour leaving her and her family exposed in a new world. Tonmawr continued down to take in water at the point where it cascaded from the rocks to tribute into a narrow stream. Satisfied and refreshed they returned as one to the flat rock den above. Tonmawr surveyed the land before her and was satisfied with the defensive location, no noise, no sign of human activity just nature at its best raw and unspoilt.

The high stepping female cubs curiosity smashed any thought of self-preservation. She retraced the path they had used to arrive at the culvert which lead her to the windfarm. She had negotiated this route two nights before with her family. Not realising that daylight was the enemy she faced it without fear and walked headlong towards innocent confrontation. The sheep trail was familiar and she skirted it with ease. A tree lined river took her away from the densely populated valley town below. Her own natural instincts were developing and assisting her journey, she now sensed the waterfalls were close as the midday sun warmed her back. She left the cover of a band of conifers in the Afan Forest Park and through deep bracken joined a stone track. Her nose lead her towards a lone farmhouse, she sat and watched with interest the comings and goings from behind a stone wall. Sheep were being loaded into a trailer, the gates corralling the herd being pushed from behind by a small black and white sheepdog. The canine was oblivious to its new visitor who's eyes followed the dance before her.

The sheep dog jumped into the tractor upon hearing the whistle from Guy Davies. The hooked up trailer bounced behind as the tractor pulled up the stone trail to higher ground with its cargo of one dozen sheep. The high stepping female cub was similar in size to the sheepdog but couldn't be further in gait. She bounded around the yard buildings searching out the scents. At an open fronted barn she settled just inside the entrance, lowered her head and lay prone behind a blue plastic container.

Sarah Davies walked through the yard holding a feed bucket for the chickens she kept at the farm. It was time to allow them to roam the yard for the afternoon. Their pen was largely open but in the shade of the barn, they craved the open yard for the afternoon sunlight. Sarah had lost too many chickens to leave them out all day, she knew they would stray and get caught under moving wheels or simply drown in the pond or water buts. She streamed the feed over the yard in the warm air, each grain lodged into the wet ground, the fowl had to work the mud to retrieve each morsel. The warm afternoon was unusual for the time of year, late winter did have its good days but was in the main wet and miserable. Sarah's fleece jacket was tied around her waist and in her red T shirt she headed to the blue container for more feed. She placed the bucket on the toe of her boot and with both hands pushed and flipped the steel clamp, releasing the lid which overturned to the floor causing Sarah to instinctively snatch out to catch it.

The high stepping female cub was cornered and as Sarah reached low for the lid the cub struck out with a claw and growled. The middle claw pierced the flesh and scooped through Sarah's forearm. Letting out a high pitched scream Sarah flinched back with force, the reaction grounding her on to the mud with the bucket flying off her toe. She instantly clamped her forearm with her right hand to stem the pain as the Panther cub retreated further into the barn. Sarah caught site of its form, almost black, short haired with an oversized head and paws, definitely larger than a domestic cat but similar in size to her sheepdog.

The high stepping female cub had settled in the far corner of the barn squeezed behind white sacks of animal feed, she was exhausted from her activities and fell into a deep sleep.

Guy Davies returned from the uplands as night fell to find his wife Sarah sat at the kitchen table, her arm in a bandage.

'Oh baby what happened to you?' Sarah relived the confrontation and unwound the bandage to reveal a crescent scar of dark red across her forearm, slightly raised and not yet sealed. Guy eyed the wound.

'Oooh that looks nasty love, it may need a stitch or two, let me take you to A&E.'

Sarah looked up and smiled at Guy. ' Don't be daft man it's only a scratch, just get me some more Germolene, it'll be ok. I still can't believe how beautiful that animal is Guy, its perfect form, crystal clear eyes, I locked the barn door so hopefully it's still in there, looked like a young cub.'

'If it is I'll send the dog in first, no wait let me call Louise Morris, she was with Annie the other day and she's the local Panther expert, she'll know what to do.'

Guy reached for his mobile phone and Sarah stopped him. 'What about Paul? He's our vet, he would be able to sedate it Guy, I don't want to hurt the poor thing plus it won't look good if we called his ex-wife first.'

Chapter 14

Tonmawr soaked in the dusk scents of her new territory. The new odours of Red Deer were strong enough to drift in the breeze from their overnight grazing in the bracken below. A Group of hinds and their calves were well established in the Brecon Beacons. The stags were fewer in number and with younger males roamed further afield to return in late summer. The female herds were capable of defending as a group, Tonmawr would need all of her strength skill and experience to fell a hind. Rabbit was less in population, not enough to sustain her family despite its reduced number. Sheep were an easier target in the wilds of Brecon as their keepers were rarely on hand. This first night would be spent surveying and marking, her cubs would follow her everywhere now, never to be left alone until they could fend for themselves. Her natural route tacked west to find a natural barrier or another predators scent. An hours amble on the high ground graduated to managed fields and tree lined deep narrow valleys, water was in abundance and provided scent cover. Passing under a bridge they continued on until the stream joined the wide expanse of the River Tawe. The watercourse mass corralled westerly progress and satisfied Tonmawr. She marked and sprayed the route as they tacked east to find the southern tree from the previous night. As the family arrived they settled to rest under cover of a thick wood. Their route to this spot had been rich and varied, plenty of cover, streams and tributaries at every turn provided natural pathways. As they groomed, Tonmawr longed for the return of her lost cub, she lingered in the hope that the cub would re-join the family.

Paul Morris arrived at the barn, walked over to his silver Range Rover and tapped the glass. Tom Price sparked from his slumber and opened the door which released the wedged empty bottle, smashing on the concrete below.

'Get the door open Paul, Ill reverse it in.'

Paul shook his head and looked down at the broken glass. ' Waste of a good Whiskey Tom, Ill drive if you don't mind'.

The roller shutter clattered open which Louise could feel vibrating through the building. Her vantage point was where Martin had first spied the Panther. She had a view of the empty cage and Toms profile silhouetted on the disappearing slats. The car backed up to the open pen and they both muscled the transport cage to the entrance, Tom lost his grip as they lowered the front end releasing a crash of steel on concrete. 'Fucks sake Tom, its wearing off as it is, careful you don't want to wake him.' Louise instantly recognised the beauty before her, the Panther was darker and smoother than Tonmawr, its shoulder stood a good two hands higher and its passive paws were double in size. No wonder Martin backed away quickly, such power. She thought. The Panther was docile yet mobile and stumbled unaware into the pen and flopped under the guiding pole and loop around its neck, Paul slipped off the loop and closed the pen door. As the roller door closed and Paul disappeared with Tom, Louise now realised her first fears that the pair were using the animal for their own gain. 'But why and what for?' She mused.

Louise prized the sheeting back with the aid of a scaffold tube, its length providing the purchase required, but the noise created was alarming to her. Martins security guard hadn't moved from his chair in the portacabin for the whole hour Louise had been patiently waiting in the shadow of the rear wall of the barn. She reached through with one hand holding her mobile and took blind images, rotating her hand in an arc. She viewed the images and readjusted her aim, this time she had a clear image stored. The sheet sprung back out as she tried to re-close the gap. The security guard Rhys opened the cabin door and feigned a patrol looking left and right whilst stretching. Conscious of her exposed position Louise soaked away into the darkness across two open fields to her car veiled on a neglected lane.

'sorry couldn't call back, home now, speak tomorrow.' Louise's text was apologetic in tone and she knew Gill would reprimand her in the morning. Heart thumping she flopped into bed and laid back exhausted. The image on her phone captivated her attention as she zoomed in and scrolled to assess the detail.

At the other end of town Paul Morris returned to the female Panther at the practice. He moved her back to the surgery table and made her comfortable, the monitors were again attached and drip administered. Paul settled into his office chair, pulled a blanket over his head and drifted off exhausted. His slumber was broken in what seemed to Paul like seconds but was in fact two hours by his mobile phone vibrating on the desk table.

'Paul sorry to bother you so late its Guy Davies.'

'Oh hello Guy that's ok what can I do for you?' Paul logged the news like he was hearing his winning numbers being read out one by one, when it reached the climax of information he spoke with a smile.

'Keep the door closed I'll be right over.' Whilst holding the solution high in the light Paul adjusted the drip feed and said to himself. 'Out with the old and in with the new.'

The high stepping female cub panged to be with her family as the realisation of solitude sunk in, destroying her will. Hunger swept her through the barn in search of a morsel or drink. She found her way back to the blue container and pawed the gap under the closed barn door. A steel bowl placed next to the bin presented welcome relief as she lapped up the sweet liquid. She finished the last drop and as her tongue pushed the bowl over her focus blurred and her head felt heavy. Her breathing rate increased suddenly and her thirst increased, as her legs gave way she looked at the glint of light burning through the opening door.

'There she's gone.' Paul Morris stepped inside the barn followed by Guy Davies who slipped over the latch without sound. Paul knelt beside the sedated cub and rolled back her eyelids revealing bright blue globes with a dark oval centre.

'Beautiful colour, think we'll call you Blue.'

Guy knelt beside Paul and stroked the cubs shoulder with the back of his hand. 'She is a beauty, presume it's a she Paul ?'

'Yes she's a she, I guess her mother is close by wondering where her cub has gone, either that or she's been rejected, far too young to be venturing out on her own. I'll take her back to the surgery Guy and inform the RSPCA. This is a first for the UK finding a live Panther.'

A knock on the barn door alerted Guy. 'Come on in Sarah its safe.'

Sarah walked over to Paul who was holding Blue in his arms and stroked the fur on her oversized paws. 'So the sedative in the sugar water worked Sarah, she will be like this for a few hours, you did the right thing calling me, hopefully we can get her rehomed in a facility nearby so you can visit her. I'll call my contact at the RSPCA wildlife centre and they can pick her up and decide where is best for her, she's a beauty isn't she?'

Sarah held the limp back legs and ran her fingers through the thick dark brown fur. 'So strong Paul these leg muscles, how did she end up here?'

'Who knows Sarah, what's important now is keeping her comfortable.'

From his vantage point Grey scrutinised the cub being loaded into Pauls silver car. He had picked up her scent the previous night and had circled the barn looking for a way in. Now he could do no more so picked up the scent trail left by the cub and headed towards The Brecon Beacons.

Tonmawr had spent the first day and night in her new territory but had not yet completed her boundary marking. With daylight fading she prepared to leave once more. Head south then east find the southernmost boundary point and work north east. She was aware also that the family had not eaten for two days. The central route south was high and barren without wildlife apart from the odd field mouse. Red Deer trails provided a natural route to flowing water but the Deer did not graze here, it was an exposed route and one to be covered quickly. The cubs were not holding her back anymore despite their hunger, the male as ever embraced each night with an adventurous spirit. The female trotted along head down but kept up with the increasing pace. A meal was required soon and Tonmawr halted the journey as they reached the southern tip of their territory. Sheep were grazing close enough to sense but they edged the Tarmac boundary where she had lost Blue, that memory sniffed out thoughts of an easy meal. Their route north and east fringed populated areas, small villages and farms scattered along water courses, which shaped their boundary. High ground was the preferred terrain for Tonmawr so she could view potential threats. There was little cover other than the occasional copse or overgrown heather embankment. Her new environment was proving to be a tough one to survive in. She sensed that her prey would have to be the large Red Deer and to achieve a kill her tactics would have to change. The male cub picked up a scent trail as Tonmawr sat and viewed the heather embankment. The low hidden trails under the knotted stems of purple heather prevented Tonmawr from following her cubs wanderings. Content she waited patiently for them to appear knowing they were not far and under cover. The cubs furrowed and scratched their way through searching the rabbit trails. The male took the lead and pounced at each twist or turn, the female pushed through the low canopy.

Grey had settled in a culvert below the tarmac border overwhelmed by the scent laden grass which the family had left behind two nights ago. He waited as they had done for the bright passing lights to fade before traversing the dual carriageway in three bounds. The area was familiar to Grey, he had stalked Tonmawrs new territory before but now it had a fresh scent. He worked left and right and found the first marked tree trunk. Its base had a deep seated tang and claw marks scared the bark, Grey pawed past the marks defining his greater height.

The cubs emerged unscarred from the heather, the male first with head held high sniffing the air to find his mother who had rested on her side but with her head level and eyes half open. The three played and groomed on the low heather and grass unaware that the males approach was accelerating, veiled by a strong northerly wind.

Tonmawr and her cubs continued north into the wind buoyed by the scent of Red Deer, exactly what Tonmawr had been longing for. A long, undulating approach with cover into the wind lead the trio to grazing ground, onto which the Deer herd had settled. The rare sight of females grazing alone held their attention, but attacking now would be fruitless. Tonmaws' tactic would be to stalk the pack for two to three days, learn their habits, assess their weaknesses and understand their relationship with the roaming lone stags. She had to steer clear of the stags who would alert the females and attack her if necessary. The herd were tranquil in comparison to the Roe Deer of the lower fields, larger and more confident they strutted the ground. The cubs were mesmerized at the sight of two dozen or more large animals before them. The male cub took in the aroma then freshened his buds with an elongated smooth tongue. As the Deer herded further north, the trio tracked a wide sweep from a distance. Grey had the family firmly in his sights, he caught the occasional bound of the female cub, or the slither of movement from Tonmawr. Since his previous encounter, the urge was to join the group and forge a hunting pair, this would take time, but the rewards were massive. Finally, Grey was maturing in thought and action. The family tracked further north, Tonmawr did not mark in case she alerted the herd. Her will was overcoming instinct in a bid to remain concealed for future hunts. If the herd sensed her now, they could be in a new territory by daybreak and lost to her for weeks. As the bird reveille opened, Tonmawr was content to move west and find comfort in their den on the rock escarpment of horseshoe ridge.

Grey pursued the family using his keen sense of smell and stopped short of the ridge base. The deep shadow of the escarpment provided perfect cover from Tonmawr and the cubs. The Red Deer also settled on the boggy ground under the cast morning shadow but the large male predator was not tempted to attack. Instead he scaled the ridgeline to seek out Tonmawr and the cubs. The entrance to the den was illuminated as the veil of night lifted, the family finished their grooming and settled to sleep. Above the den in an adjacent crevice Grey too settled and groomed himself to sleep.

Chapter 15

'Ok Tom I've got it again, the signal has come back. I guess from the co-ordinates he's settled on Horseshoe Ridge, what do you want to do?'

Tom Price remained prone, his mass cocooned in the damp twisted sheets as he contemplated his next move. 'Just stay where you are Dai I'll be up in an hour.' Toms body rolled left and an outstretched limb flapped in the darkness knocking over a glass but settling onto the bottle neck. With a hugging motion the bottle reached his whiskered lips and he glugged back the whiskey. He pressed call return and gradually focused on the name Paul Morris, watching the connect icon and hearing Pauls curt tones he muttered. ' Right Paul looks like the tracker is working and we've located the male, Dai's up there now and I'm on my way, meet me at Horseshoe Ridge just off Brecon Road there's a layby after the visitors centre, bring the gun and a transport cage.' Tom Price did not wait for a reply and crashed his head back down onto his crumpled pillow.

Paul Morris rolled his pen and watched the cub react to the ripple of the hard plastic biro, reaching out a paw and attempting to pick it up with her extended claw. Paul was relaxed as he played with the cub, the past twelve hours had been a roller-coaster of emotions, from having a lost male and a seriously ill female to finding a female cub and finding the male again. The blood sample he had taken from the cub was labelled up and prepared for DNA analysis, he had to find a match and was quietly assured that the cub was one of Tonmaws. The DNA profiler was self-testing and the auto start up would take at least one hour. 'Tom Price will have to wait' he thought. Skype flashed up on his computer screen, it was from Korea, no picture, just the name of the office used by Dr Kam.

'Hello, how can I help you?' Pauls guarded opening was typical of his recent attitude to any call from an unknown source, he was carrying so much guilt, had so many issues, threats and questions coming his way on a daily basis that his demeanour had changed from open interest to guarded secrecy.

A soft female voice bloomed out a fresh answer. ' Hi Dr Paul its Ji-a, Dr Kams daughter, are you ok to speak?'

Paul span around and picked up the cub as she lay semi-sedated on his desk, his day was getting better and better. Ji-a was a joy to speak to and lit up every room she was in. Paul had spent a heady summer with her in Seoul where she made him smile every day with her love and enthusiasm for the project.

' Ji-a, wow, it's great to hear from you, are you ok for visual I have a surprise for you?'

'Yes Dr Paul I think you will like my hair.'

Their images shared genuine happiness as Paul adjusted his position ready to show off his latest find. Ji-as' attractiveness was pure yet had a glint which suggested a wicked fun side. At thirty one she was considered old in Korean standards of availability and as such had missed the overtly commercial Korean wedding scene. Happy to date and have fun she had no intention of being a baby machine for a standard Korean male. Her father knew this and encouraged her behaviour safe in the knowledge that her siblings would continue the family line.

'Ji-a you look beautiful, I've missed your company, when are you coming over?'

'I'm at the airport now ready to check in so I arrive Gatwick, then Cardiff your time I think 07:30 on Sunday, you meet me Dr Paul?'

'Of course I will, text me your flight number and I'll be waiting outside the arrivals gate, I'll keep my surprise till you get here, safe journey Ji-a.'

Paul had a deep sense of satisfaction relaxing his shoulders as he cuddled the cub. His solo life was about to have a welcome shake up. Ji-a would not stand for Pauls lazy behaviour and would get the project back on track. The distraction from Tom Price was ruling his actions, dependant on the drugs he needed to be shaken from the pit in which he was wallowing. He stood up with the cub who in the short space of time was bonding with Pauls nature. The curiosity of Blue and her over exaggerated gait made her the perfect hook Paul thought. He coaxed her through the surgery and towards an unused room just off the cold main reception area. With a treat he enticed Blue through the open door and into a transport cage. Closing the door he whispered. 'Have a sleep and rest well, I'll be back soon'. Paul left the cub in darkness and locked up the practice ready for his meet with Tom Price.

Ji-a settled into her flight and as the seatbelt sign extinguished she opened her laptop and logged in. She allocated the eighteen hour flight as a time to complete her project scope document which was scheduled to be presented to Dr Kams clients in two weeks' time. The project would generate vast income for relatively little outlay. The concept was simple, prove that a species could be re-introduced into an environment and sustain permanent survival. Dr Kim's reputation opened doors to international governments, their protection of endangered species being high on the political agenda. The programme's success depended upon a proven project that had succeeded. Over the past five years Dr Kim and Paul Morris had worked on the Panther project. The sightings of the Panthers in an unnatural environment of the UK countryside had developed from fantasy to reality. As more reports came in of big cats Paul & Dr Kim saw an opportunity to prove their theory that if sufficient diverse numbers were introduced they could survive and thrive. The difficulty came in convincing the client that it was both ethical and that it would succeed. Generating the diverse base was proving to be the stumbling block, Dr Kim needed Paul to re-focus his efforts and get phase one completed. Ji-a re-named part one of the presentation, 'Diverse Base'. The lead in paragraph started to form; 'Two genetically separate females, four genetically separate males.' The organisation tree below the text developed to fill the screen and presented a clear concept. The next slide showed a copy of the tree and was titled 'Actual'. Its omissions were glaring except its first level which had two females and four males. Each one numbered one to six. Number one a female, soon to go under the knife to remove its dead foetus, number two was a female and its icon was blacked out indicating a death. Number three was backlit, Tonmawr, she was the success story. The female had survived completely without interference. Number four, five and six were blacked out. Number seven (Grey) was backlit. Ji-a sighed and shook her head at the poor start, she needed evidence of survival and Paul was the only person who could resurrect the plan, but she knew his state of mind was hindering the process. She recalled her father's parting words. 'If Paul cannot rebuild the base then he is finished, there will be no trace of him or the Panthers left.' The words echoed in her ears as she sipped her bottled water and started a new page. 'Resurrection' was the working title. She jotted down the plan.

Number One -terminate following birth of litter.

Number Three (Tonmawr) tag and track.

Number Seven (Grey) track

Three new males were also required plus one female, the animals could be from the surviving litter, or from Tonmawr if she were to become pregnant. The numbers did not add up and Ji-a realised that an introduction of fresh animals was required.

Another problem was tracking, which was essential to present a clear pattern of behaviour which mirrored actual patterns in the wild. It was no good to see a Panther travelling in a straight line to the nearest food source and settling, this would lead to human intervention and death. The Panthers had to develop naturally, taught by their parents, nurtured, shown the way but without the tracker evidence no client would buy their concept. Her plan in just two short weeks would be to place the trackers on all subjects, introduce the correct numbers of males and females then monitor over a two year period.

Pauls plan was to get through the day without falling asleep as he arrived at the layby next to Horseshoe Pass. Tom Price stepped out wearing a dark green waxed coat, Gumboots and flat cap, stained and grease laden the hat shone in the sunlight. Paul ignored Tom and opened the boot. He leant in and picked a rifle from the gun box. The black case lined with foam housed pockets in the lid which stored feathered darts. Paul picked a pack of ten red tipped darts and held up one to the light and gave it a circular shake. The liquid glistened and cusped to the chamber. Secure in his belt loop Paul sleeved the Czech Republic made MAO rifle and slung the loop over his right shoulder.

Chapter 16

Paul and Tom did not speak as they strode out from the layby across a fallow field towards a V shaped rock outcrop at the right finger of Horseshoe Ridge. Sitting on the rock was Dai Thomas a friend of Toms. He raised an eyebrow to acknowledge Tom as he studied his black and green laptop. The three huddled around the screen and viewed a simple image of the outline of the crest. A dark circle covering half the screen flickered and danced.

Dai sniffed, wiped the damp from his nose with the back of his hand and said. 'Can't get any more from this , it's definitely here the pings are every second, the target isn't moving, it's the signal I keep losing so the target area jumps in and out.'

Paul looked closer and replied. 'So that covers the whole of the crest which must be a mile across, we need to get closer to the centre, I need to be within fifty yards to fire the dart.'

Tom Price stood and pointed to the crest where Tonmawr, the cubs and close by Grey were resting. ' Ok let's get up on the crest, the signal will be clearer, we can work out potential dens and flush out.'

The trio grouped together for the climb and their inbuilt issues seemed to disappear as they focused on their mission. Toms shortening breath as they rose the stone trail along the ridge stifled conversation.

Dai took the lead and asked Paul. ' The signal was lost two weeks ago Paul and only re-appeared out of the blue last night, I need to reset the IP address on your computer, think it jumped to a different frequency, are you sure it's been turned on and charged all the time?'

Pauls breathing was labouring but he stuttered. 'Yes its always on, it's supposed to store all the locations, that's the whole point of this project, and that's why we bought this tracking software from you. Are you sure your equipment is up to the job?'

Dai turned, stopped and leant in close to Paul, out of earshot of Tom Price who was struggling to keep up. ' You know there's nothing wrong with the package, just keep your equipment on, I know every time you don't refresh the codes and its down to you to download the updates. This equipment is well proven and works over hundreds of square miles, as long as the user uses it as instructed.'

Paul looked round at Tom who was now only feet away. 'Come on old man not far now.' The trio rested on the crest of the escarpment and turned to view their surroundings. The steep drop below hid the Panthers location, they would know humans were close. Dai opened his laptop again and refreshed the screen.

'Ok here we go, ID #M7 is within fifty metres'. Looking over their shoulder was open ground and a clear view of over half a mile as the back of the ridge rolled away to distant tree lines. To their front was the concave rock and grass face.

Paul spoke up. 'It's likely he s bedded down below us in a crevice. We have no chance of flushing him out and getting a clear shot, our best course is to scale down to the base and wait till dusk, he'll move down to the base and we will pick him off easily.' Paul took out his field glass and spied a small copse on the flatland in front of the cliff face.

Tom had just regained his breath and protested. ' Well you're on your own, I've got stuff to sort out for tomorrow, got those Cheltenham boys coming over and I don't want to be on the wrong side of Claire. I'll see you up at the house tomorrow, just make sure you turn up with the Panther Paul.'

Paul protested. 'So how am I meant to carry a sixty kilo Panther over a mile back to the layby Tom?'

Dai shook his head. 'Don't look at me, I only came out to prove to you idiots that there was no issues with the trackers. Here it's all yours, unlike you two I've got serious work to do.'

Tom Price snatched Pauls field glass from his hand and surveyed the route from the layby over to the copse. A five bar galvanised gate at the layby led directly onto the field, the copse could be reached using a four by four. 'Right I'll be back before dusk. Paul I'll flash my light from the layby then drive the Land Rover over to meet you at the copse. This is forestry land and I've got a master key for the gate. The trio descended the western finger of the crest back towards the layby. Dai marched on with nothing to carry, he waved a hand behind without looking. Tom pulled a flask from inside his waxed coat and took a long glug spilling it down his chin, without offering a drop he screwed on the lid wiped his mouth and let out a belch. Paul shook his head and continued down, he considered why he was working with this man that he loathed and how he had got himself mixed up in such a tangled web of dependence and deceit.

As Tom lurched his red Land Rover in a spinning arc back towards the farm Paul relaxed. As he looked up at the overcast sky he stuffed waterproof clothing and water bottles beside the laptop in his back pack. Ready for the stake out he hunched up his burden and headed for the copse. It was early afternoon and Paul looked forward to the peace and solitude of the three hours before dusk spent in the copse.

Ji-a was eight hours into the first leg of her journey and awoke from a sleep that she didn't realise she had fallen into. Such was her focus that it drove her to exhaustion and her body simply took over for brief respite. A visit to the bathroom followed by an intake of water refreshed her enough to restart her presentation. She was oblivious to the busy flight and constant requests and movements from the people around her. She moved back to the presentation and linked the family tree. The environment in which they would exist and the pattern of behaviour needed to be mapped to ensure it was natural. There were still too many gaps on the second layer, only one female at the highest level was not enough. It would take another two years to develop enough diversity for the programme to work. Transporting a female from overseas was too much of a risk so it had to come from the mainland. She knew of a female on the Welsh borders but needed more direct contact with the group in that area who were tracking.

She wrote a brief email to Paul asking him to make contact again. With that in place they could start the programme with confidence. The next generations were plentiful in numbers because of her father's work with the DNA modifications. He had developed a technique which allowed the team in Korea to clone the Panther species and produce the numbers required. Their business model was to provide the service for any endangered species. Paul Morris provided the raw materials, females, to surrogate cloned Panthers.

Chapter 17

Louise had slept for more than twelve hours
and her yawning body seemed incapable of waking
but she loaded the last bag of food into the boot and
was ready. The journey to the forest lodge on a Friday
afternoon was frustrated by the throng of cars buzzing
across the town in all directions, school pick-ups,
shopping trips, long journeys home. She broke
through and settled into the winding trail to the edge
of the Brecon's where her lodge nestled amongst the
swathes of green.

As she pulled into the park of twelve cabins
she felt the world behind fall from her shoulders. The
park offered seclusion, each lodge set in half an acre
of pine covered heaven. Some neighbours rented out
their lodges but most kept the havens to themselves.
Louise pulled onto the gravel approach and nestled
the boot of her car close to the back door. The four
bedroomed two story lodge was the pick of the bunch,
its high pitched roofline was dramatically framed
with full height windows and a balcony running the
length of the gable end. It had the feel of an Alpine
ski lodge and the dimensions to match.

Louise had thought of living permanently at the lodge following her break with Paul but the daily journey would have been tedious, plus the appeal of the place was the satisfaction of arriving after a hard week of work. She had never shared good times with Paul as they purchased it off plan with money from her inheritance and by the time it was completed she and Paul had split. It was her sanctuary which she loved to share with close friends and family, they made it home.

As promised she sent a message to Martin with the location pin plus a heart. 'Be nice if you could get here before everyone arrives.' She put on her music and filled the double height lounge with soothing sounds as she prepared the log fire. The bedrooms were all made up ready as she scribbled on the kitchen planner who was coming and where to put them. The two boys in the twin room, Gill and Mike in the downstairs bedroom just off the lounge, if Jo turned up she could be in the upstairs double leaving herself to the main bedroom with Martin if he wanted to stay. Louise received a text from Jo as she scribbled on the chalkboard. 'Sorry Lou can't stay this weekend got to look after Annie may pop up Saturday afternoon x.'

She thought about how she had treated Martin over the past week and was annoyed with herself. She was so wrapped up with the Panthers and knew she had ignored him. He would sense he was being used she thought, but also she genuinely liked him and was turned on in his presence. 'Hope he turns up early.' Her needs never left her and she did want him there and then, having to wait was adding to her excitement. Ok time for a shower before everyone arrives, there was nothing more she needed to do before then.

Martin opened the message whilst sat at his desk, the week had been frantic and he was ready for the pub. He didn't expect Louise to contact him again after their night together. He sensed she was wrapped up in her own world and he was merely a convenient distraction. That wouldn't normally bother him but this time he longed to see her again. Wait he thought, let's just let her stew for a while. He did want to go up there but was waiting for a delivery which would probably not arrive until after six, if at all. He sensed that she wanted him now, and after deliberating about the delivery finally gave in. As he closed and locked the office door he heard a car pull up behind him and turned to see Claire De Motta waving at him.

'What does she want?' Martin stumped to himself. He thought it odd that she was here at this time, especially as she was here only two days ago.

'Hi Martin, glad I caught you, Im just passing on the way to stay with friends and thought I'd stop by on the off chance we could have a chat, if that's ok with you of course?'

Martin thought about brushing her off but in the light of what had been happening this week with the Panthers and his new found knowledge of Claire's past he was intrigued. ' No problem Claire, Ill put the kettle on.' Martin unlocked the cabin door and flicked on the lights, he sensed Claire's deep perfume billow in and change the stagnant air of the office. Claire set her leather handbag on the small round meeting table, muted her phone and sitting back she looked up and said.

'Im convinced that The Prices are on our side now Martin and we will have a good working relationship moving forward, Alan has indicated that he needs to cooperate better with you and your team, I don't know how you've done it Martin but he speaks highly of you.'

'Well thanks Claire, Im just doing my job and being honest with him, that's the way I work.'

'So what was that issue you spoke about the other day?'

'We had some thefts of diesel from the compound, we thought Alan might have something to do with it, but in hindsight I needed to look closer to home.'

'I can't see how Alan would have anything to do with it Martin, he's loaded.'

'That was my conclusion but he rents out that barn to Davies Transport and I know what they're like, into all sorts of scams. Then I find out our security guard is selling diesel, Pete our foreman caught him this morning filling jerry cans and it turns out he goes straight to the gym after work and offloads it. Anyway he's gone now and we have a new guy from the agency who worked for us before, someone we can trust.'

'Oh that's good Martin, so I spoke with Alan the other day and we are organising a sporting weekend on the fifteenth and he wants to invite you if you're interested? It'll be a good opportunity to meet the landowners for the next construction phase, would it be something you're comfortable with?'

Martin dreaded the thought of mixing with farmers and landowners but didn't want to dismiss the opportunity, he thought of Louise and how she detested Claire. 'Im not exactly the hunting type Claire but it would be good to meet the landowners, plus Im sure they'll be plenty of drink on offer, fifteenth that's a week tomorrow yes?' Martin replied with a smile.

Claire laughed out loud and answered with an assured tone. 'It's definitely more about the social side Martin, you don't have to get involved with the hunting.'

'Will you be there Claire, apart from Alan I don't really know anyone else?'

'Of course, Im organising the event, I'll look after you rest assured, plus it would be nice to spend some time getting to know you better, all we seem to do is work, work, work, Im not all bad Martin.'

Martin knew deep down that Claire was playing games but he was happy to indulge her, if it could help Louise in any way. ' Well then thanks I accept your offer, just let me know where and when, but leave me out of any hunting or riding horses if you don't mind.'

'No problem Martin, we have fabulous food and the company isn't all bad, plus you'll make some excellent contacts. I'll send the details over early next week.'

Claire clutched her bag and fished her keys from its depths. ' Great, I'll be down next Thursday, I've got appointments all day then its off to sort the weekend out, so I'll be in touch.'

'Ok thanks Claire speak soon.' Claire strode out of the door and with her phone pressed to her ear slid into her Range Rover and sped off.

Martin looked at his own phone and decided to text Louise. 'Be there in half hour.' His bag was already prepared in anticipation of the invite being firmed up even though he was in two minds about it, his other options for the weekend were limited.

Gill and Mike bustled around their kitchen placing food containers in cool bags, drinks and snacks in abundance were stuffed into carrier bags. 'Were only going for two nights Gill how much food do we need?'

Gill looked over to their overgrown twenty-something sons who were fixated on the fifty inch plasma screen, bobbing and weaving their cars on the same track whilst twisting their controllers as if they were actually driving. ' Really Mike, these two will demolish all this in one sitting if we let them.' Rhys and Lewis reverted back to type when visiting their parents revelling in the comfort their mother provided, food in abundance, drink and a warm home.

'Boys, me and your father are going now, what time will you be up there?'

'What times food mam?' Rhys shouted without turning.

'About eight I guess.'

'See you at eight then, we've got cameras to pick up on the way.'

'Don't be late boys and bring clean clothes I don't want you stinking Louise's place out.'

As they walked out of the door Mike shouted. 'Bring your own drink as well.'

'I'll text Lou see if she needs anything, we can pick up on the way if that's ok Mike?'

'Yeh sure we can stop at Tesco. Is that fella of hers going to be there?'

'Not sure, I hope so she's taken a real shine to him and he sounds like a good one, she needs a strong man to ground her a bit.'

Louise fresh from her shower opened the door wide for Martin. He stepped over with a smile and offered a peck on the cheek which Louise intercepted with her lips and a curling arm. 'Hey, good to see you again and thanks for the invite, this is a beautiful place Louise.'

'You're welcome and thanks for coming, are these for me?' Louise took the flowers that Martin offered and accepted the bottle of wine with a warm smile.

'Don't worry there's more in the truck I'll go and get them, is there anyone else here yet?'

'Leave them for now Martin, no just us at the moment, come in and relax I'll show you where everything is.'

The tour stopped at Louise's bedroom where she shoved Martin back onto the bed and straddled him. Her passions and frustrations took over, pulling at his clothes, they were naked within seconds.

Rhys and Lewis bundled their jeep down a narrow track which ended at the entrance to the waterfalls. Two cameras were positioned in the network of falls and streams. The retrieved memory cards were slotted into the laptop which Lewis tried to wedge onto the dashboard. Rhys looked down at his pouch of tobacco and spread the mix evenly along the oversize paper. 'Better not smoke this up there, mam will go nuts.' The black and white footage from the wildlife camera at the large pool at the base of the waterfall picked up the mist laden air. The image of fog occasionally flickered as a bird or rabbit triggered the auto filming.

'Same old shit on this one Rhys, did you find anything down there?'

Lewis span his phone around and zoomed to show Rhys the image of two footprints in the mud. Both the same outline and pattern but one was twice the size of the other.

'Think its Tonmawr but I'll have to check the scale image on the laptop, have you finished yet?'

'It's just fog and mist, which twat set the camera up here pointing at fuck all?'

'Fuck off Rhys, it was clear when I set it up. Put the other disc in from the top of the ravine, I set that at the entrance to the falls where the tracks usually are.'

The image revealed a clear crest and provided depth from a fern in the foreground, in the mid distance was the start of a stone wall. The first trigger was rabbits, bobbing along in the centre of the frame. 'Here we go Watership Down again.'

Lewis took a long drag on the joint and passed it over to Rhys, as the smoke cleared, the time flicked over on the screen twenty four hours and the rabbits appeared again. Three rabbits centred on the screen nibbling at the earth. The night light illuminated a dark feline figure that scattered the rabbits with paws outstretched, another larger cat appeared and disappeared followed by two more smaller cats. The camera once triggered continued filming for one minute. Before resting the family returned into shot, triumphant Tonmawr holding her prey followed by her equally triumphant male cub with his first kill. The high stepping female with her sister trotted off shot pouncing at the morsels.

Rhys and Lewis high fived and closed the laptop.

'C'mon we'll miss dinner, I've got the munchies now, we can pick up the other two in the morning, where did you set them up Lewis?'

'Up near Crai reservoir and Horseshoe Pass in the Beacons, its where we tracked the male last summer. It's on the way to Louise's, won't take a minute, we can download after food, I'm starving.'

As the pair approached the layby adjacent to Horshoe Pass Rhys said. 'Slow down big boy there's a car in the layby, wait a minute, I don't like this, the gates open as well, drive on Lewis, if you go another half mile there's a pull in onto an old quarry road, we can go in that way, Ill run up the back of the Crest and pick up the camera, I know exactly where it is.'

Lewis continued on and followed Bens directions which swept them along a dirt road of limestone chippings. 'Ok wait here I'll be ten minutes.' As Lewis turned the car around he shouted after him.

'Keep your phone on Rhys'. A thumbs up then Rhys disappeared into the woodland. With his eyes adjusted Rhys translated his steps into a steady jog as he broke cover the crest he was illuminated from behind with a halo of deep red from the setting sun. 'Ok where was this camera?' On the crest there was a dip of soft ground which Rhys dropped down to and skirted in a gradual fall to a rock outcrop with heather fringes. He bent down to retrieve the camera and flicked on his head torch to see the clips on the base. He retrieved the memory card and placed a new one inside. The batteries were changed and the camera repositioned. Rhys then made his way back to meet his brother leaving the head torch on until he cleared the ridge.

'So who the fuck is that Paul?' Tom Price whispered to Paul Morris. From their hide Paul Morris viewed the crest through his night scope on the rifle.

'Couldn't see his face Tom, once the light flicked on it saturated the viewer, but he picked something up and then turned and ran off.'

'Any movement now, what about the Panther as he shown any movement on the tracker?'

'Nothing yet but I'd not expect him to move unless he's waiting for the Deer to arrive, the scanner is only accurate to about five metres so he could be moving along the rocks.'

Grey had sensed human movement above him when Rhys had retrieved the camera. His senses were on high alert as he waited for Tonmawr to break cover. The cubs were restless as night fell anticipating a nocturnal venture through the territory in search of food. Tonmawr crept to the edge of the den and soaked in the dusk, she leapt down to a lower rock and the cubs followed. She waited for a few moments before bounding down the escarpment to the field below as the daylight gave way to a red night sky. Grey watched the family settle in the heather, his vision picking out the shapes amongst the deep reds and blacks of the boggy ground.

Pauls night scope had picked up the movement yet his tracker had not blipped indicating no movement. Pauls instinct led him to believe that the movement was Grey moving down the rock face. The glow from the laptop screen was shielded by Toms coat pulled over his head as he lay prone like a Victorian photographer. He whispered to Paul. 'Ok he's moving now Paul down the ridge to our right, he's taking a slow walk to the bottom, do you see him?'

'Hang on I've got movement to our left but there's more than one, wait I think it's Tonmawr, I've just seen two cubs as well. Paul did not want to lose sight of the trio and they were now within range.

Tom interrupted, 'Well he's at the bottom now heading our way as well, how manty darts have you got?'

Pauls view didn't shift as the greater prize was within his grasp. He replied to Tom. 'If I hit Tonmawr the cubs will stay, if I hit the male Tonmawr and the cubs will go, plus we can track the male now, fuck it Ill target Tonmawr.' Tom stayed beneath his veil and tracked Grey.

Tonmawr trotted with the cubs towards the copse, she felt safe in her new territory and her plan was to wait there for the Deer to arrive.

'Come on, come on keep coming, keep coming.'

Pauls aim was centred on Tonmawrs chest. He had a clear view and as Tonmawr stopped to wait for the cubs to catch up she sat proud, her chest heaving and her eyes glistening as Paul checked the range and re-focused the night scope. His warm grip caressed the rifle stock and his right index finger curled with a slight squeeze around the trigger taking up the pre-load. As the dart left the rifle Paul exhaled sure that he had hit Tonmawr. Grey had spent this time in a slow low creep to Tonmawr. He was now equidistant with Pauls rifle muzzle when Tonmawr sensed his approach and sprang to her right as the dart flew harmlessly into the night. 'Shit, shit.' Paul said through a slightly open mouth and gritted teeth. He rolled left, picked a fresh dart and loaded. As he rolled back into firing position and wiped the moisture from the lens of the night scope Tom removed his cover and illuminated the scene with the lap top screen.

'For fucks sake Tom your blinding the view.' Grey stood in the sights calmly then sensed the wave of light from the copse, reacting quicker than Pauls trigger finger he was lost into the night.

Tom pulled the veil and sat up. 'He's on the tracker Paul heading west come on lets go.' Paul folded the stock of the rifle and removed the dart.

'Not a chance Tom we could be chasing him all night for nothing, we need more people on the ground to get close enough, time to go home I think.'

Tom sighed out loud as he knew Paul was right. They trudged back to the layby as evening rain started to whip through the trees. Paul took out his phone and composed an email to Ji-a. ' Tracker back on line and positive contact with male #7. Tonmawr located so when you arrive we will have a busy time. If you agree I think we should track Tonmawr and sedate, implant a tracker and monitor. She can replace #1. What do you think?'

Chapter 18

Grey pursued Tonmawr across the open field until a line of Hawthorne forced him to stop and snuffle out the next direction. His demeanour was not one of stalk and attack but to join Tonmawr and demonstrate his intentions. Tonmawr had scrambled through the Hawthorne hedgline and was waiting with her cubs for movement to dictate they're next passage. She could hear Grey moving behind the curtain of dense twisted vegetation and let out a low deep growl to ensure Grey knew she was in control and aware. Grey found a break in the line and stepped through to present himself. It was a brave move as he exposed his mass with head down.

The cubs stood as one with their mother and viewed the large male before them. Tonmawr moved towards Grey with confidence in a left then right motion growling at each twist and baring her large curled upper incisors. Grey was submissive lounging on one side and flicking his tail up and down. Fighting her solidarity and lone hunting instinct Tonmawr had inbuilt reason to entertain the male for reproduction only and with her cubs set to accompany her for at least one more season she was in no position to entertain an affiliation which Grey signposted. It was a trust she disguised as she continued to position herself with hostility. The pursuit had lasted for four days and with the loss already of one of her cubs Tonmawr could not allow the male in too close.

Grey continued with his tender and offered a front paw exposing his soft underbelly. If Tonmawr struck now she would easily kill the male and not receive injury but her sense guided her to accept the male with a playful encounter of mock aggression and the two were now at ease. The cubs viewed the interaction but did not interfere. As Grey stood to follow Tonmawr he motioned towards the cubs but was kept at distance by a high shoulder growl from their mother. She was allowing Grey to join them but set a boundary which must not be crossed. Grey accepted the boundary and continued at a distance to follow the family deep into the night.

On the western limit of their territory the group sloped down to the river and took refreshment along the mud laden banks. Their cover was dense Willow saplings which arched and dipped into the moist steep bank. Tonmawr was the first to recognise the scent of Muntjac Deer present upstream. They thrived in the dense vegetation along the rivers due to their size, about a quarter of a Red Deer. Their group numbers were steady throughout the year as their breeding was not seasonal. This was a welcome resource for Tonmawr, leading a group of four would require strength but also tenacity and guile to stalk and provide opportunity. The Muntjac weighing twenty kilos at most were the perfect size to be dispatched and transported to a safe location. Their shorter legs would not outrun Tonmawr. Their gift though was their ability to traverse dense patches and remain camouflaged. They detected the slightest movements from predators in the undergrowth, difficult terrain for the Panthers to stalk in silence.

Grey sat with Tonmawr as they took in the scent of the Muntjac upstream. The shallow babbling river would provide a conduit for Tonmawr and the cubs to front the Muntjac and Grey would work behind the river bank flushing the prey to the shallows. The delivery had to be a natural instinctive partnership which until now remained untested. The cubs knew to follow their mother, copy her moves and only spring when they sensed the explosion of speed. Grey waited as the trio sauntered into the river and edged along its low level centre, the downstream babble covering their limbs. The water at the banks would cover the cubs backs and was strewn with twigs and fallen branches. Grey moved inland to the grazing land above the river bank. This wide arc would take the same time as the slow paddle upstream, there was no other communication just personal timing and instinctive readiness. Tonmawr and the cubs would alert the Muntjac if they arrived too soon, if Grey descended too slowly onto the river bank the Muntjac would scatter along the banks and remain hidden in the undergrowth. The dominant Doe of the group of small Deer settled the group into the fresh vegetation of late winter bulbs and bulrush which fought for moisture and light on the fringe of the final fall off into the flowing water.

Three pairs of Does and Bucks were scattered amongst the fringes of the river with two pairs of

Does with kids further upstream in more dense undergrowth. The antlers of the largest Buck clicked against the branches as he fed with a tolerance of the smaller Bucks who were close by. The kids suckled their mothers as they twitched and bobbed their heads searching out primulas from the understory. Grazing would continue well into the night until full, when they would gestate in the open grassland.

Grey paused in the long grass on the crest of the river bank and sensed the prey below. Muntjac prints slotted the moist ground leading to a bramble covered low channel which they used to access their feeding ground of dense undergrowth. Grey compressed her four pads through the upper pliable soil until a firm reaction was formed. Tensioning hind leg muscles set his spring and with a final inhale and his diaphragm taught Grey launched over the bramble and crashed through the willow spindles amongst the Muntjac. The rush of blood sprained through their static bodies before their prong spilled them in all directions, as their screaming and barking filled the night air. The largest Buck splashed mid-stream and broke the surface with a gurgled bark. Tonmawr stung him with one swipe of protracted hooks then dunked to embrace his collar. With one head twist and flick her jaw she suffocated the Buck. A tangled doe scrambled through twisted fingers of willow, her screech echoing her kids screams until falling silent under the weight of Greys paw which dwarfed her skull. His incisors clamped above her shoulder blades as he tugged the twitching body free whilst the kid burrowed deeper releasing his need for its mother. Grey reversed to the crest of the field as the remaining Muntjac diluted into the brushwood. His rendezvous followed as the trophy laden group headed towards a lightly covered glade of long grass and fern, the excited cubs jumping and grabbing to pick morsels as they trotted along.

Chapter 19

Aber-llia village deep in the Brecon Beacons crowed three houses, a disused Post Office and a gated entrance which lead a quarter-mile to Jim Prices house which had the title of Aber-llia Hall. The swept flint brickwork of the gate posts was inset with a slate nameplate boasting carved golden letters. The open wrought iron peaked gate lead the eye along a conifer fringed compacted stone driveway wide enough for two vehicles to pass. The grandeur of the driveway belied the true state of the Georgian Hall. Its frontage kept up the pretence until any guest crossed the threshold. Claire De Motta had anticipated this disappointment by erecting an oversize marquee dressed for a wedding function outside the entrance. As the Cheltenham Hunting Club members arrived they were greeted by porters and waitresses who under the close direction of Claire pandered the needs of the guests. As the visitors mingled with the Prices and other local landowners Claire ensured the drinks flowed and fostered introductions. The focal point was a central cooking area and fire pit which attracted guests with odours of fine meats being seared and a much needed heat source.

Tom Price stood on the steps of the entrance and surveyed the splendour before him. Claire moved to his side and sipped from her glass of champagne.

'Claire you certainly know how to make a silk purse from a sows ear, you wouldn't recognise my brother's house, it normally smells of damp and horse shit.'

'Someone has to bring you lot into the real world, there's money to be made from these events, its five grand a head just for the Stag hunt but we have to impress Tom and no cutting corners. We can double that figure when we introduce the Panthers, so come on give me some good news.'

Tom's smug smile put Claire at ease as he slugged from his tumbler and held the glass forward for a refill. 'I have an impressive male Panther in a cage in the back of the Land Rover, I could release him now if you want, im sure it would grab everyone's attention.'

Claire shook her head in dismay and replied. 'That's exactly what keeps you in the dark ages Tom, just stick to plan and let Paul and I deal with the Panther.'

Claire graced down the steps and caressed a member of the club with an extended hello. Adrian Miles, Chairman and Hunt Master was a tall dark haired tanned man, he kissed Claire on the cheeks and smiled into her eyes. She brushed back her deep brown thick hair and said. 'Thank you Adrian for supporting this event, as the hunt master your presence speaks volumes, I'd like to talk to you about an enhanced package which we will introduce next weekend, just to gauge your reaction and receive your valued opinion.'

Adrian's calmness and overbearing presence reduced Claire's stance to that of an excited schoolgirl meeting her male hero as he replied ' Of course Claire I'd be delighted to hear your proposal, allow me some time first to introduce you to some friends of mine, they are South American and are with us for a few days to discuss horseflesh.' Claire clattered behind Adrian's sweep into the throng of alpha males.

Jim and Alan joined Tom on the steps and the trio surveyed their surroundings. Alan was the first to raise concerns. 'So there's twelve of them, that's sixty grand for two days work not bad boys.'

Jim laughed and replied. 'Well this tent and food has cost ten then there's Claire's cut so we'll be lucky to walk away with five k each, and I've already spent twenty doing the rooms and the drawing room, so it owes me fifteen.'

Alan calmed the situation.' We haven't factored in the trophies Jim, if one of them bags a Stag there's an extra, but looking at them I can't see them hitting the barn door with a banjo. Some of them want to go on a night stalk so I'll be taking them with two of my best men. I've got them out there now tracking so as soon as I get the call we'll meet the main stag herd and come in from Cray reservoir over to The Devil's Elbow, should get a kill easily.'

Tom stifled a laugh and interjected. ' You want to watch out for Panthers at night Alan, me and Paul tracked the male Panther in the same area, plus he's tailing a female and there's cubs we've seen.'

Alan spurted his drink in shock, wiped his mouth and turned on his younger, smaller brother. 'You are such a fucking prick Tom, why didn't you tell me?'

Alans grip lifted Tom on his toes and unbalanced them both. 'Alright, alright you big twat he's on a tracker so we know exactly where he is, anyway it'll keep you entertained.'

Jim separated the pair and smiled at the audience who had sensed the commotion and raised their brows. Claire marched across with a stern look and whispered to the trio. 'What the fuck are you playing at, now fucking grow up, what the hell is this about?' Alan did his best to explain the situation and prevent Tom from butting in. Claire looked quizzically at Tom.

'So if there's a male being tracked and an untracked female what or who do you have in your truck Tom?'

'It's another male, the male out on the moor is number seven or Grey as Paul calls him, we released him again about three weeks ago but the tracker has been playing up, Dai sorted it though, the female I heard Paul call it Tonmawr, think it's from number one's first litter.'

Claire waved her hand. 'Im confused Tom, Ill speak to Paul later, now just grow up and mingle you need to try and get on with our guests.'

Chapter 20

Louise's never locked the side door to the kitchen but she was startled when Gill and Mike bundled into the kitchen. 'Shit Gills here, fuck what time is it?' Louise slid out of bed, jumped up and pulled on her jeans and sloppy jumper. She pushed and pulled her hair and ducked to see the image on the dressing room mirror. 'I'll be there now.' She shouted then giggled at Martin who was busy dressing. They both stumbled downstairs to find Gill and Mike bringing bags into the kitchen. Wine glass in hand she embraced Gill as Mike protested at the size of the bags he was carrying.

'Here let me help you.' Martin grabbed one of the carrier bags overloaded with bottles and placed it on the worktop.

Mike put the rest down and said. 'High you must be Martin, Im Mike, Gills husband.'

Martin introduced himself with a firm handshake and looked over at the embracing girls with a smile. ' Have you had your hair done Louise?' Gill accused.

'Yes , it's just had sex hair Gill, do you like it?'

Martin enjoyed the banter and loved friends coming together feeling at ease with his new acquaintances. The foursome under the leadership of Louise exchanged introductions and explanations of who was who over an ever decreasing bottle of wine. The lodge from the kitchen afforded views into the forest and absorbed the last of the daylight through floor to ceiling glass. The relaxing atmosphere took away stresses and opened up its guests. 'Come on let's sit by the fire.' Louise barefooted, sauntered towards the fire and added hardwood lumps to its heart.

Gill continued to fill the fridge and shouted across. 'The boys should be here by eight, I'll put the chilli in the oven to keep warm.'

Martin broke the ice with Mike. 'This is a beautiful lodge, love the views.'

Mike responded. ' Yeh it's the first time I've been up here, you're working on the wind turbines Gill tells me, is there much more to do?'

Martin explained the next phase as Gill and Louise settled onto the L shaped sofa and chatted about the food being prepared. Time whizzed by as the endless chit chat continued, the foursome were relaxed and unwinding with wine flowing.

Louise left the men talking and sauntered over to Gill who was preparing a salad. 'So Louise what did you find at Pauls practice last night?'

'Absolutely nothing Gill but Im so convinced he has something there, I went back to the barn later that night.'

'What the fuck Louise, you're going to get caught, and what did you see?'

'A large male Panther in a cage, here I've got some images, listen don't show Martin, let me explain to him first.'

'Gill shook her head in disbelief and viewed the still of a large male Panther, side on, lying with his mouth open sedated.' Right share them with the boys so they can upload to the database, and tell Martin!'

' Gill come on we have an hour, let's make an excuse and go back there, come on we need to know what's going on.'

'I know but we've got to keep a cool head, look I've got the analysis back from the lab, plus the boys will be here soon, it's going to be a long night so let's chill out for a while, eat and then lay everything out so we can make a sound judgement.'

Louise took in a deep breath, let out a long sigh and nodded in agreement. The odours of the bubbling chilli attracted Louise to the hob where she held up the lid and caressed the mixture. Martin sidled up behind her and kissed her neck. ' Smells good Louise, and the chilli, are you ok? You seem a little tense.'

'Too much whizzing round in my head Martin sorry, we just need to get to the bottom of what is going on with all this, Paul is acting strangely and is out on a limb, I'm afraid he'll do something stupid again.' Gill interjected their conversation.

' Martin you need to take this woman's mind of it all for a while, Ill finish off the food, take her out for some fresh air or something.'

'Good idea Gill, come on Martin I'll show you round the gardens.'

The pair opened the back door, Louise slid on her brown boots and they strolled onto a decking pathway which embraced the walls of the lodge on all sides. Wine glasses in hand they looked across the rough grass field towards the dense conifers. ' I enjoyed earlier Martin, glad you came up, how you getting on with Mike?'

'Yeah great he's a good man, so did I Louise, seem to connect well don't we?' Louise smiled and kissed Martin on the lips.

'Mikes a great guy totally down to earth and honest as the day is long, I knew you would get on.'

'Is there anything else I should know about Paul? Every time he's mentioned you go into a panic, what's the issue I thought you were long finished with that side of your life?'

Louise looked up into the night sky and answered. 'As much as I hate him and can't believe his arrogance, I still feel responsible for him in a way, I don't want any harm to come to him and feel like he's been led into something. I just need to speak to him face to face.'

Martin took her in his arms and replied. ' Whatever it is we will find out, just don't put it all on yourself, I'll help you and I'm sure Gill and Mike will back you, they're genuine people who care.'

'Martin I've not told you everything and I need to.' Louise looked into his worried expression and retold the visits to the barn and her sighting of the male.

Martin smiled and said. ' You've got nothing to fear Louise, just don't keep things from me, Im here because I want to be.'

Arm in arm they continued to stroll on the deck as headlights panned around illuminating the approach road. Louise looked back and said. 'That'll be Gills' boys, come on back inside before they eat everything in sight.'

The oblong dining table extended out to entertain eight guests with comfort, Gill set down the pot of chilli at the centre whilst Louise distributed bowls. The salads and garlic bread were filled the gaps amongst the six place settings as Lewis arched an arm over to grab four slices in one clasp. 'Hey leave some for everyone else!' Gill shouted at her son and slapped the back of his hand with a spatula. Tearing bread, salad splashing and chili being scooped was the order of the day, each guest talking, looking and serving in an orchestrated dance of hands, spoons and forks. Once the initial cravings had been satisfied the group relaxed and settled into a slower pace of picking and nibbling. The two boys could not keep their hands from the cheese coated tacos and remnants of chili sauce and continued to clear the remnants.

Martin opened two more bottles of Malbec and topped up the outstretched glasses saying to Louise. 'I haven't done this in such a long time, thanks for the invite, the food was amazing.'

'You're welcome Martin, it's good to relax and enjoy, lets raise a glass to us all and our weekend.' Cheers rang out in the room as did laughing and chat.

'So Mam what exactly are we doing this weekend, thought we were stalking tonight?' Said Rhys.

Gill wiped her lips and responded. 'I don't think anyone of us are in a fit state to go stalking tonight, anyway I want to hear about your cameras and so much has happened this week I think we need to go over everything and target the search, what you think Louise?'

'I agree Gill, come on let's leave the mess till later and go back to the sofa, we can cast to the tv and view the camera output can't we Lewis?'

Lewis had already moved to prime spot in front of the fifty inch screen and was configuring his lap top to the Chromecast. Gill brought a folder from the kitchen which contained the lab reports and her own notes. She put on her reading glasses and sorted the pages into order whilst trying to settle the group down.

'Quiet everyone the headmistress is ready.' Said Louise with a giggle.

'Thank you Louise, detention for you later. Ok just to get everyone up to speed, Louise attended the aftermath of an attack on a large female Roe Deer last Tuesday and provided the following samples; The first is a flesh sample, I've disposed of the sample now but there is a picture of it on the database.' Lewis scrolled through a file and opened an image onto the large screen, the flesh sample was scarred with a crescent shaped valley. Gill continued. 'The incision is consistent with a Panther claw but I cannot and will not speculate its size as its dependant on too many factors, so therefore I cannot attribute it to a particular Panther however if you look closely at the angle of the incision walls and extrapolate them out we can discount domestic cats. This means we can confidently log it as a Panther attack and add to the statistics. As for foreign bodies or traces in the sample I'm afraid only Roe Deer was present.' Louise looked disappointed and recalled the samples she took wishing that she had taken more to perhaps provide Gill with some Panther DNA.

Gill continued. 'The video file that you took Louise does provide some more evidence though which means that we can discount Tonmawr from carrying out the kill. Lewis could you open the next file please? I overlaid the frame capture of the incisions on the Deer's skull onto our graphics of Tonmaws jaw and soon realised that the Panther responsible for this bite was considerably larger, if you look at the link image Lewis you can see that the jaw size puts it into the male class.' The image on the screen showed an outline of the jaw in 3D and as Lewis rotated the image it was clear for all to see the Panther was at least five inches taller at the shoulder than Tonmawr.

Louise gasped at its size. ' This has to be the largest Panther we have ever seen.' Lewis zoomed in again and added.

'I overlaid the whole body against Tonmawrs size and as you can see his muscles on the shoulder are huge in comparison, almost like a different species, Mam recons I've over exaggerated the image but I've just taken standard ratios from the jaw and sized them up.'

Gill shuffled her notes and directed Lewis to the next file. As the pixels formed on the screen Gill continued. 'So this sample was the shit that Louise picked up from the barn, not much to report here except that we had traces of bone in the sample, the structure is consistent with Deer bone. DNA was extracted but we don't have a match.' Louise, subdued did not comment.

Lewis was bobbing up and down on the sofa and looked at Gill before announcing. ' This is boring shit, I've got some images from the cameras you've got to see.'

Gill looked over her reading glasses and slapped Lewis with her file before continuing. 'Wait, I still have some more information to share.' Lewis slumped back and rubbed his arm in mock pain. 'The DNA has a strain which we haven't seen in all the samples we already have. We have Tonmawrs DNA, we have her mother's DNA and we have one male unrelated DNA. That's the extent of our database boys and girls so don't get carried away thinking we are experts here, we are definitely not. I would like to say though that this DNA has an anomaly which I cannot explain.'

'Well thanks for fuck all Mam, you really strung that one out.' Rhys said and laughed out loud.

'Ok David bloody Attenborough what did you find on the cameras?' Gills response although said with venom had a hint of humour.

Lewis and Rhys settled together and opened up the first video capture. 'Ok so this is from the waterfalls, just keep watching, there she comes, Tonmawr walking into shot, followed by one, two , three cubs.' The room inched closer to the screen and wooed the vision.

Louise spoke first. 'Wow that's beautiful look how happy together they are, I guess they are about three months old?'

Martin and Mike were amazed at the images before them. 'Even though they are cubs I wouldn't like to come across them, and the mother that's definitely the one I saw by Lower Field, I can tell by the walk.'

Louise sparked up. 'That's generally how we differentiate them Martin, your quite right to pick up on that feature, each one walks in a slightly different way, their characters come through. If you could rewind please Rhys lets watch the cubs again.'

'This isn't the eighties Louise I can just select the frame.' Rhys and Lewis giggled again at the older generation.

Louise administered a slap to Rhys' arm. 'You're not too old for a wallop Rhys. Here comes the first cub, that looks like a male, he's very self-assured. Then the next she almost hops along, then there, the third with a slow loping gait, yes I'd say two females and a male cub.'

Lewis took over the laptop and brought up an image of a footprint. ' Ok so the camera at the waterfall was useless, too misty, but I did find this footprint on the bank, there are a few similar prints but this one stood out and was complete. I haven't had chance to size it up yet but it's a lot bigger than Tonmaws from memory. I think it belongs to the male we saw last summer and the male responsible for the Deer attack.'

Gill shook her head and countered. ' You cant say that for sure Lewis, it could be a different male.'

'Prepare to be shot down in flames Mam, Rhys if you will play the next file. So this is from the same camera one hour later, here comes Tonmawr, with a rabbit, then the male cub, with a rabbit, and closely followed by the two female cubs.' The images astounded the group as they took in the beautiful family enjoying their kills. The frame flickered and the new image of the same scene rolled on.

'We haven't viewed this section yet so I don't know what's going to happen.' Said Lewis.

The male known as Grey wandered up to the camera and took in its scent, as it turned to walk away its flash of grey filled the shot. Louise jumped up. ' Wait I recognise that, go back Lewis and hold the frame still.'

The image of a grey blur against a black background formed an outline. 'It's a number Gill, its, er, could you sharpen the image Lewis?'

'M7' Martin shouted out. 'It's the letter M and number 7.' As the group moved and tilted their heads they gradually spoke up in agreement.

'Your right, that's definitely M7.'Gill said.

Martin looked bemused. 'But its growing in the fur like it was born with it.'

Louise shook her head and spoke up. 'Its Freezemarking Martin, a branding iron is used, cooled in liquid nitrogen, to freeze a brand of a unique set of numbers and letters, onto a horse usually. The cold iron destroys the pigment cells on the skin so that white hairs grow within a few weeks providing a permanent identifiable mark on the horse. The freezemarking process is pain-free and the brand is usually placed under the saddle area so that it is not noticeable when the horse is ridden.

There is no need to renew the freezemark as the branded skin will permanently produce white hairs. We used to offer the service at the surgery to provide an easily identifiable unique code if stolen and allowing the horse to be traced back to the owner. However, it also acts as a useful deterant to horse thieves as it is easily visible. We had all the equipment, Im not sure if Paul still has it though.'

Gill turned to Louise ' So why the marking M7?'Louise shook her head and sat back on the sofa. Lewis loaded a new memory card into the slot on the laptop and announced.

'So this card is from the top of Horseshoe Crest, we've found tracks up there before and last summer captured an image of a large male, but, as you pointed out Mam it's the only sighting and we haven't seen him since.' The stills flicked as rabbit and bird exposed on the camera came and went. Tonmawr suddenly appeared and snatched a backward glance before trotting out of shot. The male cub appeared next followed by the loping female cub, then nothing.

'Where's the high stepping cub?' Louise exclaimed. The sequence was replayed twice, but nothing changed.

Gill spoke first, 'This was last night, Tonmawr and two cubs, The one by the falls was three nights ago, Wednesday, yes?' She looked over at Rhys for confirmation. 'So the cub has disappeared over the last couple of days.' The male Grey came into focus high on the ridge line, and disappeared from view.

Lewis jumped up and shouted. 'It's the same male he's stalking the cubs and picking them off, that's their natural instinct, he wants Tonmawr to bear his own cubs, so he'll kill the ones she's got first. That's why we keep seeing him near Tonmawr.'

Louise stood close to the screen and studied the images as Lewis toggled back frame by frame, she held up her hand as the male came into view again. 'That is definitely the same Panther I saw in the Prices barn.'

Gill joined her and they both viewed the form, Gill traced the outline. 'Such strength in the shoulders, and the hind leg is over developed, I would suggest he is from the mountain strain of Panther.'

Lewis removed the pause and allowed the file to skip to the next capture. The time was eleven eighteen a.m. Two figures walked past the camera from the side, only the legs up to the knees were visible. Lewis piped up. 'Walkers I guess, it's a popular spot, but the camera is well hidden.' Another figure arrived mid-shot but this time in full view, the overweight man staggered with hands on his knees out of breath. As he stood up his reddened face was captured in focus.

'That's Tom Price!' Louise screamed. The realization hit everyone hard that they had stumbled across a planned effort to disrupt Tonmawrs natural selection and progress.

Martin was stood leaning against the window frame watching the rain bead down to pool on the soaked deck. He turned to address the group. ' Ok everyone, this is all new to me and as an outsider I've been listening and not commenting but you need to hear this.' This opening statement drew the group to face Martin. 'You need to confront Paul and soon, it sounds to me that he is the one calling the shots and using the Prices for his own gain, whatever that is I don't know, but you all need to stop pussyfooting around and front him up, for the sake of the Panthers and that natural order thing you talk about Gill.'

Rhys nodded in agreement as Gill and Louise looked straight at each other. Rhys stood and said. ' Well you piss heads are no good, Im the only one not drinking so who's coming with me?'

'Where?' Gill questioned.

'First we go to Pauls house and take it from there, find out how he's captured a male Panther, marked it, then released it, where it is and what his intentions are, then we need to find Tonmawr up on Horseshoe Ridge, Im convinced her den is on the rock face.'

Gill & Louise rushed to the hallway and retrieved their coats. Louise announced. Martin can you come with us? Im sure Mike and Lewis will be ok.'

'Of course.' Martin replied as he finished his glass of wine. He thought it was a bad idea to go round at this time of night and would rather them waited until the morning but as he had just met these new friends he didn't want to add his opinion to the mix, far easier to go along with it for now he confirmed with his own head.

Mike stood up and motioned towards the kitchen. 'Right, do you really think crashing into Pauls house and making allegations is going to help? Im all for finding the truth but come on, listen to yourselves, he'll just deny it all. We need to catch him in the act, form a plan guys come on.'

Lewis was the first to answer following a hushed interval. ' Look we know that Tonmawr has moved her territory to Horseshoe Ridge which probably means her southern border is The Heads of the Valleys Road and West will be The River Towy, and her east is probably Devils Elbow.' Lewis walked over to the large screen and nodded at Rhys.

' When my brother wakes up, thank you, you can see on the map where our cameras have picked up the sightings and I've shown potential den locations for Tonmawr. Which means this new male, M7 or Grey has to be holed up close by. It's the male we need to catch and the only way Paul could have knowledge of its whereabouts in this vast area is through an implanted tracker.' The elders were humbled by the forethought of the youth and did not challenge his theory as Lewis continued. 'Get access to the tracker and we get the male, Tonmawr needs protection from the male, and before you butt in Mam, it's not natural for the male to suddenly appear then disappear, so Paul is interfering. There's a female with cubs out there trying to survive with a male that's been pushed onto the scene, it's not natural. Tonmawr is trying to establish a territory to raise her cubs and we need to protect her otherwise the next generation is lost. It's taken five years to get to this stage and we can't let it all go. Someone, probably Paul has captured Tonmawrs mother because we lost track of her last year suddenly, plus now he's manipulating a new male, when are you guys going to wake up and realise that we are the only people who can help prevent this happening? Let me and Rhys do some natural tracking tonight and you old gits get the tracker information from Paul.'

The group looked around at each other and muttered in agreement. Rhys and Lewis scooped up the remaining morsels from the table and left for Horseshoe Crest.

Louise flopped back onto the sofa dejected and immersed herself in her mobile phone. 'Gill can you remember when we received that dog at the practice which had a tracker fitted and we had to surgically remove it?'

'Yes it was a French Mastiff, used for breeding I believe, worth thousands. If I remember rightly it was a company in Cambridge that supplied the equipment. The owner used it as theft prevention, part of its insurance I believe. There was a local agent that supplied all the software and receivers, yes I remember now he came to the surgery with the new device for implanting but I refused to do it, I wasn't happy with the risk of infection, there didn't seem to be a sterile trail from manufacture so yes I closed him up and the breeder took him.'

Louise clutched her phone and replied. ' I don't think any of us are sober enough to drive right now, but we'll have the records at the practice, we can drop by in the morning, I'll bet it's the same kind of equipment in the Panther. We can work out Pauls whereabouts too, I'll call him and re-arrange that meet we were supposed to have in the week.'

Satisfied they had done enough the foursome settled back on the sofa and continued their evening in front of the fire. Gill mused on the facts she had delivered earlier that evening. 'Im sorry there wasn't anything conclusive Lou and I didn't mean to be harsh about the samples.'

Louise had a satisfied and relaxed smile as she turned to Gill and replied. ' That's ok I get it Gill, leave Paul to me I can gauge his mood when I speak to him and work him into providing the right information about the Panthers, he's bound to slip up and reveal something that we can use to our, and the Panthers, advantage.' Louise thought about what she would say to Paul, where to confront him and how to extract the information. Paul would protest at first but when cornered would spill information.

Chapter 21

Alan Price loaded the last of the four rifles into a steel box under the rear seat of his Subaru pick up as four of the hunting party climbed into their Range Rover. As they waited the windows started to mist up from their alcohol leaden breath. Claire De Motta stopped Alan before he drove off. ' Alan, be nice with them, make sure they all come back in one piece, and with a trophy, it's our first real test.'

Alan replied. ' We've had a positive sighting of the herd heading towards Devil's Elbow, that's about twenty minutes away so should be a quick outing, just as well, how much have they had to drink? Im more concerned that they'll crash into the back of me.'

Claire looked over to the Range Rover. ' Its sorted, one of the catering staff is driving, he's happy enough with a fifty pound bonus for a nights work plus tips.'

The convoy took half an hour to reach Devil's Elbow, which veiled in darkness and soaked with rain failed to reveal its panoramic views across the Beacons. The bend in the mountain pass provided a stone car park normally occupied by tourists. Tonight though three cars and seven males with a mission to kill wild Red Deer tarnished the beauty spot. Alan Price commanded the high stump of grass and projected his tones above the noise from the wind and rain.

'When you are ready gentlemen we will be stalking in a wide evenly spaced band no closer than ten feet from each other down towards Cray reservoir. The herd are up wind no more than twenty minutes' walk from here. As we approach the herd you can split to wider positions but on no circumstances are you to advance without first being cleared by myself or Peter Evans our head stalker. Im afraid once the first shot is fired the Deer are likely to be out of range, so between the four of you decide who takes the most likely shot. Our target will be the head Stag, a magnificent example with over eight years leading this herd, he has many suiters to carry on the herd. Good luck gentlemen and stay within the rules.'

The group fanned out as instructed and chatter diminished as they trudged through marsh and dipped to the bottom of a valley with a narrow tributary. A long step cleared the water and the rise steepened until a hand was required to assist the scramble to the next ridge. Two more undulating masses lead the group to flatter land where the Red Deer were grazing under jet black skies. Night vision scopes were attached to the rifles and their covers removed as the hunters sobered up. Now within two hundred yards the four men settled on their fronts and nestled into firing positions. Alan checked with Peter and his son and they grouped behind the armed hunters. With a slow gait Alan approached the four and offered advice. ' Ok it's all yours gentlemen, decide on your positions and capabilities and work out the shots, we will remain at a safe distance. Once you've confirmed a kill signal back to us and we will come forward with you to retrieve.'

Not a word was uttered between the four as they rose and fell during their advance. The Red Deer remained undisturbed but alert and standing. They would rarely lie or rest in the open during wet nights but keep moving as one. The relay of movement and settling by the four members of the hunting club impressed Alan who initially had dismissed the men as rich playboys with no idea how to stalk Red Deer. James Pringle being the club chairman lead the group of four. His hand signals and nods conducted the teams movements with exactness and fluidity. As they reached their final firing positions an arc had been formed in the silence. Alan had lost sight of the four but remained in position with Peter and his son. Over five minutes passed without incident until the night air was sliced open by the crack of the round leaving the barrel. In the same instant three more rounds had pierced the darkness creating echoing waves against the natural barriers over a mile away. Then silence. Alan walked forward calling out to the group who responded as one 'clear.'

'Fuck me that was close Rhys.' Lewis stood up from the hide and ranged his view towards Cray Reservoir as the rippling echoes faded into the silent night air.

'Definitely Deer rounds Lewis, I counted four shots, they would have spooked Tonmawr if she's around here.' The pair remained stood leaning on the damp frame of the hide with night scopes projected out covering the falling land towards where the Deer herd had been grazing.

'Four shots and three dead Deer Lewis, I can make out a large male, the antlers are sticking up. Look out, figures approaching from your left.' Into view six or seven figures trudged through the bog towards the humps of dead animals, now silent and still.

Alan Price knelt beside the stag and shone his penlight into the reflecting globes. ' Good shot who ever had this one, he died instantly, bullet to the spinal cord, ripped straight through.'

James Pringle pushed the antler tip with the weight of his boot which rotated the stags head up and allowed the lower jaw to spill fresh blood. ' Have this one transported straight away Mr Price if you will, I'd like the full service including delivery on a mount to the club.' The pair marched to the next body only yards from the stag, it was a female adult lying on its side as if it were sleeping.

'Enough for venison I'd suggest.' Said James as he smudged the blood from its heart across the forehead of the youngest in the group. ' Good shot for your first blood Liam, enjoy the feast.'

The third carcass was a young fully grown male with the start of soft antlers with half of its jaw missing. ' What rounds are you using Adam?' Said James with an accusing look. The muttered answer from Adam prompted a huff from the group. 'Change the weight, reduce the exit velocity, oh and adjust your sights you were lucky with that shot.'

Alan Price trotted after James and in hushed tones said. 'We will struggle to move all three animals tonight can I suggest we leave the young male to the foxes?'

James put a hand on Alans shoulder and replied. ' Absolutely my man, plus we wouldn't want to advertise such poor shooting to our South American colleagues.' The group in the dead of night packed together and worked the boggy ground with triumphant boasting and laughing up to the vehicles. Amber liquid in cut glass crystal baubles warmed the lips and fogged the moist air surrounded by the triumphant huddle.

'Look at the fucking mess those twats have left behind.' Said Lewis as he and Rhys treaded the battlefield and choked at the devastation.

' I just don't get it Lewis, where's the enjoyment in slaughtering such beautiful creatures.' Rhys shouted out 'Wankers' towards the parked cars which were over three miles away. As the mist from his breath condensed, a pair of headlights appeared in the distance.

Rhys looked over his shoulder and said. 'Come on lets head down to the river check for prints, they'll be coming to take their prizes.'

Chapter 22

The bright morning tore through the previous days mist and drizzle as if every day was like this. It lifted the spirits of Louise as she leaned on the silvered upright of the covered walkway around the lodge. These solitary moments were why she had chosen to keep the sanctuary. She pondered on the previous night's events as she caressed her solitary mug of fresh ground coffee. Louise cursed her own inbuilt alarm clock which rattled her over active imagination well before the winter sun travelled to its low arc and filtered through the evergreens bordering her property. Rhys and Lewis arrived back from their night quest and didn't notice Louise who had returned to brew more coffee in the silence of the kitchen. As they kicked off their boots and entered the side door Gill padded into the kitchen with an empty glass in search of water.

'Sore head Mam?' Gill didn't answer her eldest son but held up a warning palm and steadied herself with her left hand in front of the running tap. The boys in tandem retold their events of last night to the two hungover women.

Louise said. ' So who do you think it was out hunting the Deer?' Rhys opened the fridge and pulled out a twin pack of bacon and threw it to Lewis.

'Couldn't work out exactly who but it looked like an organised event, so I guess the Prices were there. We left and went down to the river and found something though.' Gill spluttered with her water struggling to ingest the cold liquid. Rhys' pat to her head aggravated the situation but also fired Gill into life.

'What did you find Rhys?'

'Muntjacs, one abandoned kid and a dead mother, no injuries though just dead it'd been there a day at the most. The kid was frozen to the spot so we picked it up and set it down further up the bank, it trotted off fine. No signs of Tonmawr though. We need that tracker information Louise.'

Louise had taken the bacon from Lewis and was splitting out the slices and placing them on a grill tray, she didn't look up but answered. ' Yes Lewis I know, Ill ring Paul after breakfast and work it out from there.'

Martin had heard the commotion and joined the group, followed closely by Mike.

Lewis continued. ' We moved back up to Horshoe Ridge to pick up the card we replaced last night in the camera, had a quick look and saw Tonmawr again just before sunrise. So we scaled down the face and started looking for dens. There's a crevice we couldn't reach, you could get to it if you abseiled down I guess, anyway we think Tonmawr is in there. We moved back down the ridge then waited in the copse opposite the face of the ridge, just to see if there was any movement from the den, but nothing. Oh we did find an empty bottle of Whiskey in the copse and evidence of stalkers, so I reckon The Prices were in there.

Louise's phone buzzed across the granite worktop. She reached it before the phone cascaded to the cold slate floor but not before the ringing stopped. She retrieved the missed call as she bounced back to the group who had continued with their conversation about finding the tracker.

'Hi Jo, sorry I missed you, couldn't run quick enough, what's up?' Louise's tone stopped the groups conversation and they turned to view her confused expression. 'Really, no way, that's …..'the words trailed away from the concerned faces. She returned when finished and slumped next to Gill leaning against the counter, arms fell to her side.

' What is it Louise is Jo ok?'

'Yes, sorry, yes she's fine Gill, but you're not going to believe this, she met Guy Davies, the farmer who she rents Annie's field from, well he said that he had Paul up the farm on Thursday night and he sedated a Panther cub that was locked in their barn, apparently Sue had found it and the cub had scratched her arm.'

'Oh my god Louise, where is it now? is Sue ok?' Gill answered.

Louise dragged her teeth across the corner of her mobile and continued. ' I presume so, Jo didn't say, I guess it was startled and took a swipe. Apparently Paul took the cub to the RSPCA Wildlife Centre.'

Martin and Mike shook their heads in unison and Martin spoke up. 'Sounds like we're overrun by wild animals, never thought Id ever see anything like this, I mean I've now heard of three separate sightings in a week plus the two I've seen.'

'Don't be too shocked Martin, that's what happens when humans get close and interfere with wild animals in their natural habitat.' Gill said. Louise paced around the kitchen still holding her phone and tapping it against her lower teeth then announcing.

'Ok Im going to phone Paul and find out what he's up to I've had enough of this. Guy told Jo about the cub they found, so come on, it's not difficult to work out.' Gill interrupted Louise's flow.

'That fucker has got Tonmawrs cub, but how the fuck has he done that. It sounds to me that Paul was asked to attend by Guy at the farm, he should have taken it straight to the centre, Ill phone them now, I know them, to find out if it's been brought in, then we will speak to Paul, you ok with that Lou?'

'Im just so angry Gill, he's interfering and I just can't get close to what's going on.'

Rhys bobbed down to view the bacon in the grill and motioned towards the toaster. He filled the toaster with four slices of white bread and turned the bacon in the grill. 'This won't be enough for everyone Louise.' Rhys said with a hopeful tone.

'Yes you and Lewis can have all that, I'll put some more on, anyone would think you've never been fed.'

Gill walked back from the sofa and said. ' Ok I spoke to the centre, they haven't had any visits from Paul, I didn't mention the Panther just asked if there's been anything unusual from Paul. They haven't seen him for months. So there we have it, Paul has the cub, or he's moved it on.'

Louise picked up her phone and dialled Pauls number as she looked at the kitchen clock which showed seven thirty. It rang to answer phone but she decided not to leave a message. Martin gave Louise a peck on the cheek and said. 'Im off into work for a few hours, should be finished by five, I'll give you a call and we can meet up or shall I come back here?'

Louise hadn't thought about Martin and she realised again her thoughts were elsewhere. 'Sorry, yes that's fine Martin, come back up we will probably be going for a walk late afternoon, but call me first just to make sure, oh and thanks for coming over.' Louise escorted Martin to the back door and they kissed before he left.

Gill was waiting for Louise in the kitchen. 'Well that seemed to go well Lou, he's a good man your well suited.' Mark nodded in agreement with his wife and added. ' Yeh we had a good chat last night and he's smitten with you Louise.'

Louise thanked them both and continued to prepare more bacon before answering. 'Gill are you and Mike ok here this morning, I'm going to visit Paul.'

'What are you going to say?'

Louise faced Gill and with arms folded, looked up from the grill and replied. 'Don't know yet, I hope it'll come to me when I see his face, but I'm not going to mention the cub, I'll just start the conversation about the attack at Annie's field and gauge his response.'

Mike and the boys had moved to the sofa and were tucking into the first round of bacon butties whilst flicking through the Freeview channels.

Gill moved closer to Louise and asked. ' Why don't you just front him up about the cub?'

'Because he'll deny it and clam up, trust me I know him Gill, he's like a child when questioned. You have to tease information out and then he slips up. Once he's realised that he's fucked up he'll break down and tell me everything.'

Gill continued to press. 'For what it's worth Louise, I think Paul is a lot cleverer than you think. The times I've dealt with him through work he's been extremely cautious about what he reveals, he certainly wont give up information about the cub because he must have a strong motive to be so eager to get his hands on it. Let me go to see him Louise, I can angle it differently from a more professional stance, I …..'

'No Gill!' Louise exclaimed. 'Its up to me to sort this out.'

Gill was rocked back at the vigorous response but pressed still further. 'Lou were in this together, your too emotionally involved to deal with this properly, don't push me out, let's go together.'

Louise shifted her weight from the counter top and turned away from Gill, as she bent down to turn the bacon on the grill she croaked an answer. ' I've got to do this on my own, no offence Gill but leave it to me.'

Gill sensed the anxiety in Louise's reply. 'Is there something your not telling me Lou?'

Louise continued to tend the sizzling bacon, her hair shrouded the welling tears as she rolled her lips tight. She was torn between revealing the truth to Gill and continuing with her defence. A deep nasal inhale sided with defence as she fished. ' No, why?'

177

'It's just every time I mention speaking to Paul you clam up and push me out, what's going on are you still seeing him is that it?'

Louise's relief translated to a nervous laugh as she shook her head.

'Well what the fuck is it then?'

'Gill stop fretting, there's nothing going on with Paul and me, but as I said, I know him in a way you'll never understand, I can tell when he's lying and I know we'll have a better chance of finding out what he's involved in if you leave it to me.'

Gills frustration and anger ebbed as the pair hugged then made up the batch of bacon rolls.

Mike looked up as the warm stacked plates and bacon rolls were placed on the coffee table. ' So what's the plan girls, I take it from your bickering you've sorted everything out and we can relax and enjoy the rest of the weekend?'

A smile and glance to Mike from Gill as she tucked into her breakfast settled the group. The satisfying feeling from the nutrition also calmed Louise's nerves and allowed her mind to focus on the next steps.

'Rhys did you say Tonmaws den was on Horshoe Ridge on the rock face?'

'Looks like it, yes, I guess you could reach it from the base, maybe worth securing a rope from above, it's a scramble really but there are some dodgy parts to the climb.'

Lewis wiped his mouth with the back of his hand and added. 'I wouldn't want to disturb them during the day, I think we should go back to the copse at dusk and wait for them to leave, then scale it, but what's the point, once we confirm them leaving there's nothing much to see in the den?'

Gill nodded in agreement and said. ' I guess that means you boys will be sleeping most of the day, well Lewis could you find out more about the tracker first? I've got some information at the practice so Ill pop down and get the files, Ill give that rep a ring as well, find out what I can.'

Chapter 23

From their vantage point Tonmawr and Grey watched the Deer slither along the grass being dragged behind a Land Rover and disappear out of site. An hour of still darkness without movement proved sufficient time for Grey to rise and edge forward. As Tonmawr and her cubs remained prone Grey galloped to the abandoned carcass. Stopping short Grey took in the air and looked up to Tonmawr who by now was standing tall as a look out. Grey tore at the underbelly and managed to slide the body to the cover of a ditch. Satisfied with the location Tonmawr bounded with her cubs to join Grey. Her instinct pushed her close but she remained at a respectful distance to honour the larger males position at the swelling abdomen. The cubs stayed tight to her side and observed the feeding, knowing it was not their catch. As Grey rolled away licking his paws he offered a signal to Tonmawr and the cubs that it was their turn to eat. Within an hour all viable meat to support the predators had been consumed. Traces of gristle and bone would be picked by Crows and Magpies. The skin and fur would be taken too by the insects and grubs until the carcass blended into the soil. Opportunity rarely feeds but tonight the group were satisfied without the expense of energy.

Trust between the unlikely paring was now loosely cemented by the trowel of sharing two catches. Grey had made the distinct transition from a lone predator to a group member. His ingrained desire to hunt solo had been modified to include others. Without a traditional upbringing, mother, siblings and occasional sparing with his father, Grey was adapted to his changing environment.

The rewards were increasing. For two nights they had eaten well without disbursing valuable energy. The relationship was akin to a mother son and siblings situation which Grey was comfortable with. The desire to mate was growing stronger as he moved into his third season but Tonmawr was not receptive. Choosing instead to maintain a hierarchy of control and a defensive stance. She continued to distrust this relationship with a strong sense of protection but also enjoyed the strength in numbers. Tonmawr for the first time directed her cubs back to the den without fearing an attack from Grey allowing him to mark the rear of the caravan. As they reached their den Grey had followed close and sat upright at the entrance. The cubs curled into the darkness at the rear of the den and eyed the large male, curiosity prevented them from settling down. Tonmawr approached Grey and moved in to take scent. It was her grooming tongue that noticed the hard plastic collar fitted to Grey. Unaware of its origin and it being alien to her previous male encounters Tonmawr growled and tugged with her incisors at the matt black mass. It afforded little movement and irritated Grey who contracted his neck and on one paw stretched to cup its underside in an attempt to relieve himself of the tracker.

A parting growl and lifting of her head signalled to Grey that he was not welcome in the den. He bounded to his upper lair and settled before sunrise warmed the day.

Paul Morris had not slept and continued to be enthralled by the tracker movements on the laptop. As the movement stopped he reviewed the nights events. From his encounter at the copse he could follow the movement west to the river and back towards the den. He marked each turn point and noted the star forming as the male hunted, alone surely he thought. The most unusual point was no movement between midnight and four a.m. Had the signal been lost? Or was he simply resting? The movement returned Grey to Horseshoe Ridge at the centre point, elevation unknown. As Paul annotated the screenshot he rubbed his tired eyes and opened his desk draw for the fourth time that night.

The silver foil was by now a crumpled labyrinth which split as Paul stretched and pulled it apart in search of cocaine. The dust mixed with draw debris would not satisfy the craving. Paul scrolled his contacts and disregarding the time called Tom Price. It was seven o'clock on a Saturday morning and with alcohol fuelled sleep Tom Price did not answer. Pauls desperate search led him to the glove box of his silver Range Rover which despite false hope was devoid of the drug he craved. His mobile phone dropped from his shirt pocket to the litter strewn foot well as he stretched prone to close the glove box, as he cursed he sensed the proximity of a figure. Through a crooked arm and half open driver's door he could make out dark jeans and the hem of a green coat.

'Hello Paul, can we talk?'

'Claire! Yes, sure it's early for you isn't it?

'Busy times Paul, you look like shit have you slept?'

Paul glanced in the rear view mirror and smoothed his thatch in an attempt to look presentable, the matted locks and stubble merged over an insipid membrane. He shifted off the seat and slammed the drivers door shut before heading to the main front door which he had left wide open. Heightened realisation of the decrepit state of his practice building smacked him square in the face. His blurred vision caused by drug dependency hid the reality which Claire reacted to with a hand covering her mouth as the damp animal odour enveloped the pair.

'You need to clean up your act Paul, this place disgusts me. I've invested heavily and this is how you treat it?'

Paul shuffled through the corridor and rested at his desk. 'I take it you're here to discuss arrangements for tonight with the Panther?'

Claire retained the shield of her coat despite the stifling heat of the windowless surgery. 'Ok remind me, from the start, what is happening with all the Panthers supposedly under your care?'

Paul shook his head and rubbed both temples with the back of closed fists before taking a deep breath and facing Claire's imposing glare. ' My original plan was to take the female #1 to the house but as you probably know her pregnancy has complications, she has a dead foetus which could cost her life and it needs removing. I've consulted Dr Kim and he's sending over assistance so we can perform the procedure tomorrow. We have three males available but as they are fully grown Im reluctant to show them uncaged. Grey #7 is mobile, being tracked and I know his whereabouts however I have reservations about bringing him in. It'll take a good team and a couple of days to dart him and transport to the house. Plus he is stalking a female, Tonmawr, who is from #1s first litter. She is completely wild, never been captive and would be totally unsuitable. Also she has three cubs, one of which has become estranged, more by good fortune, I managed to capture her, she's in my care. Which leads us back to the males, they are from #1s fourth litter. The only captive litter to survive into adulthood.'

Claire pieced together the situation and replied. ' All we are trying to do tonight is present a healthy Panther to the hunting club and entice them into joining a live hunt next weekend, as for trophies the feisty male in a cage is perfect.'

Relieved Paul replied. 'Tom Price has the male in a cage already, I need to fit the tracking device and work out a hunt route. Do you need me there tonight Claire to demonstrate the Panther?'

Claire loosened her jacket and passed a sealed black plastic envelope to Paul. ' If you can stay awake, yes I do, this should help, sort yourself out Paul.' Paul was embarrassed at his condition but could not function without the cocaine, he was trying to juggle too many balls. The cracks were fully formed and could not be closed, he was close to a breakdown and he knew it. 'Claire do we have to introduce this hunt, Im trying to progress the Panther programme for Dr Kim and that will bring in far more money once it's up and running.'

'That's the problem Paul, its going to be years before that money comes in, in the meantime I need to recover fifty grand and this is the solution.' Satisfied with the situation Claire dusted her hands and made for the exit. Before leaving she turned and asked Paul. 'That ex-wife of yours, Louise? She's been snooping around at Alan Prices farm buildings. Sort her out Paul we don't need any more distractions, apparently she's become the local expert on Panthers and is on to something.'

Paul did not reply, his swallow prevented the use of his voice box and his dry mouth held his lips tight.

Louise towel dried her hair and shook it around her shoulders allowing the wet tips to release droplets down her back. With her body fully awake and fresh clean underwear on she felt good. As she reflected on her night with Martin, a squeeze of her thighs brought a smile to her face. Dressed and full of positive thoughts she returned to Gill before making her way to Pauls surgery, certain that he would be there.

Gill was deep in conversation with Rhys and Lewis at the laptop on the coffee table. Without looking up she beckoned Louise. I think we may have a way in Lou look at this.'

Gill with frequent interruptions from Lewis to correct her technical inaccuracies described the GPS system.

'So we looked in more detail at the footage from the cameras and if you remember we focused on the grey mark and deduced it was a number, 7, what we failed to notice was the dark shadow under his jaw, Lewis took a still from the video and sharpened up the image, you can make out the transmitter and collar.'

Rhys leaned over and moved the laptop around and continued. 'I think it's an IBB GPS system, I used the same on a research programme at Uni last summer, they are the latest and best for gathering data and can pinpoint the subject to within five metres, the battery technology gives twenty eight days of data depending on the transmitter frequency set up. The data is linked to a mobile network with a secure IP address but commonly linked to a mobile phone. '

Louise sensed the next step and asked. 'So if we get access to the mobile phone its linked to we could receive the data?'

Rhys interjected ' Yeh but you need the APP and the software, which I've downloaded to this laptop. You need to get hold of Pauls phone and link to it, he probably wont realise its linked. The only other option is to hack into his IP address on his laptop or PC, but that's more risky as we could interrupt the data flow and it changes the address.'

Louise shook her head.' Ok, Ok that's too technical for me and it sounds risky.'

Gill prompted Louise. ' If you can get hold of his phone for five minutes you can link to your mobile and Lewis will do the rest.'

Paul Morris had taken the cocaine and was in full flow cleaning his office surgery and moving into the corridor with the mop as Louise entered through the unlocked main entrance.

'Hello, Paul are you there?'

The mop fell from its perch and splashed opaque liquid over Pauls shoes as he startled a response.

'Louise! What are you doing here?'

'Nice to see you as well Paul, don't you remember we were supposed to meet the other night and you didn't show up, well I was passing and saw your car so here I am.'

Pauls confused state failed to make sense of the situation as he apologised and ushered Louise towards the reception area away from the cub and #1.

Louise started the conversation with updates on their children to put him at ease. The estranged couples common bond fostered a compliant and open discussion putting them both at ease. Louise's thoughts were working hard in the background as she listened to Paul.

'I've heard you were called out to Guys farm something about a Panther cub?'

'Ah yes, I was going to call you to let you know but it's been so busy here.'

Louise looked around and could see no evidence of clients, patients or staff, only abandonment.

'I did want to see it to take a DNA sample so we can confirm if its related to Tonmawr, plus I bet its cute as anything so would love to see it, but I guess it's at the RSPCA Wildlife Centre now?'

'Err yes, they picked it up yesterday, but err not sure if it went to the Swansea centre, oh wait I think they took it up to Bristol, not sure.'

Louise looked away and took a deep breath. 'You Fucking Liar, don't you think we checked Paul, where the fuck is it?'

'Get out Louise, this is none of your business, how dare you accuse me of lying, Im a professional and how I deal with the Panthers is no concern of yours ,oh and may I remind you that there is an injunction preventing you from being within half a mile of Alan Prices property and indeed this surgery building, so get the fuck out before I call the Police.'

Pauls reddened face and diluted pupils shook Louise into submission but she managed a reply. 'Paul you're a mess and whatever your mixed up in I can help you, just be honest with me, what are you doing with the cub, it belongs back with its mother before it's too late. Look what happened to the first Panther, she's disappeared now and her legacy gone, all that hard work for nothing, just let me help you Paul.'

Pauls anger boiled over and he stood bearing over Louise. ' I don't need your help Louise, and may I also remind you that you started the captive programme and then abandoned me, so just Fuck off now, get out, out!'

Louise flooded with tears pulled her arms in close and ran out of the doors to bright sunlight and the comfort of her car where protected and cocooned she sobbed. As she composed herself deflated she opened her window to breath in the fresh air. The noise at first was low in tone and difficult to make out then it linked into the cars speakers and sounded loud, ending in Pauls answer phone message. ' Surely he hasn't left the door unlocked?' Louise thought. She kicked open her door and made one step to the passenger door of Pauls Range Rover, it opened and spilled rubbish to the tarmac. She located the phone and cancelled the call. 'Come on, come on, think

Louise, think.' She recalled Lewis's instructions and side by side linked Pauls phone to hers, then placed it back amongst the debris and edged the door closed.

Chapter 24

The Prices family country home had been transformed from a respectable house into a commercial operation pampering to strangers. Where once children had played and land owners provided a stable life for their wards there was now decadence and an open disregard for sustainability. The Prices had pawned out their inheritance and whored out their land. After a day's hunting the Cheltenham Club were in high spirits, the younger element were cavorting around the snooker table half dressed and high on cocaine. The hired staff fought to keep up their service of cocktails and canapé's. Alistair Bunce bounded through the panelled doorway almost knocking over a waitress in her teens, barely strong enough to carry the tray of empty and broken glasses. His enormous frame brushed her aside without recognition, and with arms triumphantly held high announced. ' She wasn't worth twenty never mind the two-hundred it cost me.' The reaction was uproar and laughter as he re-joined the group. The billiard room was saturated with cigar and cigarette smoke. It billowed under the low lights above the green cloth, and layered a blue grey interweaving screen across the room. Alistair Bunce hushed the audience as his quarry entered the room in her underwear. The two hundred pounds he paid her bought not only his own satisfaction but the chance for her to earn more from his friends. Tom Price knew his guests well, he knew their needs and he provided Swansea's best for an evening of pleasure.

The drawing room was rather more sedate although the atmosphere as arrogant. Conversations around the fire centred around the ability to retell a story louder and more outrageous than the last. The South American contingent were becoming bored and the chairman Adrian Miles could sense their disdain. Claire Da Motta's timing could not have been better.

Claire circled the wing backed chairs caressing the bulbous shoulders of deep red and tan leather. Adrian looked up and invited her over the threshold onto the thick woollen pile of symmetrical patterns with an outline of deep crimson. The change in height caught her heal and caused her knee to drop, as her arm extended out to steady her falling frame a large warm hand cupped her side and steadied the imbalance. 'So sorry, Mr ...?'

'Snr Flores, Bautista or Bo if you prefer Miss ?'

'Claire, Claire De Motta, thank you for sparing me the embarrassment of a fall.'

Adrian Miles was stood by now offering a gesture and smile to assist if he could. The formal introductions and brief resumes were expertly flavoured by Adrian as he conducted the group back down to their seats. The bores had been uprooted by a raised eyebrow and inaudible comment from Adrian, smarting, they made their excuses and left the group. The large group naturally filtered down to Adrian, Bo and his confident Bruno Vargas, with Claire being afforded the focal chair to which the men faced with relieved anticipation.

Claire was now ready to accept the flirtatious gestures and compliments from the strongest trio she had ever sat with. Her black cocktail dress hem followed the curves from hamstring over thigh, dipping then rising again to her right crossed leg, the curve dropped a line to her bottom. Her pointed black stiletto formed a barrier as it thrust forward, a high arch of flesh took the eye upwards to her tanned knee. She wet her lips with a fresh glass of prosecco and with a hand that was within reach of Adrian's draped veined muscular forearm, which Claire caressed before she opened her gambit.

'I trust you and your guests are satisfied with the event so far?'

Adrian reached his left hand over his body to touch Clair's fingers which had retained their touch on his right forearm. 'Bo, Bruno are you happy with the hunt?'

Bruno edged forward on his low seated chair and twiddled his cufflink before answering. ' The sport is good Claire and the hospitality as good as any country house I have visited.'

Bo laughed out loud and interjected. 'Bruno this is the only country house you have ever visited.' Claire smiled and raised her glass in a mock toast to the house.

Adrian relayed the day's events and encouraged Bo and Bruno to retell their experiences to Claire before asking. ' Claire you mentioned an enhanced package yesterday, would you care to elaborate?'

Claire seized the moment and invited Adrian to join her at the stables. A glint in Bos eyes delayed the visit as he tied his gaze to Claire and began his tried and tested routine to flatter and entice Claire into a deeper more private discussion later that evening. Claire responded with a signal which hooked Bo, it was a subtle turn of the head and slight opening of the mouth and caress of her own waist drawing a curve up and over her breast to adjust the bra strap whilst her eyes were fixed on Bos torso. As Adrian and Claire made their excuses she leant in close to Bo as he rose, preventing him from rising fully, her height in ascendance she held his arm at the elbow and said. 'Snr Flores I look forward to a more detailed conversation with you after dinner, Im sure I could provide you with some favourable introductions.'

Paul Morris sat on the transport cage at the stables waiting for Claire to arrive. He had manoeuvred the male Panther into a wood lined pen more akin to housing a pedigree stallion. Its oak tops were stained a deep sienna, brass fixings held the door firm and the opening where a horse would normally look out and bob its head into a feed bag provided an ideal view of the Panther , now circling its enclosure.

The new tag had been fitted to the Panthers thick neck, a smaller tracker which blended well with the dark ruffles. Pauls laptop and mobile were working hard to link and configure the tracker to which he allocated the sign #M8. Transport sedatives ebbed away from the large male predator as he clawed the wooden walls, his paws rested on the rounded tops and touched the protruding black iron bars which rodded up to the panelled roof. He tested the strength of the enclosure by pushing up with his hind legs forcing front pads into the oak which remained compact. The door provided clear daylight through the U shaped cut out. The Panther weighed up a leap to squeeze an escape route. The first attempt rocked the iron bolt that connected oak to ribbed concrete. The gap though enticing was too small and high for his shoulder frame to slip through. The knock back and fall onto fresh hey relapsed the Panthers energy. He circled and settled in the far corner, contrasting light and dark perfectly.

As Claire and Adrian entered the stable corridor Paul Morris looked up at the regal couple. Their air was confident and marked as if arriving to open a new hospital wing. With the laptop whirring Paul set it to one side and greeted them with a firm handshake. Claire spoke first. ' May I introduce Dr Paul Morris, Paul this is Adrian Miles Chairman of the Cheltenham Hunting Club.' Claire tells me you have an interesting animal for us to discuss?'

Claire dusted her hem and urged Paul to speak up with a smile and nod.

'Walk this way Adrian you can see for yourself.' The Panther had already built a mental image of the predators in its midst. He could not escape so must prepare for attack. A simple decision reached based upon his surroundings. The three separate scents, one being familiar suggested he would be attacked. He prepared for a leap, back paws shuffled through the hey and wedged the skirt of oak and colder concrete, front legs limp, resting on the spring of straw. As the clip clop, shuffle and scrape approached he launched at the door and thumped hard with weighty pads growling an explosion of anger before landing side on maximising his high shoulder, low head turned up eyes intensifying the contrast of saturated black and glazed blue. Adrian cowered as Claire grinned over his convex back at a smiling Paul. 'Bullfighting was something I did not expect Dr Morris, he must weigh over two tons, Bo and Bruno will be impressed though I can't see it catching on in Wales, or do you plan to export?'

Paul peeped over the yoke and beckoned Adrian. 'Take a closer look'.

As a child would be transfixed by a wild animal at the zoo Adrian miles was frozen to the spot as he followed the circling Panther with diluted pupils. 'Magnificent specimen, a Panther I presume? It has the shoulders of a Lion, and the collar?'

Paul explained the tracker before Claire stepped in. ' Our proposition Adrian is to provide your club with an exclusive Panther Hunt right here in the Brecon Beacons. We will provide the guide, tracking equipment and transport, your prize is there in front of you and with careful management there are other Panthers to hunt. Ultimately the choice is yours, but obviously that comes at a cost.'

Adrian's eyes remained glued to the Panther but replied with confidence. ' I presume you would prepare and mount the trophy as well?'

Paul Morris stepped closer. ' Of course, all part of the service, however we must insist upon discretion, this will be strictly by personal invitation and each hunter must be personally vetted by yourself.'

'Of course Dr Morris, our club is exclusive, you have my word. Could you explain the mechanics of the hunt?'

'Quite simply we track the animal using the GPS to within five metres, and you put a team of four within half a mile. We are aware of the Panthers habits and routes so after release he will settle in an area after two or three days, he then settles into a stalking routine at dusk and through the night, often the same Deer trails you are used to. From there we remain at a discreet distance and keep in radio contact with yourselves. You then have roughly eight hours to track and kill.'

'And the cost Claire, I presume you are dealing with that element?'

Claire struggled to control her heart beat as she took a deep breath. ' I'd suggest we have an introductory hunt this week with yourselves for a nominal fee of say thirty thousand a head and from there you can work out your expenses, a cost for future guests could then be agreed to accommodate your cut Adrian.

Adrian nodded in agreement as his fingers dropped from their resting place at the top of the gate.

Chapter 25

Martin Quinn arrived back at the lodge just before five pm, his Saturday at the wind farm afforded him the luxury of an uninterrupted catch up of the workload for the following week, planning, scheduling and deliveries sorted he returned his thoughts to Louise. Her car had moved and was facing nose in to the lodge, she's been out he deduced. Before leaving his truck he reflected on the previous night, his enjoyment and relaxation with a woman he desired was exciting his body, he wanted more but there was a niggling doubt in his mind, was Louise being honest with him? Was she just using him? He felt she was being genuine but the distraction of the Panther was strong, he knew it was her passion, he also sensed she needed his steadying influence, would the two work together he thought?

His doubts were soon levelled as Louise bounded from the back door to greet him with a fling of arms and deep sensual kiss. 'God I missed you today. How was work? We have had some developments come on in.' Martin sensed it again, elation and a smothering of love quickly followed by a re-focus on the Panther.

The kitchen was buzzing with excitement as the pair hand in hand breezed in. 'Let me see, let me see.' Gill cried as if a child.

' Wait Mam it's still loading, it takes a while there's twice the amount of data, could do with more memory.' Lewis replied.

Martin joined the throng and asked. ' What is it ,what have you found?'

'If Mam stops refreshing the screen and let it load, I'll show you Martin!' Lewis's frustrations at the errant childlike behaviour were boiling over.

'So we managed to gain access to the tracker and have been following Grey for three hours, he hasn't moved from Horseshoe Ridge but in the last ten minutes he's moved in short bursts in around his den. At the same time we received a notification of another tracker with the code #M8, that hasn't moved its up at Aber-llia in a farmhouse, Rhys is trying to ID the address.'

'It's registered to Jim Price, Aber-llia House it's called.' Rhys shouted over.

Mike offered Martin a cold beer from the fridge and rested on the counter next to him.

'When they get their minds on the job they get results, not a bad team eh?'

Martin responded. 'Im impressed guys, I won't ask how you managed this but my money is on Louise carrying out some dodgy dealings.'

Mike clinked his bottle to Martins and confirmed his comments with a nod and closed lipped smile.

'I want to see Grey, we should go now, come on.' Gills excitement was boiling over. Louise was quiet and hovering around her shoulders. Lewis persuaded Gill to wait until darkness provided a veil before the teams expedition.

Louise was deep in thought about the outing. Tonmawr was her primary goal, would Grey lead them to her and her cubs? Would her lost cub be re-united with her family?

Gill broke her concentration. ' This is great news Lou, you did well getting the phone, What shall we do when we locate Grey?'

Louise pondered on the question as she didn't have an answer. The reality was that Grey was the key to locating Tonmawr. ' Not sure Gill, ideally we need to locate Tonmawr and Grey is the most viable method but then what?'

Lewis listened to the conversation and butted in. ' You're at it again, look its simple. We locate Grey, sedate him and remove the collar. We locate Tonmawr sedate her and fit the collar. That way once we rescue the cub we can re-unite the family.'

Louise shook her head. ' Simple? Really Lewis that's not an easy task. Your assuming that Paul doesn't find her first, and just as an aside, how do we rescue the cub?'

Martin chipped in. ' We need to rescue the cub, that's got to be our first job.'

Gill returned from the hallway and zipped up her waterproof jacket.' Ok so were all agreed, tonight we locate Grey and try to locate Tonmawr and that's all. Let's observe and learn their behaviour, trust me we need to understand their characters, the tracker is a massive help but it only tells us one thing, location.

We need to understand their agendas, we can learn a lot from observations. So we take three vehicles and position ourselves around the dens, when they move we move as one keeping distance and cover. Lewis & Rhys you take the closest point, Lou and Martin south and me with Mike north. Keep the Watsap chat open so we can all communicate. Well come on lets go, this is the closest any of us have ever been to these beautiful amazing animals, lets enjoy the experience.'

Louise knew different, she squirmed in silence at her involvement three years ago with Paul.

Tonmawr rose at dusk and followed the same ritual, taking in the scent of the evening air, small steps to the den entrance and still undercover work out the wind direction. The male cub followed Tonmawrs hind legs and took in the bouquet of the damp drizzle. The drizzle helped and hindered the group. It disguised their scent but also masked their prey and more importantly their predators.

Grey had left his perch above Tonmawr before dusk to take water from the pooled falls at the ridge bottom. The bedrock jutted up before the ridge faultline creating a natural spring which saturated the foreground and melted into reed filled bog. The tuft islands jutted above the waterline of the high water table. The clear shallow water refreshed Grey and the tuft was soft as he waited for Tonmawr to join him.

Tonmawrs priority this wet evening was to complete her survey and remark the boundaries. Hunger was not an issue, but if the opportunity should arise, she would take it. She also needed a secondary den within her territory, which would require a lot of ground to be covered this night. Her cubs were ready, but would Grey follow? He would sense it was not a hunt and probably lose interest as his instincts were more focused on prey. Tonmawr felt more at ease in the damp conditions, she glided with ease amongst thick vegetation. Heather and briar did not penetrate her dense fur nor did it seem to impede her progress. Her raw sienna colouring soaked in the moisture of the night, her darker spots were shaped as smudged paw prints each one nudging into the next with a circumference of sienna. Silver lengths fringed the crevice between her toes and were shooting from her underbelly as it arched to the muscle of her upper hind legs. These glints formed her frame and provided clues as to her age and size when viewed from a distance. Her proportioned neck and head sprouted silver whiskers which extended beyond the width of her rounded shoulders and drooped at the tips to cradle moist droplets. Her forehead and crown between delicate ears afforded deeper ripples of dense short pelt creating patterns which formed images of tonal faces.

As she walked with a low head her shoulder blades jutted higher than her spine in opposing triangular punches. The loose skin between sifted the drizzle to produce balls of water which pooled then ran forward and cascaded from the upper leg muscles as they loosened on the forward flick of her toes. The bow of her front legs was pronounced enough to create a rounded silhouette from the front view, more pronounced than her cubs suggesting a greater weight being carried on her bulbous paws.

Grey soaked in these features as Tonmawr crept down the rock face to join him to take in water. The cubs puppeteered by their spring steps bounced behind their mother, excited at the sight of the large male. Grey lay with front paws crossed. His darker form revealed a more pronounced melanism. The differences between his markings and background colour could not be distinguished providing him with a jet black appearance from far.

Tonmawr checked the signals from her surroundings and decided to head due south across the open barren landscape. The night mist of the high ground would provide the optimal natural cover in an otherwise exposed journey. Grey waited for the family to form their train and followed just out of the restricted vision. The route meandered the contours of the undulating earth and provided few markers apart from rock outcrops. Before the masses reduced a man-made rock pile with a wooden post atop sprang from the high point. Scent of humans remained from the hill walkers where they had taken rest at their conquest of Fan Nedd. The cubs rooted around its base for crumbs of discarded sandwiches and snacks. No den was to be found here, nor any trace of prey.

Tonmawr marked the rounded stones for future reference. Grey had caught up and circled the outcrop, it was an area he had not visited before but took less interest. Grey moved on first, he had picked up a scent and moved downhill to investigate further. Tonmawr picked up the same scent as the blustery air swirled around the high point, the cubs moved in close to her as she bounded after Grey. Their plunge south stopped at the high stone wall of a hump backed bridge which crossed a shallow boulder strewn tributary. The underside of the arch was the source of the scent which sparked Grey to move.

The rotting carcass of a swollen Yew half in the river was wedged tight where dressed stone met flowing water. Tonmawr guided her cubs away from the waterline, aware of the potential for the diseased liquid to enter their bodies. Grey had no such awareness and waded closer to the corpse. Tonmawr padded the bank whilst warning Grey with a nasal tone of a high pitch. The cubs copied their mothers concerned call willing Grey to move away.

He continued to approach drawn in by the potential of a free supper. The undercut of the river pushed its level higher than Greys shoulder forcing him to withdraw. Soaked by the contaminated water Grey waded back to the bank and shook his sodden coat. He was out of breath from the physical exertion of his failed mission.

Tonmawr was losing faith in Grey and was clear of the exposed single tracked road which traversed the river before Grey recovered enough to look up. Tonmawr traversed the river upstream where it shallowed to a lazy trickle of current. She continued along its natural path south in search of a den. Central location within her territory was perfect as a bolt hole when required.

The unpredictable nature of the humans created the need to disappear in an instant away from potential search routes. Tonmawr had observed the humans habits of travelling level ground and their dogs routine of fanning away from natural courses but not too far from their masters calls and whistles. Higher ground, difficult terrain with escape routes and flowing water were the desired features Tonmawr searched out for.

Satisfied she was centrally located Tonmawr paused at a rare natural den. The feature was trivial from all approaches and looked like nothing more than a reed bog forming a bowl but it hid a natural rock lined deep scar at its centre. Where it met the bog the rocks adopted the colour of the reeds. The fault caused by change in strata and a shifting event deep in the past provided a shallow protected ledge. The winter grass beetled on each side, the thick weave held up the overhang and was dry on its underside. This rare feature amongst featureless terrain delighted Tonmawr.

She entered the tunnel of moss and ochre grass and pawed its wall. The soil was dry and its ledge wide enough to lay on. The male cub joined her and rolled on his back and scratched the itch between his shoulders. The female cub followed but didn't notice the dark cold stream at the bottom and shook her dampened paws. The trio retraced their steps without marking until they reached the river bank. Tonmawr marked the largest rock and scarred its moss with pressure from her mass through extended claws. Grey had picked up their scent and re-united himself with Tonmawr after a forced cleansing as he traversed the same lazy meanderings of the shallow river.

Martins truck was planted on the edge of the hill walkers car park at the base of Fan Nedd. An embossed vertical plywood map allowed the finger to trace a fluted route to the summit of over nine hundred feet. Louise took shelter with Martin under the slope of the three featherboard slats which peaked the information board. Martin shielded his phone from the rain and waited for the group chat to start. Louise had the location beacon for #M7 dancing on her screen as she rotated from portrait to landscape.

'Come on for fucks sake.' She snarled. Martin giggled at her frustrations and suggested enabling auto rotate, which she duly did.

Gill and Mark sat in their car watching the same views at the entrance to the quarry just north of Horseshoe Crest. The steam from their damp waterproof jackets had misted the windows and provided Mark with a blank canvas on which to draw a comedy cock, Gill reprimanded him with a slap to the arm then giggled.

Rhys and Lewis trudged through the bog at the base of the escarpment and through a night scope Lewis eyed the rock face close to the crest. The horizontal lines created by the layers of rock were spliced vertically from a millennia of erosion which created stepped routes. The location of #M7 indicated Grey had moved two miles south of their location and was stationary. ' Do you want to go up to the den Lewis, its where Grey was an hour ago?'

'Nah, let Mam come in from the north and wait at the crest, she can pick up the memory card from the field camera as well.' Rhys agreed and the pair turned away from the steep gradient and headed south. Lewis opened the group chat and directed Gill and Mike to the crest of horseshoe ridge.

Louise asked Rhys where she and Martin should go. ' Stay put, when we have Grey in sight I'll let you know which way he's heading, you should see the direction on your App but it takes a while to update, we can see him real-time on the laptop.'

From the edge of the bog Rhys and Lewis followed the contours south and skirted the rise of Bryn Melyn, the peak of almost five hundred metres covered in cloud to its base. The ground opened up before them as a fresh wind blew the mist north. Four silvered horizontal beams marked the start point at the style to traverse the stock fence and ushered the pair on an inside track marked by an undulating dry stone wall. At regular intervals the four foot high wall had collapsed into the shifting bog as water found its natural course. In years gone by the stock wall would have been maintained to prevent the sheep from escaping. The effort and time ploughed into the upkeep of the wall over scores of years lost now to a wire stock fence requiring no such attention.

The path up to the Cairn atop Fan Nedd was a steady incline on firm ground, not a prestigious or popular walk as Pen-y Fan, the highest peak in the Brecon's favoured by charity walks and day trippers. As they reached the Trig point Lewis circled the lower stones just as Tonmawr had done only one hour before him. 'I can't understand why Grey would come up here, there's no prey, no water, nothing.'

Rhys rested on a large flat stone which had toppled from the monolith and rolled a cigarette.

' Can't you smell it Lewis?'

'Cat Piss?' Lewis replied.

'It's fresh and its female, that's why Grey was here, he's tracking Tonmawr. We might be in luck and catch a glimpse of the cubs.' The image on the lap top screen illuminated their faces with a green tinge. The track Grey marked on the screen provided their route down. Rhys folded the laptop. ' We need to save the battery till we get back, Ill use the phone App for a while, he's about five minutes in front and stationary near the old lime works, looks like where the track crosses a stream. Come on.'

The pair like fell runners scuttled down the cobbled path with ease until they reached the stream. The boulder strewn waterway was shallow, Rhys bounded across in three steps and sunk into the far bank, a controlled fall, resting to support the night scope which focused on the underside of the hump as the track before him rose and fell. 'Can you see him Lewis?'

Lewis's camera focused on the right shoulder of Grey as the animal shook the remaining moisture from his back. 'Yes got a good shot, it's definitely Grey, M7 clear as a bell on his shoulder.' The pair followed Greys bounds across tussocks of thick grass and reed stalks until the grains of the night scopes saturated their view.

'Ok he's heading towards Louise and Martin.'

'Don't worry no one will see you Louise, its pitch black out there and in any case were in the middle of nowhere on a rainy Saturday night.' Chuckled Martin.

As Louise squatted down to wee she used her left hand to steady her balance on the back bumper of the truck. Martin picked up her phone to acknowledge Lewis's instructions but didn't explain Louise's absence. As the screen cleared he expected the cursor on the tracker App to appear, as he pressed refresh a message flashed which he inadvertently opened.

'Hi Louise its Paul, feel really bad about earlier, I shouldn't have shouted at you it's not your fault, can we meet up tomorrow I need your help.'

The tracker App came into view again as Louise climbed into the passenger seat. 'That's so much better Martin, sorry when you've gotta go, you've gotta go, especially at my time of life.'

'That's ok I warded off the marauding masses charging over the hill.' Martin replied then added. ' That was Lewis he wants us to head across to the high ground south of the peak, do you know the way? Oh and a message came up, something about a meet tomorrow, sorry didn't mean to read it, it all flashed up together.'

'That's ok, yes we'll follow the tracker route, it's not far, we can go on foot from here, just let me see the message a minute, hang on.' Her pallor gave away her obvious shock.

'Ok nothing important Ill deal with it tomorrow, ready for a stroll in the dark? Your eyes will adjust very quickly. Most people think they need torches at night but you'll be surprised how well you can adapt.'

Louise strode out along the single track road with Martin close by her side. She felt safe with Martin being so close but her thoughts were stifling any conversation. 'What could Paul want? The text sounded desperate. Has he had a change of heart about the cub?'

The south side of Fann Nedd was a featureless gentle descent fading into a rounded crest over a mile wide. Tributaries fingered through the wild grass, not visible until a foot sunk in. As the tracks of flowing water neared the roadway greener vegetation sprouted. Louise stopped at a moss layered style overgrown at its base with strands of ochre grass.

Without words she gripped the post and slid her left boot onto the first step, a single foot knee bend tested its reaction before she slung her legs over, looked down at Martin and whispered. 'Ok so there's a trail over this field according to the map and I believe at the midpoint is where we should find Grey.' As Louise dropped into the bog Martin followed over the style and asked. ' What do we do if we see him?' The opening ground and cleared mist allowed their dilated pupils to absorb the tonal contrast of sky and land.

'We stay quiet and still, keep low, he will probably sense us before we see him.'

As they reached the midpoint of the field dancing orange flecks of the dual carriageway hung like a chain across the distant southern horizon of Nedd Valley. The derelict remnant of a stone corner wall drew the pair in as it portrayed a triangular dark mass before them.

'Let's wait here, we've got a good view all around and it will provide some cover.' Louise said as she opened the group chat to relay their position.

Lewis replied and informed Louise that Grey was now further south, at the river into which the tributaries flowed. As they reluctantly got up from the relative comfort of the stone wall Martin grabbed Louise's arm and placed his finger on his lips. Louise stifled a gasp as from nowhere Tonmawr appeared followed by the two cubs. In clear view only twenty feet away the trio cantered past into the saturated darkness.

'Lewis, Lewis, Tonmawr and the cubs, heading towards Greys location!'

Lewis replied. ' Were too far to get there in time, you'll have to go. Grey hasn't moved for five minutes, hurry Louise.' Relieved at the instruction Martin jumped up and with Louise in arm and gave chase.

The adrenalin pushed their pace until Louise reached the same style she had carefully tested only twenty minutes ago. With a push and step she bounded the hurdle and landed with ease. Martin struggled to keep up but as she looked back he waved her on.

Louise crossed the Tarmac and followed the tributary deep into the Nedd valley pausing as the flowing water became audible. The view before her was cluttered by Hawthorne branches and leafless Willow splines but she could make out the feline shapes.

Grey approached Tonmawr and lowered his head allowing her to groom him. Louise observed the interaction with amazement. She expected an aggressive stance from Tonmawr to protect her cubs but was delighted to see the opposite. In the dark quiet Louise felt at ease as she watched the group settle under the branches. Her view was improving as she crawled closer on her elbows, her damp cotton coat soaked through to her skin. Her advance was deadly quiet, no manmade fibre noise. The crawl brought her to within ten feet of the group. As the willow trunk rose from the angled ground she stopped with an uninterrupted arc of vision looking down on the group. She was tempted to record the events but the potential to expose her position was too great. The two cubs rolled together in a playful wrestle. Their size, Louise thought, put them at three months, maybe four. She could sense Tonmawr was content with their behaviour as she lay with her head and neck upright.

Louise's thoughts turned to the high stepping female cub and how she could re-unite her with her family, time was running out, Tonmawr would reject the cub, maybe even Grey would kill it? Grey was less relaxed, he paced and sniffed the soil, pawing and scratching the ground.

Louise tried to work out how a normally solitary life had changed to a group existence . Perhaps instinct was not that embedded in Grey, had he not had the right upbringing to hunt alone, was he too young? Surely he couldn't be their father? Louise dismissed that thought and observed his size in comparison to other males she had encountered. Grey had a distinctively larger frame, his hind leg muscles were overdeveloped and his shoulder width more pronounced, just how Gill had pointed out on the video images last night.

Tonmawr sprung up to her feet and with an elongated stretch sniffed the night air, Louise looked her directly in the eye. Tonmawr appeared to be looking directly back at her, motionless. Grey followed suit and lined up by her side, head and shoulders above her head. The cubs sidled between the pair. A mass of taught legs and focused eyes. Louise's heart raced, she felt as prey would at the moment of attack. As one, sixteen paws twisted and gripped before high tails bobbed into the dark. It was then Louise heard Martins Gortex trousers grate behind her. ' Wow you look like you've found a pot of gold.'

Louise remained on her back and beamed at Martin.

'I just did Martin, it was beautiful, Grey was here with Tonmawr and the two cubs, all together like a family, so relaxed, so content. They heard you coming well before I did. We have to get that cub back to her Martin, it's so unfair what Paul has done.'

The surgery lights were off apart from the emergency exit as Louise entered the rear fire door determined this time to find what she was looking for. Her quest was supported fully by Martin who by her side provided the strength she needed on her shoulder. They strode out to the reception area, ignoring Pauls surgery room. Her father's old room reminded her of better times when Louise would pretend to understand his diagnoses and advice as he treated the pets with the upmost care and consideration. School holidays were spent by his side, learning, playing, helping. Her father never lost his temper, became frustrated nor ignored her. The high stepping female cub did not move from her repose until Louise knelt beside the cage and said.

'Hey there beautiful, just look at you, we need to get you to your mother.' The cub snarled in retreat but did not swipe. The pair knew they had to move quickly. Louise had messaged Paul an hour ago at eleven -thirty pm but had not received a reply. He could arrive at any time.

Chapter 26

Paul Morris struggled to focus on the arrivals board as it refreshed and confirmed 'on time' for the flight from Amsterdam. Ji-a was on the connecting flight, the final leg of her long haul from Seoul. Paul had half an hour to wait until the plane landed plus immigration probably an hour he thought. Cardiff arrivals had little comfort for his thumping headache, the lights were bright, the announcements piercing and the nagging irritation of his car in the short stay car park, he had to move it. In the dead of night with no distractions Paul functioned well. It was the mild irritations through the day which clouded his judgement and drove him to addiction. He approached the barrier just in time to avoid the ten pound charge and decided to drive out of the parking area to a layby along the approach to the airport. He could watch the Easy Jet flight arrive, the first one of an overcast dark Sunday morning, whilst the cocaine took effect.

Ji-a breezed through an empty customs hall and without hold luggage to disrupt her passage she was stood outside within ten minutes of the plane landing. Paul was relieved to see her as he had been away from his surgery for too long. The cub needed feeding, #M8 was still in his transport cage at Aber-llia house and the pregnant females drip would be empty in half an hour. Ji-a bounced up into the passenger seat, leant over and embraced Paul before starting. ' Well if I knew customs would be that easy I would have brought a female Panther or at least a cub.'

'If only it were that easy, so good to see you Ji-a, I hope you don't mind but we need to go straight to my practice, the female has deteriated overnight.'

Ji-a was relieved to hear the plan, she was anxious to start straight away to determine the next stage. The journey back was interrupted by a pit stop at Pauls favourite café for a full Welsh breakfast. Ji-a revelled at the flavours and textures, the fresh ingredients cooked before her opened up a new world of sensory excitement, far away from the drudge of water filled carbohydrates and flavourless meat substitutes.

Satisfied and eager Ji-a and Paul arrived at the practice ready to perform the C-section on #1.

'I doubt if she will survive the procedure Paul, her BP is too low, do you have blood substitute?' Paul did not care about the female, he knew he had a replacement in the cub who within one year would be ready.

'I have no substitute blood Ji-a, we must try our best with the routine medicines we have here Im afraid.'

The Panther was barely sedated as they did not want to induce heart failure, she lay exhausted and forlorn in the hands of a Vet who did not care for her welfare. The incision produced little blood and as she entered the sack clear liquid oozed onto the green cloth darkening the seams. The dead foetus was pulled and its cord sealed within seconds. Ji-a was prepared and did care. Her expert technique amazed Paul, her knowledge of the Panthers anatomy was intimate. She examined the remaining three lives which were thriving and when satisfied closed up the mother. Ji-a sat at the end of the table as Paul adopted the role of assistant attending to the cleaning and clearing of the surgical tools. Ji-a held the back left foot of the Panther in her right palm. The lifeless limb dwarfed her own arm and her fingers were hidden by the mass of the Panthers paw. Without looking up she asked Paul. 'What was the surprise you promised Paul?'

Paul felt excitement at the prospect of showing Ji-a his surprise and hadn't even checked on the cub since they arrived back. He disappeared to the front of the building and eased open the door to his mentors office. His first thought was that he had moved the cage to a different room the night before. Then the realisation hit him hard, the cub had gone. He spun around on his heal held his head with both hands and thumped it repeating.

'No, No , no, that fucking bitch.' His pace decelerated as he reached the surgery door, he paused before slipping in, being careful not to disturb Ji-a who was nursing the resting mother.

'Oh it was nothing important Ji-a, just wanted to show you how well the male predator was doing but he's still up at the house, so maybe tomorrow.' Pauls anger and frustration was well hidden, Ji-a sensed there was an issue and replied.

'You must be tired, you need to rest, I've some test results to analyse, plus I need to link in to father in Seoul. There's nothing you can do here, why don't you go home for a while Paul?'

Relieved Paul agreed, he loved how Ji-a had a knack of knowing his moods without ridiculing him like other women did. He thanked her and leant in to kiss her head, Ji-a looked up and smiled. 'Go on get some rest, I'll see you later this afternoon, maybe you could bring me a Pizza in from that place we went to on my last visit?'

'Ah yes, I remember, no problem, thank you Ji-a I don't know what I'd do without you.' Paul recalled her last visit with fondness and a yearning he hadn't felt for a number of months. He had resisted her advances then but regretted doing so when she left. He was surprised that she showed an interest when he was at his all-time low and did not read the signs that Ji-a had a crush on him. Believing she was just being nice, he didn't want to play his hand and be rejected or ridiculed. Ji-a had taken it in her stride and with a pragmatic approach moved her emotions on. Pauls focus changed to Louise as he left the building and jumped into his car. He resisted the temptation to call her, instead he sped towards her house in the village.

'So exactly what are we going to do with her ?' Gill asked Louise.

'Nothing today, Gill, we need to work this one out and not rush into it.'

'Ok but what about Paul? When he realises it's gone he'll call the police and send them straight to you.'

Louise had not stopped to think since she and Martin rescued the cub from Pauls practice. She soaked in the gravity of what they had done but didn't have a plan. She fell into the sofa and looked up for inspiration. Martin flopped beside her and asked. 'I think we need to move the cage from the back of my truck, where do you want to put her?'

Louise suggested the garage, Gill endorsed the choice and exchanged places with Martin. She mirrored Louise's relaxed body and glared at the same spot on the vaulted ceiling. Louise turned to Gill and smiled. She was comfortable about the situation and felt in control. Her thoughts drifted away reliving the few minutes with the Panthers, their interaction surprised her but more than ever she felt confident the cub would be accepted back.

' Don't worry about Paul and the Police Gill, what would he say to them? My ex stole an illegally held Panther?'

Gill shook her head and replied. ' All he has to say is that you were on his property, then bang! They can charge you.'

'He wouldn't Gill, he's a coward, time for us to focus on the cub and how we are going to re-unite the family.'

'Whilst you were all having fun chasing Panthers myself and Mike manged to access the den up on Horseshoe ridge. We started at the base and followed the vertical ridges until we got to the rock face. I stopped but Mike scrambled up and found the den. Its quite large and well covered, here look at the photos.' The shadowed images revealed a pyramid interior of slate walls, heather roots strangled the smooth floor. Gill swiped through the gallery and continued. ' As you can see, despite Mikes crap photos, its low on home comforts but its dry and large enough for them to stretch out. I think if we can get to it with the cub, leave it there with some food just before daybreak she will stay and wait for Tonmawrs return. What do you think?'

' Sounds perfect Gill, I'd have expected remnants of kills and fur but I guess this isn't The Lion King!' The pair Looked at each other and laughed, then as one jumped up.

Gill grasped Louise's hands and said. 'Come on let's have a look at the cub.'

Louise bobbed down next to the cage and beckoned the cub with a morsel of dry dog food but the cub remained wedged in the corner with her front paws outstretched supporting her body. The cubs head twisted from side to side and fixated its glare on the biscuit as Louise rotated her hand. A yawn revealed the underdeveloped teeth which were translucent at their tips. Gill joined Louise low down and said. ' No more than three months old I'd say.' Louise's fascination fixated her observations of the cub. She traced the line from her oversize paws up her powerful legs to a broad chest and full neck. The soft down of her ruffled neck needed to be comforted though Louise. She held her palm against the transport cage mesh, wide enough to poke one of her slender fingers through, she considered the consequences and retracted. The cub was intrigued and stepped forward and took in Louise's scent. The cage was large enough for the cub to walk in small circles which she duly did whilst maintaining eye contact with Louise.

' Don't create a bond Lou, it won't help her when we take her back tomorrow afternoon.' Louise knew the bond had been created already, her experience with Tonmawr and the cubs siblings was wild and natural yet the high stepping female cub she had rescued from certain death played with her heart. Could she risk returning the cub? The chance of rejection was ever present. Could she persuade Gill to change her plan, which in her head Louise knew was the right option. Gill stood and stretched before announcing. 'Ok I'm off to make breakfast and get some sleep, its been a long night. There's some steak in the fridge ill leave it out to warm, if you could tear it into strips and feed her in an hour Louise?'

'Sure, how are we going to sedate the cub Gill to carry her up to the den?'

Gill considered her options before replying. ' I'll mix up a mild sedative in a drink or some raw meat that should be enough, I wouldn't like to try and pin her down for an injection, she's a wild animal Lou and we need to remember that.'

Martin passed Gill at the adjoining door to the garage from the house and asked her. 'Do you think Paul will cause a fuss over this Gill?'

'I don't think so Martin, but you need to stop getting involved in stunts like that. Louise has her own agenda and takes unnecessary risks. She has nothing to lose but you do, your job?'

' I get it Gill, but she's very impulsive and I just want to help.'

'Maybe but that will be her undoing, look we all care about these animals and we all want to ensure they have a chance of surviving in this environment, that's what we need to focus on, not scoring points over her ex. I've told Lou as much, let's concentrate now on getting the cub back then leave them to it. If they bond then great, but if they don't its natures way and we shouldn't interfere.'

Martin stood at the door and watched Louise lead the cub around its confines with her hand on the mesh. The slow click, click, click as her fingernails connected each square intrigued the cub. Incremental steps were drawing the cub closer and closer to full contact. Martin leant in and wrapped his arm around Louise's shoulder before whispering. ' Im going home for some rest and to change, call me when your free later this afternoon. Do you need anything bringing back, food, drink?'

Louise looked up and smiled. ' Ok, thank you Martin, I couldn't have done this without you, please don't think Im ignoring you. I think were ok for food, oh could you pop into my house on your way back, there's a box of wine and some Gin in the kitchen, I think we might be alone this evening so we could spend a little time together, its been a busy couple of nights so time to relax a bit?'

Martin eased his thoughts and moved away from the defensive feelings that had been creeping in. ' Now that sounds a good idea. Yeh we need it, I've got work first thing Monday but I could go straight from here if that's ok?'

Louise kissed him on the lips and whispered. ' Oh yes please, take my car, its unlocked and the keys are in it, the house keys are on there too, just watch the front door lock you have to pull up the handle or it sticks.'

Alone now with the cub Louise locked the access door to the house from the inside and sat cross-legged in the semi-darkness on the concrete floor. Without distractions she felt at ease with the cub as it pawed at the door of her prison. Louise looked around for toys to entertain the cub, she spotted a coil of data cable, soft and pliable. Uncoiling it she extended the plastic socket end into the cage through the bottom rung towards the cubs paw. Come on, come on, she urged as the clip dragged along the cage floor catching the man-made fibres of the thin layer of carpet. As the clip danced, the cub extended a claw and tugged its recoil. The tension translated to Louise's finger tips as if she were touching the wild paw. One claw had such strength she mused, as the cub grasped it fully in both paws and rolled onto her back offering it up to Louise. The satin soft fur now touched Louise's forefinger allowing a gentle caress with her fingernail of the cubs toes. Content with progress Louise talked to the beauty before her and encouraged further contact through the barrier. ' Wait baby, I'll get you some food.'

Louise returned with the steak on a dinner plate cut into finger sized strips, blood pooling and oozing its underside. She dabbed her fingertips into the crimson liquid and rested them on the bars at shoulder height for the cub. Her circling increased in speed as she ebbed closer to the dripping blood. She licked the lower bars then followed the trail up to touch Louise. The first touch drew Louise's breath in deep to her lungs as the static discharged and she snatched her hand back as if bitten. The cubs nose felt the same intense click causing a sneeze and shake. ' Oooh I'm sorry baby, let's try again.'

The first slither was pushed through the bars with ease, the cubs bright blue eyes widened as she sucked and smacked her lips. Hungry for more of the same taste she stepped from side to side and willed Louise for the next morsel. With the bloodied plate now waiting on the floor outside the cage, Louise released the upper bolt and slid the safety bar from the door of the cage. All it needed now was a bump to open. Louise withdrew and sat again cross-legged waiting for the cub to advance. Without delay she nudged the wire mesh and it arced open.

Louise's heart raced in anticipation as the confident steps were taken without hesitation. The cub squatted down to eat but remained taught as each strip was smacked up, whiskers twitching and ears flickering. Louise's soothed tones of encouragement did not disturb the cub but as she rocked from cross-legs forward onto her elbows the cub broke her feast and focused on the movement. With the plate licked clean and scraping on the concrete floor Louise unclenched her hands and projected them out wide, each palm cradling the last strips of raw steak.

The cub strutted to her left hand and took away the meat with her incisors, returning to the plate where she adopted her previous position. The repeat to Louise's right hand and back to the plate raised a giggle. With her arms remaining still the cub returned to lick clean her palm. A strong kneading tested her reaction as her palm was pushed by the cubs warm tongue. Then the other palm was treated to the same feline embrace, followed by a brush against a sweating forehead, it was then Louise realised it was too late.

Chapter 27

Martin Quinn stopped in the middle of Louise's street and tried to recall the house number, then he recognised the light green paint of the sash window frames and stained glass front door. He decided to go straight to her house before going home as he felt sleep would come quickly and cloud his memory. The stone bay fronted houses each had a token garden to the front not big enough to park a car. He spotted a gap three doors down where a silver Range Rover had just left. In the house memories of their first night made him feel warm, the comfort of her neat welcoming home reminded him in layout of his mother's home in Ireland. The front door there was always unlocked and the kitchen never empty. This kitchen was quiet and empty except for a well-stocked drinks fridge. He found the wine box and the Gin and wondered if they would fit in his fridge. As he searched for a bag the front door bell sounded an unfamiliar ring.

'Oh, could I speak to Louise?' Paul Morris stepped back from the door as he asked the question.

Martin replied ' Sorry she's not here anything I can do to help?'

' When will she be back I need to see her?'

Martin wondered who it was and was feeling reluctant to divulge any information to the stranger. ' Im not sure, I can pass on a message or you could ring her, who shall I say called?'

'It's Paul, her ex-husband, Im sure I just saw her car pull up, and who are you? Is she inside?'

Martin expected a more self-assured man from the descriptions Louise had given him but instead felt confident as he viewed Pauls dishevelled, diminutive figure.

'Im Just here to pick up a couple of things, I'm her friend Martin, do you not have her mobile number?' Martin noticed a change in his stance as Paul Morris folded his arms and leaned in closer.

'Yes but we had arranged to meet here, so Ill wait if you don't mind.'

Martin looked behind himself into the hallway, he picked up the 'bag for life' containing the drinks, spread the keys between his fingers and found the front door key.

'Well Im leaving now, if I see her I'll tell her you came around.' Martin pulled the door closed, double locked it and moved towards the road. The few short steps were interrupted by Paul Morris's hand which reached out and grabbed Martins right arm. Martin looked down at Pauls hand, lifted up his own taught arm which was holding the bag and said. 'Think you should let go Paul.'

Paul dropped his grip but stayed close as he looked up into Martins glaring eyes. 'Wait you're

Martin Quinn from the windmills construction site yes?'

Martin felt he didn't want to get into an exchange with Paul Morris but was not surprised that Paul knew him, he must have been kept up to date by Alan Price and probably half the people in The Crown. Martin had learnt that nothing goes unnoticed in this village.

' Like I said, ring Louise, goodbye Paul.' Martin brushed Paul aside, his height and weight overcoming the slight resistance. Paul followed Martin down the street, Martin could sense his steps were closing in so turned to confront him.

'You Know she's using you Martin, just to get access to Alan Prices barn, she'll carry on using you and get you wrapped up in her illegal activities, I'd be careful, could cost you your job.'

Martin realised that Paul knew a lot more than he should, who was providing the information? Was it Alan Price? It must be he deduced.

' I've got CCTV of your truck at my practice last night and evidence of a break in, one phone call Martin and your locked up.'

Martin knew he was right about the CCTV but the rest Paul would have to make up, he could say he was lost or just parked up for a rest on the way to the construction site as it was close by. He put the shopping bag down and with a grab and twist of Pauls thick collar Martin lifted him onto his toes. 'Threaten me again you piece of shit and you won't be walking again.'

Paul cowered under the strength of Martins grip and collapsed as he was released. 'Listen Martin, what she took is too vulnerable to survive, it needs special care and returning to the wild, Louise doesn't have the expertise to deal with that, I'm trying to help her, just ask her to call me, we can meet up and sort this out. You do know it was Louise that started all this, don't you?'

Martins surprised look registered with Paul who raised a condescending smile.

'Oh she failed to mention that small detail to you then. Well just remind her she has a responsibility to sort this mess out Martin.'

The Passat fired up first time, Martin left Paul stood on the pavement with his arms outstretched shouting through the closed window. 'Fucking prick' Martin said to himself as he pulled out and headed the short distance to his house. Martin sensed Louise was holding something back but he didn't know what it was, he made up his mind to confront her on his return to the lodge.

Chapter 28

Rhys and Lewis surfaced just after midday to the calls from Gill who had prepared a Sunday lunch with Louise's help. The pair had busied themselves in the kitchen after Louise had teased the cub back into its cage with tender morsels of raw chicken breast.

' There's enough for Martin, is he coming back?'

'Yes, I'll text him to remind him about the wine.'

Louise felt they were getting back on track with the Panthers, they could relax for a while and re-unite the cub in due course she thought.

Rhys picked at the cooked chicken on the carving plate and said. ' So I've just been in to see the cub, she's sleeping, when are we taking her back Mam?'

Gill slapped Rhys with the wooded spoon, the gravy was thickening and left a dollop on Bens wrist which he licked off. ' Tomorrow, afternoon, we cant leave it any longer, Ill sedate her first then Ill need you and Lewis to carry her up the ridge. We could do with putting a tracker on first though.'

Rhys continued to scout for food and replied. ' What if we sedate Grey and take his collar? We know where he is, Lewis you still got the App open?'

Lewis was sat before the large flat screen and shouted back. 'Yeh he's back in the same place Horshoe ridge, hasn't moved all day. We watched him return with Tonmawr and the cubs this morning, have you still got the gun Mam?'

Gill looked over and replied. ' No I didn't renew my licence and it was a loan gun anyway.'

Louise sparked up and contemplated a reply, she could get one from Paul, if he ever spoke to her again that is, she considered. She picked up her phone to text Martin and noticed three missed calls from him. 'Shit Id better ring him'.

' Hi Martin, sorry had missed calls from this morning, Sunday Dinner is nearly ready everything ok?'

'Err yes, and no, Im on my way up with the wine I'll talk to you when I get there.'

Louise was confused and by Martins tone worried as to what he might say.

'Ok see you soon.' She returned with an optimistic tenor. Louise stood behind Lewis in the living area, she kneaded the back of the sofa as she watched Lewis zoom in on the location where Grey had settled. Lewis brought up the location of #M8 to see if it had moved.

' So this is the past twenty four hours movement map of #M8, whatever that might be. Well if it's a Panther its got a chauffeur, it started off at Aber-llia House then this morning had a run out to, let me see, Melin Street in Tonmawr, now it's on the edge of the industrial estate on Fern Lane.'

Gill was listening and shouted over. 'That's your street Louise and Fern Lane is Pauls Practice.'

Lewis continued. ' It was at Melin Street between eight and nine a.m.' He looked up at Louise for an explanation.

' Don't look at me Lewis I've been here all this time!'

' Alright Louise keep your pants on.' Lewis returned to the screen with a scolded expression and swapped files to reveal Greys pattern of behaviour.

Gill was drawn in to protect her son from Louise's manner. ' I don't think Lewis was accusing you of anything Lou but don't you think it's odd?'

Louise felt her anger build, hear she was again protecting Paul, he crept in to her mind moulded her thinking and made her look a fool. How could he still do that? She took a deep breath and responded.

' Its Paul, got to be, maybe he has a tracker in his car which he left turned on, I can't see him transporting a Panther around the village. He's obviously looking for me, he knows I took the Panther, probably on his way up here now.'

Lewis chipped in. ' Well if he is the trackers still at his practice building, it hasn't moved for hours.'

Gill put an arm around Louise, showing her appreciation Louise lifted her hand to Gills and said. 'Why does that man make me feel like this, I go to pieces when I hear his name. If he turns up here Gill will you send him away? I can't bear the thought of speaking to him, I'll just crumble.'

'I'll send Mike, he knows how to handle him.' Said Gill.

Louise was anxious to speak to Martin and thought about what he might have to say, then it dawned on her, he must have spoken to Paul. What did Paul say ? The last forty eight hours were taking their toll on Louise, she felt exhausted, her head was spinning with questions and her temper was frayed. It's all about Paul she thought, I have to find out what's motivating him, what his agenda is, why he wants the cub so badly, what is he doing with Grey. She racked her brains and drifted back to when they were together working at the practice. She recalled exciting times when the Panther first came to them whilst out walking one glorious Sunday afternoon at the waterfalls.

It appeared as they sat in the shade under the willows with the sound of the falls and the wind in the trees. Paul had returned from the car park with prepared sandwiches and two bottles of Budweiser. The female was fully grown and waded up the river to rest across the pool from where they were lying. Louise remembered the Panther grooming herself, cleaning her paws and nibbling at her soft pads. Paul and Louise's whispered discussions centred around how to capture the animal and study her in more detail. They had both had to deal with the aftermath of a Panther attack. Calls from farmers were on the increase to deal with sheep either dead or badly injured by the claw of the new apex predator. Deer were also found but less of a concern to the farmers. Louise had studied the news reports and web sites devoted to the 'Big Cats' and had become preoccupied with them.

Paul had shown a more clinical approach and liaised with his colleagues to share information about the origins of the predator. This lead him to Dr Kam in Seoul University who at the time was providing research opportunities for endangered apex predators. As Louise reviewed her past the answers to her questions were starting to form.

Paul slid away and returned with his rifle loaded with a dart. His first shot hit the Panthers right leg causing it to jump up and tear the dart from its flesh. Pauls second dart sunk deep into the hind quarters and they both watched as she stumbled and slowed before collapsing into the boulder strewn shallows. Louise cradled the Panthers soaking head and shoulders whilst Paul hauled the mass of its body onto his left shoulder. Louise guided Paul through the shallows and up the dry banking to their Range Rover where the Panther was placed in the back, along with Louise still supporting its head.

The next few days were spent observing the Panther in their makeshift compound at the stables adjoining the surgery. They did not have a detailed plan but knew the best outcome would be to release the Panther back in to its habitat. It showed no signs of malnutrition or injury. The Panther was surviving well. Pauls tests revealed that the Panther was pregnant and Louise recalled the excitement she felt. Paul made enquiries about a tracking device and they decided to fit a device and release the Panther back into its chosen habitat. Louise recalled the intense emotions she felt the day before they drove back to the waterfalls. Louise would monitor the Panther using the tracker and in time see the cubs flourish, naturally.

Then the memory resurfaced with a bang. It was the same weekend that Dr Kam had visited and that bitch Claire De Motta turned up for the dinner party. She felt that the plan she had formulated with Paul had been hijacked by Dr Kam, he wanted to keep the Panther for longer and carry out more tests. They talked about DNA profiling and discussed in depth various methods of extraction, Louise did not understand fully the significance of their plan. After many drinks and a seething anger building Louise retired early to bed. When she awoke their plan to take the Panther back to its environment had changed. Paul insisted on the tests but wouldn't reveal their content or reason. In late afternoon as Paul left for the hunt ball Louise feigned a migraine and sent him off on his own. This time of reflection had cleared Louise's thoughts, she now realised Pauls motivation, DNA profiling and extraction, with a live surrogate in captivity, cloning would be the next step.

She hauled the Panther cage into the back of her Passat estate car and threw a blanket over the top before driving back to the waterfalls. She backed the car close to the river and waited for nightfall. The release was without incident, one brief look back as the Panther landed on wet grass and she was gone, forever she thought.

Paul did not return that night, he announced his intention to work with Dr Kam in Seoul after his anger overboiled at Louise's actions. The trust had gone, she could not prove that he had been with Claire but she knew in her heart he had spent the night with her. Bank Holiday Monday Hunt followed and Louise attended but in a drunken state she made a public spectacle of herself. Never again she remembered would she allow herself to be treated that way.

'Louise, you still with us?' Gill shook Louise's shoulder and placed a glass of cold crisp white wine in her hand.

' Sorry, I must have drifted off, I needed that.' Louise wiped her mouth with the back of her hand and stretched out her free arm.

'Thank Martin for the wine, he's in the kitchen, doesn't look happy.' Gill whispered.

Louise walked over to Martin and on tip toes placed a kiss on his cheek and her palm on his chest. 'Hi, you ok? Thanks for the wine.'

Martin replied. 'I think we need to have a chat in private, shall we go out front?'

Louise grabbed his hand and padded out to the decked area, her dry feet soaked in the damp cover of the grooved deck. She leaned in and focused on Martins words as he recited his encounter with Paul earlier that day. The pause at the climax of events remained silent as Louise had no response. Martin summarised his dilemma with a pointed question. ' So is it true, are you using me?'

Louise didn't have to think about her response and she resisted the temptation to defend herself with a return question. ' No Martin I'm not, but I don't blame you for thinking that way. Im so wrapped up in this that I sometimes forget my manners and expect too much. As I told you at the start my concern is the welfare of the Panthers and to prevent human interference.' Louise felt a great sense of relief and thought she was off the hook.

Martin did not change his gaze into the distance and responded with a deeper question. ' He said you were responsible for this mess and that you started it, what did he mean by that? '

' I can only guess he's referring to three years ago when me and Paul had a Panther in our care and I released it back into the environment.'

'You never mentioned that before Louise, what else are you hiding?'

'Nothing Martin, and bear in mind we've only just met, I doubt you've told me everything about your past?'

' Fair enough Louise, a bit harsh I guess, look, I get that your wrapped up in this and you need space and time to deal with the cub, probably best if I leave you to it for a few days.'

Louise started to well up as she could sense what was coming next. It was a feeling that had repeated since her split from Paul, she would get to know someone and when they got to know the real Louise, her passions, her commitments, it would scare them off. ' Ok your probably right Martin, Ill call you later in the week.'

Louise stayed outside as Martin returned to the kitchen and said his goodbyes without breaking stride. Gill slid the door and joined Louise, she topped up her glass and in silence they stared into the woodland.

Chapter 29

Tonmawr returned to Horseshoe Ridge with her cubs but without Grey. Her encounter in the night with the human reminded Tonmawr how fragile their existence was. Although it was an insignificant event and the human did not get close, the fact that Tonmawr allowed her cubs to be within sight of the human reinforced her primary goal-protect and survive. The distraction of Grey blurred her focus, she was adopting the male predator as if he was one of her cubs. It was time to revert her stance and keep Grey at a distance. Tonmawr knew a human had visited the den, it's scent was different from the one she encountered last night but was as strong. This unnerved her and she found it difficult to rest as the night gave way to the red morning sky. Her cubs were becoming more adventurous, they fought each other with greater vigour, their appetites were voracious.

Grey remained at the copse opposite the ridge and waited for the first grains of light to arrive in the hope of an opportunity to fell a curious early morning rabbit or stray doe. His energy ebbed since the feast of the shot Deer which was gifted two nights ago. His hunger for a kill drove him to stay in the open during daylight, it overrode the need to hide and stay safe. The opposite of Tonmawr who would not stray away from the den during daylight. It was a tactic that was working well, there were few occasions when she saw a human, let alone was seen. The early warning in her first year, the searing bullet which clipped her shoulder was a valuable lesson. The memory, embedded, formed her behaviour, that coupled with the loss of her first litter kept her alive and free. Grey had no such lessons, until he was confronted by Grey at the waterfall. He felt the full power of a mature adult yet he still did not have the armour required to survive in the human world.

Tonmawr would remain at a distance, allow Grey to move on, despite the early promise of the Muntjac kill where their teamwork lead to success. Letting him take the risks and attract the humans would assist in her protection of her cubs, as long as they could keep their distance. Greys boredom surfaced at full daylight when he panted into the bright sunlight straight across the bog to the foot of the crest to scale the rocks to his den. He had gained nothing waiting for a passing morsel, but lost cover returning home.

Rhys and Lewis had watched him travel across the open ground and confirmed the tracker accuracy as it depicted his pace on the laptop screen. Their camera set up behind the claw of the ridge enabled a full screen high definition video to be shot in good light.

Grey stood at the entrance to Tonmawrs den, the deep scar in the rock pushed a full ten feet into the cool dry darkness. Time enough for Tonmawr to detect the movement and react, which she did with unusual aggression. She launched at Grey and managed to land a swipe of her right claws across Greys chin. Not enough depth to cause a serious injury, but blood was drawn and the message delivered. Grey withdrew and hopped up the rock to find refuge in his smaller lair.

Tonmawr considered abandoning the den but needed to find a suitable alternative first. Grey was content following the cubs and his instinct was to move on further afield, the brief feeling of group had only lasted a few days and now his basic instincts were returning. The cubs settled to sleep deep in the recess of their den and were unaware of the change in atmosphere between their mother and Grey.

Rhys and Lewis reviewed their video capture and were amazed at the power of Grey as he bounded up the rocks. They noted his brief disappearance into Tonmawrs den but could not distinguish the actual entrance. As he re-appeared scolded the image blurred and faded as he jumped up to his own lair.

Louise slept for an hour on the sofa after lunch. By the time she fully woke Rhys had cleared the kitchen under the instruction from Gill and was packing his clothes in his jeep. Gill brought out some left over food wrapped in a tin foil package. 'Go easy on Louise I think she's just split with Martin.' Rhys received the package and replied.

' Well that didn't last long, he seemed alright as well. So when are we taking the cub back to its Mother?'

'I'll speak to Louise, but we should do it tonight, can you come back later and monitor Grey? Once he's gone with Tonmawr and the other cubs we can take her up, well, you and Lewis can carry her up.'

Rhys nodded and said. 'I'll go straight to the ridge at six, you can bring the cub to the car park at the back of the quarry, we should be able to carry her from there.'

Gill thanked Rhys and hugged her son before returning to Louise. Sat cross-legged on the garage floor Louise stared at the sleeping cub as Gill tiptoed in and sat beside her. A whispering finger to the lips and a nod set the volume for Gill to start. ' She's beautiful, so dark, but she needs to be taken back Lou.'

Louise sighed and replied. ' I know Gill, sooner rather than later, but can we monitor in any way, what about tagging?'

' I haven't got access to anything as sophisticated as the system on Grey but I do have access to pet trackers, we sell them at the surgery. The battery lasts about five days if they are on permanently but if we just access the signal when we need to then I guess we'd get about a month, that's all we need just to ensure she has bonded, that usually happens straight away, we'll know within a day or two.'

Louise nodded in agreement as she continued to look at the cub.

Gill hugged her and said 'I'll leave you to it, we are packing up and going home for a while, I'll be back about five with Lewis, I need to get the sedatives and Mike needs to get his stuff sorted for work tomorrow. Rhys is going to meet us up at the ridge, see you later.'

The silence and solitude focused Louise's thoughts. She knew Gills plan was right but felt there was still a danger that Paul would interfere if Grey continued to follow the family. It was a situation that she never imagined would affect the wellbeing of the cubs. Animals which are lone hunters had bonded in a way not seen before, but why? Louise surmised that the male, Grey, had not evolved in the same way as Tonmawr, he must have been introduced to the wild without the benefit of parental nurturing. No steady learning of behaviour no play with siblings, unnatural. 'I must protect you.' She said under her breath to the cub who slept oblivious to the forthcoming events.

The tracker will help her she thought, she could follow and monitor over the next week or so until satisfied, but would that be enough? She suspected Pauls motives were to introduce the Panthers in greater numbers as part of a programme, something related to the programme in Seoul, but what exactly were they trying to achieve? She decided that she had to confront Paul again, without the support of Martin.

Louise returned to the kitchen, the house was empty of chatter and movement, her friends gone and the atmosphere cold. At this low ebb she decided to call Paul, stop the waiting game she thought. To her surprise Paul answered on the first ring. ' At last, you've come to your senses, so where is the cub Louise?'

'She's safe and in our care, and that's where she's staying until you come clean and tell me what you're up to.' Replied Louise, shaking.

'Do you realise that she will be rejected if you try to return her Louise?'

Pauls knowledge of the animals put Louise on the back foot. He had the knack of cutting her dead with his comments taking her right back to when they were together and he bullied any situation where veterinary decisions were made. He continued. ' We are carrying out a re-introduction programme in Seoul and Grey is part of that programme, as a comparison study. Granted it's not legal in this country Louise but its ethical and we are controlling and monitoring Greys exposure. This isn't some fantasy game Louise, it's a serious study.'

Louise gathered her thoughts, he hasn't told me anything I don't already know, so she replied. ' Well it is affecting Tonmawr, natural or not Greys presence has an impact on the environment, her behaviour is being modified by Grey whether you wanted it or not.'

'Ok I accept that Louise but the impact is minimal and in the bigger picture it will help us understand the progress of the predators in our environment as well. They will never be accepted here, but you know as well as I do that they can survive without negative impact on the rural community.'

Louise was falling under the controlling influence of Pauls argument and replied. ' So how are we going to resolve this Paul?'

' Louise I want to help to keep Tonmawr flourishing, she has two cubs with her, Grey will soon move on he's curious that's all. So we leave Tonmawr to nurture her cubs and bring them to independence. I'll continue to monitor Grey and track his movements to help with the Seoul programme. The cub you have can be useful too, if you want to help with the programme?'

Louise felt a sudden pang, that she might be able to keep the cub.

' What do you mean Paul?'

'Work with me again Louise, you know the practice well enough, the cub needs to remain in captivity, we could work together, you look after her whilst I carry out the research and tests. I bring Grey back in from time to time to analyse his bloods and wellbeing to compare with similar specimens in Seoul so you could help with that also. I know I haven't been the best husband Lou, but we were good together, let's put the bad behind us and work together, nothing else.'

Louise was taken in and felt excited at the prospect but could not quite believe him, although the feelings took her back to the exciting times she spent with Paul before it all went wrong.

The quiet spell was broken by Paul. 'Time is against us Louise, what do you say?'

Louise with a reluctant sigh agreed to bring the cub to the surgery that afternoon. 'I'll be there about four o'clock Paul' She said, followed by a dab from her thumb to end the call. Louise had an hour to prepare the cub for moving, without Gill it would be difficult.

She texted Gill. 'Hi Gill can we postpone our plan for later. V.tired. Can do it tomo? Cub will be ok till then xxx.' Lies, lies, lies, she said to herself. The return text satisfied Louise. ' ok good idea think we all need a rest spk soon xxx.'

Ji-a washed her hands at the stainless deep square, her shortness pushed her elbows high in order to reach the pad on the tap lever. Satisfied with the readings on the monitor she smiled at Pauls gaze as he stood at the open door of the surgery. ' Did you have a good rest Dr Paul?'

Paul straightened and replied. ' I think it's your turn now Ji-a, come on I'll take you to my place you can shower and rest a while, I'll come back here and look after mother.'

' Yes I need to rest and change clothes.'

In the car Ji-a updated Paul on the mothers status. 'So her vital signs have returned to normal, I spoke with my father and he reviewed the data, he is a happy man. He asked what about number seven, Grey you have named him?'

Paul was feeling in control again, his ego now started to take over. 'Grey is being monitored and controlled, in fact we shall introduce number eight, another apex male next Saturday to start the rival interaction study. Also I have a natural female with cubs under my control. She has a well-established territory and is nurturing her cubs with great success.'

Ji-a looked at Paul with wide eyes and an open mouth. 'We had no idea Paul, we thought you had only one male, this is fantastic news, why didn't you tell us?'

Pauls smug grin would have irritated Louise as she knew it was a sign of his ego rising but Ji-a did not recognise Pauls subtle expressions. 'Like most things in life Ji-a you should be certain before advertising your achievements.'

'Paul this information is invaluable to our programme in Seoul, when can we see the data?'

Pauls bragging was again about to be his undoing so he deflected the request. ' One day at a time Ji-a as your father would say, we have to focus on number one.'

Chapter 30

Claire De Mota pushed the heels of her hands along her warm hips and arched her back which curled her gaze towards Adrian Miles' dark haired chest. He sensed her waking, extending strong arms to touch the headboard. ' Haven't slept that well in such a long time, how about you?'

'Same Adrian I think we used most of our energy last night, I guess its late?' Claire woke her phone focussing on the screen. 'Think we missed breakfast its ten thirty.' Adrian rolled out of bed and wandered to the en-suite. Claire watched his muscular torso expand in its stretch and followed the padding feet with a satisfied gaze. He called from the bathroom. ' I hope our hosts don't think bad of us Claire, I would like to formalise our arrangements for next weekend before I head back.' She joined him in the bathroom leaning across to turn on the shower. As the temperature rose and steam billowed Claire beckoned her lover.

' Care to join me Adrian?'

Alan and Tom Price sat warming next to the open fire, Tom already nursing a crystal glass with amber liquid. He offered the decanter to Bautista Flores, and asked. 'If you would prefer to deal direct with us we could arrange a more tailored package, with more options on the girls?'

Bo raised a hand to refuse the whiskey and replied. ' That is very kind Tom but we have a favourable arrangement with the Cheltenham club which we have built over a number of years. Ah Adrian, glad you could join us at last.'

With Claire following close behind Adrian Miles nodded with an apologetic smile. 'Alan would you care to join Claire and myself for a strole? Bo I'll be ready to take you back to Cheltenham in half an hour if you would care to meet me at the car. Tom I trust you can keep our guests entertained and ensure their luggage is taken care of ?'

Within a few short words Adrian had directed proceedings. Tom tensioned and lifted his feet to rise from the leather wing backed chair but was held from a terse response by Claire's interruption. 'Tom why don't you show Snr Flores the stables, there is a Gelding which Im sure he would be interested to see.'

As the group dispersed in different directions Adrian whispered a thank you to Claire. 'You need to keep your brother under control Alan, I will deal directly with Claire regarding our visits.' Alan Price bowed behind the towering frame of Adrian Miles and replied. 'Of course, now what did you want to discuss?'

' The Panther hunt next weekend, I'd like to firm up the arrangements and understand your plan to track the beast, it's a risky encounter which could turn into a damp squid, I'm not convinced the vet, err

Paul, is capable of setting the field, so what is your plan?'

Alan had no idea of how to set up the hunt let alone manage the Panther. His experience lay with Deer stalking but he was quick to sense the concern in Adrian's question. 'As with all blood sport Adrian nothing is certain, however a Panther brings in a few extra challenges. The satisfaction is in the kill rather than the chase I think.'

Claire guided the trio through the marquee and stopped to pick the remnants of fruit from the breakfast display before adding. ' The Panther will be hunting its prey, Red Deer, so a similar method of stalking as Paul explained last night would be suitable.'

Alan agreed even though he wasn't party to that conversation before adding. ' A standard format for Deer wouldn't work here, I think with the tracking device we need to approach from three directions each group covering an arc, if we approach from two or one direction it would be a chase to nothing, not my idea of a hunt. However that has its risks, especially when a shot is called, we all need to be in direct communication and a lead must direct the shot.'

'So Claire do you think we are ready?' Adrian disguised his intimate knowledge of the woman before him, switching his manner to customer -client relationship.

' In principal Adrian yes, we have the ingredients the hardware, the setting, but as Alan suggested the method needs fine tuning, I'd recommend we carry out a number of practice hunts or trials before next Saturday. Are you available this evening Alan?'

'Good idea Claire, we can set up for this evening, I'll call Paul to arrange a time. That will give us the opportunity to iron out any issues by Saturday.'

Adrian Miles appeared satisfied with the conclusion of the conversation, he shook hands with Alan Price then embraced Claire before taking the short walk to his car.

Alan looked at Claire and asked. ' How the fuck are we going to pull this one off Claire? I haven't a clue how to track a Panther let alone direct a kill.'

The pair returned to the drawing room of the house and settled into the wing-backed chairs to discuss the plan for the evening. Tom returned, now unsteady on his feet as the alcohol level returned to his normal for a Sunday lunchtime. Claire took out her mobile and dialled Paul Morris. 'We need you at the house this evening, bring the tranquiliser kit.'

Paul Morris was sat at home having returned from his encounter with Martin Quinn at Louise's house. 'I can't just drop everything for you Claire, what is all this about?'

'Just fucking get hear by six o'clock.' Claire replied as she turned to Tom Price who had fallen into his chair and was staring from a slumped position at Claire's bare legs. She was wearing the same cocktail dress from the night before. 'Keep your eyes up Tom you filthy bastard.'

Claire set the tone for the meeting with her manner, the Price brothers sat to attention. Following a lengthy discussion Claire stood and returned to the master suite to change into her hunting attire.

The gravelled drive way of Aber-llia House was covered with four by fours spewing diesel fumes into the clear dark night. The convoy gripped and pushed the stones to the grass as it tore through the gated entrance on its way to Horseshoe Ridge. The lead vehicle, a Subaru pickup driven by Alan Price slewed around the narrow road towards the Forestry Commission gateway on the lee of the ridge. The road provided access to the copse of deciduous trees facing the steep escarpment of Horseshoe Ridge. Alans brother Tom held the laptop, the tracker icon #M7 was centred on the screen.

As night fell the icon moved, indicating that Grey was on the move. Tom opened the steel box behind his seat and took out the Deer hunting rifle. The matt black barrel of the Ruger was sleeved by Tom and the carrier slung over his shoulder. Winchester Deer rounds were counted out and pushed into the carrier inside his tweed coat. Alan Price waited in silence then replaced his brother at the gun box. His rifle was already sleeved but he took it out and checked the mechanism and the nightscope for security. Satisfied he filled his outer pockets with rounds. Standing in the dusk to dark conditioned their vision for night hunting. Five miles to the south on the fringe of the Beacons Paul Morris and Claire De Motta sat on the tailgate of her Range Rover. Claire eyed her Sako 75 deer hunting rifle stock and caressed the engraved block tracing her fingertip around the scroll of her initials. Her rifle was a gift from the Cheltenham Club at last year's Christmas Ball. She had never culled a Deer and was anxious to break her duck. The blood smeared across her olive skin would excite her and allow her to be accepted as a hunter, in a male dominated world this would add to her sex appeal, already she was courted by the upper echelons of Cheltenham society. Raising her game to talk at events from experience was her goal.

Paul Morris took the tranquiliser rifle, pistol and darts from their case and sleeved them in less exotic covers. Black, waterproof and functional was all that mattered this night. The plan developed over the afternoon was to track Grey whilst he explored his territory to search out the Red Deer herds. The experienced men who prepared Deer hunts would track the herd. No driving, beating, or interference, let them come together naturally. If Grey failed to kill a Deer then Alan, Tom or Claire were to shoot a doe. Paul Morris would then wait for Grey to return to feast on the doe. He would get close enough to dart the Panther. This test would be the blueprint for Saturdays real hunt where the club members would then kill the Panther and have their first predator trophy.

Peter Evans the head stalker received a call from Alan Price that everyone was in place and Grey was heading south west. Peter was watching the main herd sat on the scrubland which fringed the open moorland.

They had rested there since the middle of the afternoon when the brief low sun had warmed the ground. Peter Evans aimed his rifle at the largest body a male stag who was feeding away from the main herd. His scope focused on the stags fully grown antlers which were scared and chipped. As the dusk drifted away to a dark clear sky the herd rose and headed to the open moor in search of fresh grazing.

Peter called Alan Price who relayed the direction to Claire. The tailgate closed with a blip of her remote key fob and the pair set off North towards the grazing herd. Tom Price lead his brother on the trail of Grey having closed the laptop and secured it in the Subaru. His mobile phone now replicated the tracking software and indicated the direction. As they followed, the distance between Grey and their own position increased at each refresh.

Grey had no direction indicator to follow other than his natural stalking route which ebbed left and right over half a mile in a zig-zag. The route would cover four times the distance of Alan and Tom and with good fortune would cross the Deer's path. The scent of the Deer was strong enough to leave markers for Grey, he would then follow the scent trail until he had a visual indication of the herd. Two hours into the night Grey had picked up the first fresh scent. He curtailed his ebb and flow straightening his course to run parallel and upwind of the herd.

The herd settled to feed on the head of a rise in the ground, vison in all directions was uninterrupted. The herd were safe from predators both animal and human. A shot from lower ground was never accurate. The rising muzzle and firing position was the most difficult to judge distance as no reference point behind the target was available. An attack from the Panther would be spotted well before it could reach the herd. The stag knew this from experience, that is he had never experienced it from this position of strength. Sudden falling and deaths within his herd were confined to more enclosed surroundings such as woodland and watercourses.

These areas were approached with more caution and the Deer did not linger or rest when in woodland or taking water.

Grey curled his tail around the ample trunk of the fir which marked the edge of the man-made forest. He could not see the herd but the subtle noises transmitted down to the wall of trees from the open higher ground. The scent was drifting down the slopes. He was satisfied that the herd had stopped to graze and took the opportunity to rest. His patience surprised Alan and Tom who had remained downwind of Grey, their advantage being the tracker, the marker hadn't moved for three hours. He called Claire and instructed her and Paul to take a wide arc and remain south of the herd. Peter Evans and his son were to remain to the east. All angles were now covered and all they had to do was wait for the herd to move on.

Tonmawr had waited for Grey to leave his den and move south, the pattern she created some two nights ago. The cubs were anxious to follow but would not move until their mother lead the way. She would follow Grey at a distance, watch his pattern, learn his habits to prepare herself for the inevitable parting. As the scent of Grey fell to nothing it was replaced by human scent. She caught the brief light and sound of The Prices following Grey. Tonmawr bounded down the rocks but halfway down the crest turned and climbed to the top and headed in the opposite direction towards the quarry road.

Rhys and Lewis had been sat waiting for their mother to call for an hour. Their arrangement was to meet her here at six. They arrived early to take the opportunity to smoke a joint. Rhys called his mother at six-fifteen. Gill explained that the night had been called off and they were doing it tomorrow. 'Well thanks for letting me know Mam!' Rhys tossed his phone onto the dash board. The backlight diffused through the windscreen illuminating Tonmawrs globes. 'Lewis there's Tonmawr and the cubs!' They passed in front of their car and disappeared into the quarry compound. Lewis checked the tracker on Grey and realised he was seven miles in the opposite direction high up in the forestry. 'Well they must have had a fall out, Grey is miles away.' Rhys yawned and fired up the engine, food, fast food beckoned, as they tore out of the car park in search of their own nourishment.

Claire strode with a confidence that unnerved Paul Morris, her purposeful gait swept up the steep incline leaving him falling behind with each step. Her athletic form covered in dark tweed made no sound, her experience of stalking and beating made the tracking seem effortless. Paul had no such experience, he was more likely to be called to an incident or be on hand to sedate an animal. Covering miles of open ground in silence at night was alien to him. Claire paused at the fir tree border and raised her weapon, viewing the open ground to her front through the night scope fitted to the rifle. The curved silhouette of her extended hip posture was raw and female, it excited Paul, he recalled the night she leant with the same position naked against the frame of the bedroom door, minus the rifle. Claire sensed his approach and dropped a hand palm down behind her, beckoning Paul to remain in her shadow. 'What is it Claire?' whispered Paul.

Claire turned to his ear and responded. 'The Deer on the hill, just as Alan said, that means Grey is in these woods probably only a few yards from us.' Paul checked his phone tracker and tapped Claire on the shoulder.

' Probably more like hundred yards over there.' Paul directed Claire's gaze through the forest to her right. The fir trees stood fifty feet in height and were packed together only feet apart. Their pattern was randomly spaced but planted with a purpose to maximise speed of growth and minimise the outcrops of branches. This patch would be felled within two years then replanted. The ground underfoot bore the knee height severed trunks of the previous generation and supported little groundcover. Perfect for predators to lie in wait. Scent was masked by the pine , wind disrupted and moisture shielded by the year round canopy. Their patience must match that of the Deer and Grey, although Grey was becoming more impatient. He heard Claire and Paul approach the treeline but could not deduce their scent through the pine.

Claire dropped to the ground and shuffled her body to a firing position with elbows nestled and her right knee bent up to her chest. The view through her scope was stable, the night vision over two-hundred yards did not reveal much detail but the dark mass against the lighter background provided enough contrast for Claire to mark her target. She had to regulate her breathing as her excitement pushed up her heartrate. Deep inhales through her nose and low long exhales through her open mouth condensed her breath until she controlled her lust for her first blood. Paul sat behind her supporting the weight of his upper body on a fir trunk and called Alan to confirm they were in position. Claire told Paul to relay that she had a shot on the stag and would take it on Alans call.

' What do you reckon Tom, we've been here for an hour, Grey hasn't moved and the herd are gonna move soon?' Tom remained prone, his night scope trained on the Stag from the north, he knew Claire had the more favourable shot.

'As much as it grips my shit let the bitch take the Stag.' The herd did not rely on the ageing Stag as younger males were starting to encroach the group and raise interest from the older females. The Stag was dominant but would soon be ousted.

Peter confirmed Claire's position as they arrived from the east but pointed out that they would have to gralloch the stag in the field then come back with their Land Rover to transport the beast back to the house. Alan agreed with the plan, take the Stag ,remove its bowls then retreat, this would allow Grey time to approach the stag. This would then provide the Cheltenham Club their opportunity on Saturday. If it worked tonight it would work on Saturday he repeated to Tom. With them all in agreement Alan gave the instruction to Claire to take the Stag.

Claire removed her finger from the trigger and wiped her sweating palm on the dry tweed covering her elevated buttock, she caressed her fingers around the dial on the scope and adjusted the focus. As she did the stag stopped the lick of its behind and skipped from the hill towards her position causing the herd to prong after him. Paul offered a caution. 'Let them settle again.'

Claire's breathing shortened yet again billowing condensed breath which clouded the lens. 'Wait, breathe.' She said to herself.

Her trigger hand caressed the carved initials on the lock, her index finger took up the lag on the curved trigger, its tension held back. One squeeze, that's all it required, waiting for the Stags head to raise above the cross hairs, her breathing settled. A shot to the mass of upper chest was required. The tip of the barrel moved with her inhale and lifted the tip, as she exhaled the fall came to the mass of the chest. Squeeze, twist her left arm and hand in the opposite coil, head statuesque. The round left the rock solid barrel and followed through Claire's imaginary line to the heart of the stag. The animal fell before the noise registered and echoed in her head as if someone had taken the shot a micro second before her. She looked around for confirmation it was her. Paul rolled to her side and said. 'Excellent shot Claire.' Her face erupted and blossomed, heat pulsed, exuberant energy took over as she sprung from her block. Claire raised the scope to view her prize, motionless the stag remained on its side, head held off the turf by its majestic antlers.

Grey bolted deep into the wood at the noise, bounding across stumps and branches before cutting north. His curiosity and memory of the sharp crack from the rifle led him to a free supper on the last occasion. This recall pushed a return circle into his navigation, find the high ground and view the aftermath. The spokes of the hunting wheel radiated to the hub where a once great leader lay without his hareem, without his presence and without life. Claire's triumph infected the group who congratulated her shot. Peter the most experienced tracker offered his review. ' You showed patience and didn't flinch when he moved down, shot clean through the heart, I watched him fall, perfect.'

Claire beamed her smile back and thanked the group. Peter knelt beside the head and with his left hand gripped the base of the antlers. As the head rose he unsheathed his bone handled curved blade. Feeling down the sternum the point entered the body and disappeared to its hilt. With a twist and tilt an opening was made out of which expelled damp air and little blood. His hand reached inside and pulled a tube of pale blue which was severed and tied in one motion. The back end was severed and carved, tied in the same manner. 'Ready Claire? Come on, hold the blade and move it up to the cavity at the knot, I'll hold it taught, just watch my hand as you break through'. Claire followed Peters instruction and felt the blade lift the skin from its underside, keeping the tension she sliced through from anus to throat without stopping. The grey and red gut fell under its own weight to the damp ground. As the blood spilled Alan Price cupped the warm liquid and wiped his palm dry on Claire's left cheek.

Tom Price embraced Claire and offered a 'well done girl.' The group toasted from a flask passed around. Paul remained low and scanned the circumference of their view with his night scope. The herd had long since left their leader. They would not have even seen their stag fall but reacted as individuals to the crack of the rifle and disappeared on differing lines to regroup when clear of the scent.

Paul Morris reviewed his tracker. 'No sight of Grey, his signal shows his position deep in the forest north of the hill top where the stag was first targeted.'

Alan offered his advice. ' Hopefully Grey is watching us and waiting to move in so let's move out and set up an arc of field as before.' He eyed up to the crest and realised their positions would have to change adding. 'If we swap positions and set up as if we were to take another shot at the Deer.'

Peter offered advice. 'The high ground is too exposed, a silhouette would alert the Panther, I'd suggest we move closer below the horizon, its risky though as arcs will cross. If we move positions east and west and leave the woodside without an arc then no one can get caught in the crossfire.'

Tom looked confused. 'I thought we were just targeting and not shooting?'

Paul Morris piped up. 'I hope were not thinking of shooting Grey tonight that's not what we agreed.'

Alan Price raised a hand. 'Calm down Paul, no one is going to shoot Grey, unless we are attacked of course, just targeting and learning his movements so we can advise the hunt group on Saturday. Ok, is everyone clear, keep in contact and be patient, this Panther will wait for as long as it takes to feel safe enough to take the bait.'

Chapter 31

Tonmawr dipped into the shallows of the limestone quarry pool, the milk covering her fur in the sediment. The cubs followed, tasted the opaque liquid and spitted out, for the first and last time they would experience the taste of lime, a lesson learned. Content with her covering Tonmawr did not shake when she left the water but allowed the liquid to soak in. Her scent covered she turned south past her den in search of Grey.

Claire settled into position as instructed by Alan, still revelling in her achievement. Paul was less excited by the situation, he was neglecting Ji-a who he had left alone at home. Ji-a would want to return to the surgery to check on #1. Pauls phone was logged into the tracker, its battery was down to 15%. He needed to speak to Ji-a.

'Claire, Im going back to the car, this phone is about to die. Alan has Grey on his tracker, I'll be back in half an hour.' Claire looked concerned as she would be left on her own without communication with Alan. ' Really, can't you wait, what about Alan and Peter'

'I need my phone to be available Claire, Ji-a is caring for the other Panthers at the surgery, I'll be as quick as I can.'

Claire pursed her lips and replied. ' Be quick, and let Alan know, send him a text ask him to send one of Peters men down here, I don't want to be on my own.'

'No problem, Ill text him now, don't worry I won't be long, I've a spare battery in the car.'

Ji-a was awoken by the call from Paul. Her flight from Seoul and the surgery carried out on the pregnant Panther had taken their toll on her slight frame. Her reply was guilt ridden as she had been away from her patient for eight hours, she was anxious to return to the practice. 'But Dr Paul, I need to get back to the surgery, I'll take a taxi.'

Paul wanted to be with her and was trapped by Claire and the Price brothers, he knew his loyalty lay with the programme, to provide a sustainable group of Panthers and secure much needed long term income. This distraction was interfering but he couldn't break the cycle of cocaine, and his cash flow problem. Claire provided both and had a hold he longed to break. ' There's a spare key to the surgery in the hall way draw Ji-a, I'll be with you as soon as I can. I've been called out to a sick horse at one of my farmer clients, sorry to leave you alone, call me when you get there.' The lies were now extending out to Ji-a and it added to the stress, trying to remember what he had said to who. The sooner he could finish this hunt the better he thought.

Peter joined Claire at the edge of the forest in silence, the experienced tracker startled her as he tapped her shoulder. The pair lay in silence waiting for Grey to appear. Tom and Alan were also set in a shallow ditch on the slope of the hill. The gutted stags mass was visible below them.

Ji-a arrived at the surgery within half an hour of speaking to Paul. She checked the Panthers vital signs and logged the time on her chart. She viewed the drip and realised it would require changing soon. She left the surgery and found the storeroom at the rear of the building. The steel cabinet behind the door banged as she swung open the storeroom door. This same cabinet was firmly locked when she entered the store earlier that afternoon, she remembered her last visit when Paul showed her his tranquilizer gun and hunting rifle. A broken open card box blocked the cabinet door as she tried to close it. .20 Winchester emblazoned the white box, she noted it was empty as she placed it back in the cabinet and closed the door. Why would he take the weapons on a call out to a horse she thought.

The saline solutions were kept in cold store, again she was surprised at the lack of stock, this was the last one. The Panthers eyes opened and closed under heavy lids as the snap of the connector allowed the flow of liquid to resume into her forlorn body. She called Paul but it went straight to answerphone.

' Hi its Ji-a, we are out of saline Paul, the last one will keep her going for eight hours, maybe twelve if I reduce, could you order or pick up in the morning please. Oh I forgot, your gun cabinet was left open Dr Paul, you have the guns I presume. Anyway call me and let me know when you are coming back.'

Claire checked her phone, no missed calls, no messages. Paul had been gone for over an hour. She messaged Alan to ask if he was with him. Nothing. Peter tapped Claire's shoulder and pointed towards the far edge of the tree line. Claire raised her aim and viewed the angle, Grey appeared in her view standing tall with his nose taking in the drifting scent of the Stags blood. Alan had his sights set on Grey, his elevated position provided an exaggerated view of the Panthers sleek length. Its back bone extending through a high tail. 'What a magnificent animal Tom, I'd be proud to have that stuffed and mounted at the house. Paul has more of these males doesn't he?' Tom had the same view and admired the feline through his rifle sights.

'Yes he's got another two, don't suppose he'd miss this one, do you ?' Alan grinned at Tom before resting his cross hairs on Greys upper body mass.

Greys curiosity pushed his body closer to the stag. The flavour from two nights ago when he tasted the red doe near Horseshoe Ridge lingered on his buds. With a lick of his nose he freed his senses to take in the environment. He sensed human which checked his progress towards the stag and returned him to the relative safety of the tree line. As he settled, Tonmawr looked down on him from high on the hill. Her vantage point was chosen when she picked up Greys scent, her cubs were cautioned to remain still with a nudge and deep growl. Tonmawr needed to observe Greys behaviour from a distance, she wanted to see his next move so she could plan her exit from the territory. The failure to settle in this new land was not borne out of lack of opportunity but from interference, human and the unnatural behaviour of Grey. He was unlike other males she had encountered.

Claire tracked the male predator back into the tree line. Her patience was wearing thin, she was cold and was angry with Paul who had still not reappeared. Peter offered encouragement. ' Something spooked him, maybe it's our scent, the wind has whipped up again and its coming from the North, if he caught a whiff from Tom hell never come back.'

Claire liked Peters calm manner and his subtle humour, she smiled in agreement about Toms odour. 'Be patient the Panther will come back out.'

Alan Price saw him reappear first from the middle of the tree line, within twenty yards of Claire's position. His trot built slowly to a full sprint as Grey attacked the dead stag. The pouncing blow would have killed a live stag outright, the force of Greys body shook the ground and made the hunters feel insignificant. The grips on their weapons tightened as Greys power toppled the stag exposing the spilled organs. Grey gripped and turned to assault again and pounced on the lifeless mane tearing a tuft and snapping the neck. The ferocious attack was unnecessary but proved to Grey that there was no threat from the stag.

Claire was aghast and in her tremoring hands she struggled to focus her sights. Grey attempted to move the stag away from its position but failed. He settled at the underside and took his first chunk of meat with a ferocious snap of his incisors. The tearing was audible and soon the crack of ribs followed as he dug deeper into the cavity of the chest for the heart and lungs.

Tonmawr was tempted to join him as she did previously but remained steadfast. She had a view of the two humans lying prone in a shallow ditch below her. Lower down the hillside at the tree line from where Tonmawr had appeared another movement attracted her attention.

The muzzle caught the dull light for only a split second but was enough to alert her peripheral vision. Within the tree line the rifle was being held by steady hands now. The preloaded weapon targeted the neck of Grey. It was a straight forward shot if taken as Grey was lying prone feeding. As his head tore another morsel the body remained still. Breathing steady, squeeze firmly in one movement and hold the stock with a twist inward. The bullet left the barrel and struck Grey in the jaw sending splinters of bone up through his head, the high velocity void behind the round dragged the splintered head with it as Grey jolted and the remains of his skull fell to the earth.

The crack of the shot started the race for Tonmawr, her speed left the cubs but they soon picked up her reaction and followed her sprint to the North. She saw Greys head explode before she heard the crack from the rifles bullet.

Alan Price shouted down, bellowing to stop firing as two more rounds pierced the night air. The hunters approached Grey and the Stag from three directions, talking their way in confirming all were present. Paul Morris appeared from nowhere, and knelt before the shattered skull of grey. ' What have you done? Why? Who did this?'

The silence from the hunters was broken by Claire who's heart was pounding. 'I fired two rounds after the first one hit Grey, I just reacted, sorry and fired.' Peter put a comforting hand on her shoulder and offered an explanation. ' It's a natural reaction don't worry Claire.'

Alan lifted the Panthers head and looked at Tom. 'Not much of a display left for the house.'

Tom replied. 'Well it wasn't me who fired first.' The group focused on Paul who held up his hands. 'Well don't look at me I'd just come back from the car.'

Alan looked directly at Paul. 'We need to clear this mess up, Peter get the Landrover and remove the Stag and Panther back to the house. Well one good thing Claire we've proved our tactic works and we're good for Saturday.'

Paul grabbed Alans arm and shouted. 'And what exactly do you intend to shoot on Saturday?'

Tom pulled Pauls hand from his brother and gripped Pauls lapel. 'Another one of your precious Panthers Paul, just remember who's running this ok!'

Paul looked at Claire for support. 'You have five days to get another Panther ready and out in the field Paul, take me back to the house now please, Peter will sort out the Panther.' Without breaking stride Claire continued towards the treeline with Paul stumbling behind her.

The rifle tip was still warm as she held the barrel whilst unscrewing the night scope. Out of breath Louise stowed Paul Morris's rifle in the boot of her Passat under the cover of a horse blanket. She rolled the car down the forest track without lights on and only started the engine as she cleared the first bend and headed back to her lodge, mission accomplished.

Chapter 32

'Im so sorry Ji-a for leaving you for so long, how is the mother?' Pauls words were so quiet that Ji-a strained to hear the lies through his apology.

'We need to re-stock Paul, can you call the supplier now please?'

'I already have, they will be here just after ten a.m.'

Where were you last night Paul? You need to change you are covered in blood.'

'Sorry Ji-a, I'll wait for the delivery then go home to change, it was a long night helping one of my clients.'

'Your gun cabinet is open and you should keep it locked, why did you take the guns?'

'I needed the tranquiliser gun, I always take it, just in case.'

'And your hunting rifle?'

'Hunting rifle? No, that's in the cabinet.'

'No its not Paul, the cabinet is empty.'

Paul dropped from his chair and ran down the corridor to the storeroom. The door crashed against the gun cabinet as he pushed his way in. Seeing the cabinet empty Paul fell to his knees and thumped the cold steel with both fists. ' That fucking bitch has done it again, that's it she's finished.' He pulled his mobile and pressed call to Louise.

The call did not come as a surprise to Louise, she had been awake all night, unable to rest after killing Grey. The vision of the animal eating then falling lifeless revolved in her head. Could I have done it differently? Why didn't I just sedate him, and remove him to a different territory? The questions revolved , the answers did not come. Whichever way she looked at it there was only one way to protect Tonmawr and her cubs. She had to eliminate all of the cloned Panthers. She knew Paul must have access to more Panthers, or was he keeping them hidden at the surgery? The one place she did not look was the old stables at the practice, were they hidden there? Or were they up at Alan Prices farm buildings? Louise missed Martins calming influence. She needed Gill as well to guide her, but knew that she would be against her tactics. She was alone, fighting to save Tonmawr, fighting to sustain the natural order.

'Yes Paul, what do you want?' Louise said in a firm voice.

'We agreed yesterday that you would bring the cub to the surgery and you arrived without it. Then you steel my hunting rifle and shoot dead Grey. What the fuck is going on Louise, I thought we agreed to work together on this?'

'It's never going to work Paul, its interfering with the natural order, Tonmawr is running scared and needs her cub, these cloned Panthers are causing havoc and before you know it the authorities will get involved and that will be the end of the Panthers existence. They don't need humans to interfere, they have been surviving without causing any issues until you introduced an unnatural Panther. How many more are there Paul, who's paying you?'

'You have no idea Louise, I thought you understood the programme yesterday, Ji-a and Dr Kam have an international programme which is accepted, the Panthers in our care are an integral part of that programme.'

' Well take your programme out of our back yard Paul, it's not your playground.' Louise hung up before Paul could reply. She was satisfied that he wouldn't report the gun missing, he had too much to lose.

Paul returned to the surgery and turned to ease the worry on Ji-as face. 'It's ok Ji-a, I had the rifle at my house in the cabinet, just remembered.' Ji-a did not respond but continued to study the charts before her on the magnetic board. She scrolled through the monitor and noted changes in the vital signs of #1 on the chart before turning to Paul.

'I have spoken with father this morning, he has decided to move the programme to our colleagues in Norfolk. They are arranging transport this week so it is vital we stabilise#1. Also the two male Panthers in the stables, they will be moved,#M8 and #M9.'

'Ji-a no you can't do this, we are so close to success, please give me a couple of more weeks, the data is coming in it all looks good.'

'Paul I took a swab from you jacket, that is Panther blood, what has happened to #7, Grey?'

The realisation of the situation should have culled his appetite for lies but Paul resorted to more deceit. 'He was injured, caught in a poachers trap, I had no choice Ji-a.' Paul removed the tracker from his bag, covered in blood he wiped it clean with blue roll, opened the battery case and disconnected the supply.

Ji-a lifted the collar and replied. 'So sad, another Panther gone, he was the first of our enhanced embryos, we had developed the gene for more power in the legs, it was meant to be introduced in Honduras, the government there want to re-introduce their species to the mountain region to assist with the conservation. They have deposited a large grant to our company to develop a mammal which will be introduced in the region.'

'But don't they have natural predators, mountain lions and cougars?' Paul realised the gravity of the situation, the funding so hard to come by was there in abundance, his share would solve all his problems.

'That is their problem Paul, natural predators have died out as their territories have been developed for the ever growing population. Their prey are ruining the remaining forest, so we have provided them a solution. Grey was our first enhanced male, there are two others left at the right stage of development.' We can't take any more risks, we must be ready to deliver the two males into their new habitat before the rainy season start. The proving of Greys ability to survive in the wild was the key to the first delivery. That data will now have to be, how you say, invented.'

Paul clutched at a solution to tag #M8 and release him, he would satisfy Claire's hunt and Ji-a's needs, his suggestion was dismissed instantly. 'No Paul it is too much of a risk to the programme, father has made up his mind. The remaining two males will be transported to Norfolk by the end of the week. In the meantime we need to ensure #1 stabilises to ensure her pregnancy will go full term.'

'And what happens to the cubs, there are two females and two males, are they of the same gene?'

'The females will be the new surrogates in time, we need them for future gene and clone development. We are not saying that this can't be done with your help here at the practice Paul, but for the next few months work will be co-ordinated at Norfolk. Their facilities are excellent, you should come with me to look this week.'

'Ji-a we've worked so well together over the past two years, I can't see why we have to move everything to Norfolk.'

'Paul take a look around, it is not good, you need help of a different kind, this will help you to regroup and improve the facility, then we can work together again. In the meantime father is adamant, the Panthers move to Norfolk.'

Pauls world was collapsing around him, his lies and deceit could not help him now. He needed to act if he was to save anything. He thanked Ji-a for her honesty and said goodbye. 'I'll be back this afternoon Ji-a, I'll bring you a pizza?'

'Thank you Paul that will be nice, I've got this under control don't worry, I'll take care of the delivery as well.' Paul raised a smile and trudged to his car for the journey home. Before he started the engine he was overwhelmed and broke down sobbing, out of control, the cocaine was taken too quickly causing him to cough and catch his breath.

Watsons vet supply van pulled alongside Pauls silver car, the delivery girl waved to Paul and he pointed her towards the reception and provided a thumbs up sign to which she acknowledged with a smile. Paul jammed his car into reverse and sped off. As he reached his home he didn't recognise Claire's white Range Rover Evoque billowing fumes into the cold air. As he put the key to his front door Claire and Tom Price appeared. ' Paul we need to talk, inside if you don't mind.'

The pair did not wait for an answer and pushed past Paul, walked into his kitchen and sat at the bar stools. 'What is it Claire? I need a shower and some rest.'

'We have worked out the schedule for this week and need you to deliver the two male Panthers up to Alans barn. The tags need fitting and activating today. Alan and Tom will take over from there.'

'But they need sedating before release, plus they are not conditioned yet.'

Claire replied. ' No more Paul, we are taking control of this. Get yourself sorted out and the Panthers delivered, sedated with tags activated by this evening.'

Chapter 33

Louise broke her mental block by opening an ice cold bottle of white wine. The crisp dry liquid soothed not only her taste buds but her mind as well. The relaxing effect of the first glass opened her mind to the possibility of a satisfying outcome to the problem of Tonmawr and her estranged cub. Gill barged into the moment with a long Hi which echoed from the hall way through the kitchen and rested on the far wall of the expansive living area. Louise instructed her to grab a glass and another bottle on her way through.

'You picked a good day to take off, it was bedlam at the surgery, every cat in the neighbourhood seemed to have the same cough.'

'Glad I missed it Gill.' Louise stood too quick and steadied her wobble on the arm of the sofa. 'Cheers, here's to a successful reunion tonight, any news from Rhys or Lewis?'

They are on their way over, Mike is working late so won't be coming, is Martin, have you spoke to him, he seemed a bit peeved yesterday what happened?'

'I guess I did my usual and ignored him most of the weekend, too wrapped up in the Panther, probably shouldn't have invited him up, but I do hope we can spend more time together, I do like him and mmmm he does things to me I haven't felt for such a long time.'

'Tell me more Louise.' The pair settled with their glasses and giggled like it was their school lunch break until Rhys and Lewis clattered into the kitchen. Louise directed them to the fridge for a beer with a threatening warning not to touch her wine.

Rhys flopped next to the pair and shook his head at the empty wine bottle on the coffee table. ' How many have you had Mam?' The giggling continued as Rhys composed himself. 'So, Greys' tracker has gone off, this morning about ten o'clock, it also remained constant overnight at Crai Moore, just off the forestry road. We went and had a look this afternoon…'

Louise almost choked on her wine as she spurted out. ' What did you find?'

'Alright keep your pants on Louise.' Returned Rhys. ' Blood, lots of it, soaked into the grass, also there were Landrover tracks backed right up to the spot, oh and drag marks where they must have tied and pulled whatever it was. We took a sample of the blood Mam, oh and Lewis picked up bone fragments from the same area, sharp and jagged like they were smashed and splintered.'

Louise stuttered and her mouth dried, she wanted to tell Gill, get it off her chest, but how would she react? Better to tell her now before she found out. No keep quiet, let it play out she concluded. After a soft sip to wet her pallet she answered. 'It sounds to me that Grey has been taken by Paul and the Prices, probably shot knowing Tom Price.'

Gill looked confused by the news and spoke up. 'Why would they do that? What is their game? Or is that what their game is, shooting Panthers for sport? It wouldn't surprise me, so that means Tonmawr could be next.'

Louise felt that Gill was getting too close to the truth, so replied.

' If that's the case, which I tend to agree with Gill, then they must need the trackers to get close, Tonmawr has never been in captivity to our knowledge and doesn't carry a tracker, they could never stalk her, she's too experienced, she would spot them a mile off.' Louise realised her error as soon as the words left her mouth, she had encountered and observed Tonmawr by chance when she passed by her and Martin on the moor.

Rhys edged forward on the sofa and added. 'We can only deal with what we know, Grey has gone, off the scene for now, we have a cub to return and we know Tonmawrs habitat. What's the chance of sedating Tonmawr Mam so we can fit a tag?'

Gill stood and pointed her finger in the air. 'Wait, I've got something for you to look at.' She skated in her socks over the slate floor and returned with a sliding stop holding a small white cardboard box.

' Here I have a brand new fully charged Pet tracker, plug and play, comes with a security collar and the battery lasts one month. I smiled and shook my puppies at the rep so it's a free demo.' Gill replicated a boob shuffle and cupped her breasts for effect. Louise laughed out loud, Rhys and Lewis feigned sickness and scolded their Mam.

'That's disgusting Mam! Let me see it.' Rhys grabbed the box. Louise felt she had to bring something to the occasion.

'Ok so I have a confession, I retrieved ahem, the dart gun including sedatives from Pauls surgery yesterday.'

'So much for being too tired Lou?' Gill quizzed, knowing that she had cancelled last night's attempt to return the cub. To Louise's surprise Gill did not press further. Louise hated herself for lying, and knew that Gill would remember and bring her to account later, like her own conscious seemed uncapable of. Deeper and deeper her mind was falling into the chaos of lies. She needed to come clean but did not want to jeopardise their mission. She had to focus on returning the cub and allowing Tonmawr and her family to resume their life together. She knew time was against them, but at least Grey was gone and nothing was left to interfere with the natural progression and growth of Tonmawr and her cubs.

'So we return to Horseshoe Ridge at dusk, wait for Tonmawr to leave, if we observe from different vantage points we will spot her, then what?' Lewis asked.

Louise pondered the question but kept falling into the trap of what comes first, sedation and fit the tracker? Seemed to her the logical step otherwise the cub would be returned into the unknown and potentially lost. The other option would be to fit the tracker to the cub which she thought warranted further discussion.

Gill was the first to pick up on this idea. ' I suppose that's the safest option, then we don't have to interfere with Tonmawr, just remember though the cub will grow so how do we remove the collar, we would have to dart four Panthers to remove the collar.' Louise loved the way Gill looked at the bigger picture, the consequences, the outcomes. Medical training she presumed conditioned her thought process to preserve life. This enlightened outlook was why she needed Gill, Louise thought. Also a reason not to tell her about Grey, it goes against all that Gill Stands for.

Rhys chipped in 'Tonmawr is more likely to reject the cub if she's wearing a collar.'

Louise noted dusk was fast approaching and was conscious that the cub needed feeding and sedating before they left. ' Ok guys we need to move, and quickly.' She emphasised the point by skipping over to the light switch, switching the room from fading grey to a clear white downlight which straightened the groups backs as the images from the floor to ceiling glass reflected their shapes.

The cub raised her trapped body from its blanket and padded around the transport cage. Lewis held a dead rabbit by its hind legs. The cub recognised the odour and licked its own mussel, tasting the air. The low light of the garage steadied the atmosphere, Lewis's whispered tones reached Gill and Louise. 'Road kill, picked it up on the way its fresh, the first thing Tonmawr will look for is what the cub has been eating, what it smells of, if she doesn't recognise her scent then the cub has had it.'

Gill mixed the solution of sedative in a metal bowl with a plastic spatula. 'This will take effect instantly so let her eat the rabbit first.'

Louise enticed the cub to the locked door of the cage and smiled to Gill as she opened a small gap. She held Lewis and Gill back with an outstretched palm then beckoned Lewis over with the rabbit. Lewis tossed it into the cage and Louise eased the door closed. The cub pawed at the dead animal, he lifted and pushed, leant in and sniffed before her jaws clamped on the rabbits neck and lifted it to her preferred dining spot in the corner, shielding her mealtime from the prying eyes. The rabbit was finished within two minutes, the tearing of flesh and fur being spat were the only sounds. Bone and fur were nibbled at but soon the cub stopped her picking in search of refreshment. Gill had already placed the bowl inside the cage, the cub lapped and lapped, before a head haze translated to her hips and she collapsed to the floor, head lolling and tongue out.

'Ok let's head up to the ridge, Lewis can you carry the cub please.' Louise instructed. Gill stayed by Louise's side as she locked the front door and opened the boot of her Passat.

'Lou is the dart gun hear?' Louise remembered the hunting rifle was wrapped in the same blanket as the dart gun, and panicked.

' Err yes let me sort it out its err behind the seat I think, why don't you go up with Lewis.'

'That's ok I'd rather come with you, those boys play the music too loud and smoke, even though they think I don't know.' Louise steered Gill to the passenger seat and asked.

'How long will the sedative last Gill?'

'About twelve hours now he has a full stomach, Im really not sure how Tonmawr will react to finding her cub in the den, hopefully the shock won't be too great. I've no experience of this but I did speak to Lucy at the wildlife centre last night. She tried it with fox cubs, not a good outcome Im afraid.'

Louise had transferred her longing to keep the cub to a need now to return her. It was a fleeting desire she thought, brought on by her love of the animals and the feeling of abandonment that surfaced within her body. Tonight was the night to put all of that right. Remove the need to lie, allow Tonmawr to develop naturally, go back to her life, maybe even resurrect her relationship with Martin. It all sounded ideal to Louise but the nagging cord that pulled was Paul. She knew this would not be the end, Paul had another agenda, what it was she could not work out. She needed to clear up this loose end otherwise she knew Paul would be back interfering with the Panthers.

The cub slid down into a deep sleep offering no resistance to the drugs administered. Lewis lifted her into his arms feeling the weight. Her tail trailed to the ground from Lewis's hip, Rhys lifted it and curled it under Lewis's arm. He pulled the blanket over her head then lifted the empty cage and followed the pair outside to the Landrover.

Gill lifted the cubs eyelid and observed the relaxed iris, bright blue and moist. The collar was slipped around its warm neck and secured with a fold and pull of the security tab. Gill tugged to check the seal, satisfied she ruffled the deep, thick fur and joined Louise in her car. With a look in her mirror

Louise was satisfied they were all ready and drove at cortege speed from the sanctuary of her lodge. In silence the journey meandered through back lanes and forest tracks before turning into the quarry road, she found a spot in the trees large enough for two vehicles then turned to Gill. 'Ok here we go, let's get her back to her family.'

'I've activated the tracker, it should appear as a text to your number as well Louise, just follow the link and it will install the App.'

Tonmawrs view of the killing of Grey cemented her instinctive distrust of humans. Her curious nature never took over her primary predisposition to protect and survive. The den amidst a barren moor without the comforts of Horseshoe Ridge provided the temporary refuge required to lay low. The low-slung ceiling of the den, soil underside of the tufts of grass, prevented a stretch. The light through the day did not arc into the refuge, its overhang cut it off from the warmth of the midday sun. The hideout frustrated the cubs, they had nothing to amuse them, not a breath of wind, tumbling leaf or insect crawling. Their hunger rumbled on through the day, waiting, dozing, curling up tight, playful paws. Tonmawr was content with the solitude and quiet, no need to check for predators, no requirement to leave their bolthole, until the air cooled and the grey light faded to black.

At Horshoe Ridge the transition from dull afternoon to dark was seamless, witnessed by Louise and Gill laying in the copse. Rhys and Lewis waited on the top side, their distant view of the horizon offered a slot of grey below the black mass of cloud.

The WhatsApp group chat opened with Rhys informing the assembly that he was returning to the Landrover to pick up the cub. Gill replied to leave her for another hour, they had to be sure that Tonmawr had left the den. By the time they had arrived the mix of day and dusk confused the body clock as the distinctive time periods mulled into one.

Lewis replied that Tonmawr had probably left already as they arrived in the midst of dusk. Patience from the boys was wearing thin, they wanted action so informed the girls that they were checking the field camera on the head of the ridge then fetching the cub.

'Im concerned about the tracker on the cub Louise.' Gill announced.

'Why?' replied Louise, relieved at the break in silence.

Without taking her eyes from the ridge she continued. ' At some point we need to take it off, and as I said earlier if this reunion is a success she will be at Tonmawrs side for another eighteen months at the least.'

Louise sensed Gills concern and replied. 'I've read about a study in Patagonia, the cubs tend to start wandering at six months so there may be an opportunity, if the tracker lasts that long.'

'Im wondering what we are gaining from putting the tracker on at all, why don't we put her back without the collar and leave her to it?' Gill answered.

Louise reverted to her selfish side as she took in the consequence of no contact with the cub, if rejected it would die, no rescue, no RSPCA, no contact. She thought that the cub would be rejected as Tonmawr, now on her own and with Grey out of the game, would deepen her survival instinct and leave no room for the cub.

Lewis sent a message that they were ready to scale the escarpment. Louise picked up the tracker movement to the right of the copse at the toe of the ridge. Lewis had fashioned a carrier from a back pack, Rhys opened the zip after lifting it onto his brothers back and attached a length of rope to the cubs collar. The first third of the ridge was covered as if out for a stroll, then the increase in gradient forced the two boys to keep three points in contact as they scaled the rocks. Gill turned to Louise. 'This is where I stopped and Mike took over, the rocks don't get much sun and are extremely slippery.' The outlines of the humps appeared then fell from the view scopes as the scramble turned into a vertical climb. Lewis was in front of Rhys, the lower climber watched each step above him and loosened the rope or brought it in depending on his progress. The climb was comfortable for the boys but the damp rocks steadied their ascent, each boot or hand required a shuffle and test before the transfer of weight. The cub did not stir despite the irregular jerks of movement. Their arrival at the den entrance was confirmed by Lewis via his phone. Louise refreshed the tracker and noted the position, she saved the location and stored it on her Google maps also.

Lewis unclipped the belt of the rucksack and eased the pressure of its weight from his lumbar. He shuffled to sit with his feet dangling over the ledge and eased the shoulder straps until the weight transferred to the floor at the entrance to the den. The bag tilted as the cub slumped to the bottom of the bag and fell against the inward sloping wall. Rhys pommelled up to join his brother. The den floor had a natural drain afforded by a fissure in the bed rock which funnelled the moisture away from the bowl of the sanctuary. The pungent odour left by the family of Panthers stuck in the brothers pallets. The matted fur from the cubs released during their play fights and grooming coated the damp veranda and balled into the dry recesses. This was Panther territory and the brothers felt exposed.

A field camera was set up at the entrance, high, attached to a thick stem of heather root.

Lewis reached into the rucksack with both arms and cupped the Panther as Rhys held on to the bottom of the bag. With a twist he placed the cub on the dry floor then shuffled on his knees whilst guiding the limp warm body to the recess. He was careful to support the head as if handing a baby back to its mother. The cubs whiskers were cradled and set down on its paws facing the entrance. Satisfied there was no other predators the brothers slid to the edge and eased themselves down the escarpment leaving the lone cub exposed to whatever or whoever visited.

They slumped next to Gill in the relative warmth of the copse. Rhys brushed the damp fur from his canvas trousers and announced. 'We need to take it in turns to monitor the cub overnight until Tonmawr returns, any chance I could go back first and get changed?'

Louise replied. 'That's a good idea Rhys if we take three hour stints, in pairs?'

'Glad you said that Lou, didn't want to be out here on my own.' Added Gill.

Chapter 34

The large male predator with tag #M8 prowled his captive space anxious to escape into the clear air which drifted through the parted window of Tom Prices Landrover. An identical clone mirrored the display of eager anticipation. Its frozen mark on the right shoulder displayed M9. The growth rate had surprised Tom Price, when he last saw the Panthers only two weeks ago there was plenty of standing room in the cages. Now their spines brushed the wire mesh as if scrubbing it clean. Their pacing translated movement to the chassis of the vehicle inducing a rock.

Alan looked at his brother Tom as he joined him in the cab. 'Feisty pair Tom.'

'I'll be standing well back with two loaded guns when we release them.' Tom answered.

Claire De Motta cruised behind the Panthers with Adrian Miles at her side. 'Glad you could make it Adrian, I think after our successful trial last night you'll be impressed with the hunt.'

Adrian reached a hand over to her knee and ran his palm over the curve of her leg to her inner thigh. 'When you showed me the footage of the Panther feeding I had to come Claire, magnificent beast.' Claire returned with a satisfying closed mouth smile and guided his hand deeper.

Adrian's eyes widened as he continued. 'I've spoken with Bo and Bruno Vargas, they scolded me for not introducing the Panther on Saturday night and positively begged me to return here tomorrow for the hunt. So I agreed, they have deposited fifty grand into my account and will produce the balance tomorrow before the hunt starts. This could be the start of something big Claire, once they return to Argentina and brag to their family we will be inundated with requests. This land is so raw Claire, the rain, the terrain, it all adds to the appeal.'

Peter Evans had been tracking the Deer herd since first light and followed their migration to higher ground, the bleakest spot of the Brecon's where snow peaks remained most of the year. Now in late winter the snow had compacted and persisted in the undulations which never acknowledged the suns low beams. Sheep farmers would return in the coming weeks as shoots broke through and the meltwater released its nutrition to the thin layer of topsoil. The ancient glacier bowl now in the temperate zone was remote enough for the Stags and Doe's to relax. The herd never accepted the crack of gunfire, spooked for days until fading memories calmed them.

This was familiar territory for Peter, the majority of illegal hunts were under these skies due to their remoteness and vast flat top terrain. Herds could be viewed from distance, corralled and guided to even the most inept hunters. Hides had been established over many years and were providing a shelter for Peter as he awaited the Prices.

Claire and Alan Price leaned over each wing of the Evoque and eyed their phones. Alan turned to Adrian Miles. ' Mr Miles we have a herd ready, Tom will release one of the Panthers a mile down wind. Same drill as last night, we monitor the Panthers progress via the tracker whilst holding an arc of fire on the herd. If he attacks, all the better. If not we will despatch a doe or stag then await the Panthers arrival to feed. This will be the point tomorrow where your guests would despatch their trophy Panther. Clear?'

'A Panther kill of a Deer would be the most favourable outcome Mr Price, however I understand the frailties and I like the backup plan. Did it work well last night?'

Alan Price looked at Claire first before answering. Her downward expression tailored Alans response. 'Not as well as we had have hoped for Mr Miles, we had to despatch a Panther due to its proximity to an occupied building, however tonight's herd is over ten miles from the closest farm.' Adrian Miles did not look surprised and accepted the response with a smile and nod.

The group agreed with the plan and returned to their vehicles for the journey to meet with Peter Evans at the hide. Tom Price was in position to the north of Pen Y Fan. He had rumbled over the last cattle grid before the tarmac turned to stone and through a normally locked gate. The wind curled around the bowl and stirred the coniferous lip pushing their strained tips over. Tom backed the vehicle under the fringe and opened the tailgate to face the open rise of the highest peak of the Brecon Beacons. The scent of Deer drifted down into the bowl and soaked into the conifer wall. The barrier being the start point for the Panther to begin its hunt, and be hunted. Its demeanour of agitated craving for freedom worried Tom. He had been instructed to release M8 but could not recall which one was which. The pair were identical in form, scent, age and character.

As he pondered the choice he recalled the sedated animals being fitted with collars by Paul Morris. M8 had the dirty collar he recalled. Shining his penlight into the cages prompted a reaction of turning and turning from the animals. M8 snarled at Tom Price, its ferocity pushed Tom back. His eventual conclusion was correct, M8 the feisty one. He took the extended tube with a hook from the side of the cage. The security bar was pushed up away from the swing of the cage door. Next he had to reach the latch and lift then pull. The cam of the hinge prevented the animal from pushing the door open if the security bar had been left off.

This final movement to release the predator was done with ease by Paul, he had the knack. Tom Price had not watched the demonstration, he had been more interested in watching Claire. As he struggled, M8 become more and more agitated.

Alan Price made the call to Tom that all were in position, and to release the predator M8. The wind whipped the open tailgate of Toms Landrover as he swung the cage door open, the Panthers lightning reaction at the paw width gap banged the door against the higher tailgate, reacting and bouncing back with force. The rebound trapped its paw and the high pitched reaction caused Tom to fall back dropping his hooked bar to the floor. The rotund mass struggled to stand on the uneven ground as the cage door released from its lock and slewed open.

The Panther recovered from its pain and in an instant bounded to the soft turf. Toms palms dug as deep as his heals dug but the excavating movements failed to move him away from the paws pacing toward him. The look before pounce, a solid mass of head with upturned lip revealing the incisors at their full length. Tom gave up his escape and moved his hands to protect his head and face, rolling to the side in one movement curling in a ball. M8 sensed his power and control had overcome the irritating whimpering of his captor. He patrolled around the lump wallowing and kicking in the mud. With disdain the Panther pushed his front paws, span around and bounded into the open ground.

'Weve got movement Alan.' Called Claire.

'Quiet' whispered Peter as he eyed the herd through camouflaged field glasses. The hide had a panoramic view of the descending valley spliced by a deep tributary. The near vertical banks required a careful footing before a bound to take the weight of a human with all the hunting attire and weapons. Peter watched as Claire, Alan and Adrian descended to the lower vantage point as the cutting opened out to join a larger tributary.

Natural vegetation was sparse in these exposed moors, no room for shelter, no room to hide. Slow deliberate steps were required to ensure the Deer were not spooked. The hide was an uncovered bund of tufted grass where the poachers would lay prone, their heads shielded by the swaying ochre stalks on the head of the mound.

The trio settled side by side. Adrian took the prime position on the right. He had an uninterrupted view of the lower reaches of the moor. The bowl protected the herd from predators as the wide open ground provided an early warning plus escape could be afforded in any direction. The females bobbed and twitched as they nibbled and snatched at the sparse grassland. Their tails circled in a twitching dance, each movement caching the eye of its neighbour. A constant playing out of a well-rehearsed visual tune provided comfort in numbers and an early warning system.

When the twitching and movement stopped it signalled a warning to the rest of the herd as the animal would freeze to take in its information. As the focus honed in on the first responder the herd would mobilise as one then scatter.

The poachers took their time to set their sights. Claire was anxious to follow up her first kill and lay on the incline with a confidence which settled her nerves. Her rifle focused on one doe, then the next, adjusting, breathing and settling in her elbows. In this position amongst men she felt powerful, accepted and at one with her quarry. Alan was at ease and ready for a long session waiting for the predator to make its move. His conversation with Adrian centred around the old days of fox hunting, Deer stalking and the freedom afforded to the privileged few. Their Masonic relations surfaced with a brief mention of common acquaintances and loose invitations. Claire soaked in their chat and realised she could never be part of that world.

Tom Price had overcome his shattered nerves with a long slug from his flask and a chain of cigarettes. He topped up the leather bound silver flask from a bottle of Grouse stored under the driver's seat of his Land Rover. The screen of the laptop placed on the empty passenger seat refreshed M8's position. Tom had not even turned on the engine as he gazed at the random circling of the Panther since his release. Thirst, Tom thought, the Panther is searching for water. Relief was found at the base of Pen y Fan where a once lazy brook had to fight around the steep chaos of the east face of the large hill. The babble sped to a cascade of crashing water searching for a course to join the larger river below. Here on a perch of wet granite the Panther took refreshment as the aroma drifting from the bowl where the herd were grazing soaked his senses.

Alan was alerted to the movement via text from Tom, the Panther was moving towards the trios position. If he continued on this track they would have to move, and move quickly. Peter suggested they move now as he had expected the Panther to arrive in the centre of the bowl from his release position. Alan took the lead standing tall to search out a new position before calling Peter. 'Were moving east there's a rock outcrop behind us with a view of the upper reaches of the bowl to your position at the North, we will have no view of the spout so won't see the Panther until he is right on the herd, what's your view like of the approach Peter?

'Its poor Alan, we won't see his approach until the last minute, shouldn't affect the herd though, just wait is the best policy, if the herd are going to be spooked shall we take one of them now?'

Alan pondered the issue and turned to Claire. ' Your call Claire.'

Suddenly Claire was being asked what to do next, was Alan being genuine or trying to set her up for a fall? She thought. She stood and looked to the north through her scope and danced the sight between does grazing then lowered her sights before replying. 'In my limited experience of these situations Alan I would gladly follow your lead. I guess every situation is different but if we stick to our plan and take down a doe then we are in control. If we wait for the Panther and he fails then we have nothing but a long distance chase.'

Adrian with his arms folded viewed the exchange and looked to Alan for his response. Alan knew Claire had returned his volley and took a moment before responding. 'My thoughts exactly Claire, if we are all in agreement we'll move to a new firing position before the Panther arrives and take down a doe, Adrian if you would like to take the lead shot?'

Adrian grinned a response. 'Excellent Alan, lead on.' Alan relayed the new position to Peter and instructed him to hold fire, Adrian would take the animal.

Refreshed and eager M8 bounded towards the herd, with only three miles to cover he would arrive within minutes.

Adrian preferred a kneeling position for firing. His experience in the army as an officer rarely surfaced however now he felt in control of the situation and secured his left shoulder into the rockface and squatted with his left elbow resting on a locked knee. Without warning the doe fell followed by the echoing crack from the bullet. Its twitching stopped and the herd bolted North towards the hide where Peter was observing. The dozen led by the dominant stag were in full gallop as they flew past him. In flight they were as silent as they were grazing, hooves tipped the soft ground leaving a trail of indents across a natural trail.

Tonmawr had moved to the lee of Pen Y Fan in search of prey. The family of three did not hear the crack from the rifle, its sound masked by the low rhythmic hum of the wind farm on the adjacent hillside. Their progress was halted by the sight of the herd still in full flight and closing in fast. Tonmawr ushered her cubs from their path and resisted the temptation to attack. The stags would overrun Tonmawr but the trailing younger does might be worth following she pondered.

The cubs were excited by the encounter and motioned to follow the herd, the male cub trotted a few yards and looked back for an encouraging acknowledgement from his mother. Tonmawr content that no one was around bounded past her cub and followed the herd at pace. The trio had needed some action and this even if it did not provide a reward would be good practice for the cubs. They continued in pursuit until the herd felt safe enough to settle and graze once more. Tonmawr halted deep in the bulbus grass, and waited, her cubs either side copied her low form.

M8 was by now approaching the fallen doe, Claire and Adrian remained at the rock observing the animal, waiting for the Panther to appear. Alan had joined Peter in the hide and settled, satisfied the plan was being repeated. As M8 arrived at the bowl Adrian spotted his arrival and nodded to Claire. He viewed the prowling gait of the Panther, a low profile with its tail tucked and head pointed in line with the ground.

'He's beautiful Claire, so tempting to take a shot don't you think?'

Claire feared a repeat of last night, the adrenalin pumped and the temptation was overwhelming. She too felt compelled to fire and take her own trophy. 'Yes Adrian, but let's wait for your guests tomorrow, they will be as equally excited I hope.'

M8 stopped twenty yards from the dead animal, its heat rising and drifting in mist towards the Panther as if filtering from the kitchen to a hungry table full of guests awaiting their call for dinner. The wait stopped as the Panther stood tall, he stretched his neck and lifted his muzzle high checking the area for predators, looking, listening and smelling the air.

Adrian had replaced his rifle with a high powered camera , its focus picking the fragments of light cast across the form before him. The imitation clicks from the digital lens rolled and took full frames with clarity and depth. In the low light images were difficult to capture but with the latest technology, that Adrian could easily afford, his equipment made the shots as simple as an instamatic at the beach.

The poachers expected M8 to pounce and confirm the animal was dead with a ferocious attack. Instead the Panther, from his statuesque stance bounded past the bleeding doe. A heavier more carnal scent had swamped his focus, a female Panthers scent had drifted down from Tonmawrs position. It was an instinctive drive for the male, he had not felt it before, but it was the strongest urge he had felt in his brief captive life.

He had to find it no matter what was in front of him. Alan looked to Peter, Claire looked to Adrian. Both sets in disbelief, their understanding and plan shattered, but they didn't know why. Peter offered an explanation. 'He must have smelt us, he knows our scent, we are too close, another lesson learned Alan.'

Claire's excitement boiled over. 'Come on, we've got to follow, Tom can wait further north and guide us.'

Alan shook his head. 'More like pick us up when we're flat out knackered.'

Adrian picked up on Claire's ambition. 'This is the whole point Alan, the chase, Im sure you old ones could follow up in the vehicles, come on Claire I'm with you.'

As excited school kids on a paper chase the pair strode out in pursuit of the Panther unaware that its motives were far more determined than their own.

Tonmawr eyed a young doe grazing the fringes of the groups selected patch. As if nothing had happened previously the herds forgotten minds reverted to foraging for succulence amongst the brackish, bleak moor. Their transition of five miles took no more than one hour and brought them to within sight of Horseshoe Ridge. A welcome sight too for Tonmawr, her preferred den. The herds migration blew a favourable wind for the family.

M8 gripped the scent tight and did not waver, her progress restricted by endless checking and criss-crossing to ensure his vectors were on course. The southerly wind favoured Tonmaws stalking of the herd but equally favoured the male predators quest to find his female.

The male cub eyed the same doe as his mother. Their shared stalking technique was developing into teamwork. The mother shuffled and crabbed until the pair had opposing lines of attack with the doe at the centre. Tonmawr sprung first, low fast and hard she accelerated and did not need to rise until upon the senseless doe. The Stag had seen her and with his suiter turned to defend the doe. Tonmawr did not waiver, she pinned the doe with one paw, already concussed by the flying punch of jaw to its neck. The stag barked, feigning a rush, barking and waving its antlers. The male cubs thirst for action brought him to his mother's side baring his curved incisors and snarling at the stag. The standoff ended abruptly as the stag withdrew to leave his doe to the mouths of the predators.

The Doe in its second year was similar in shoulder height to Tonmawr. She tested its weight with a pull using her clenched jaw around the Doe's rump. It moved with ease and brought the cubs to follow its trailing head as it bobbed along the ground. Tonmawr scolded the cubs as they hindered her progress with their nibbling and clawing. Horseshoe Ridge in the distance was too far to drag the animal. Tonmawr had eyed its ridge and realised it was too far, but to stay exposed would leave her open to humans. Her instinct to find cover drove the family towards the ridge, but their track guided them towards the copse at its base, the journey of gentle undulations could be covered without hindrance as long as the cubs stopped pulling in the opposite direction.

Chapter 35

Louise and Gill welcomed the text from Rhys that he was walking towards the copse to take over their watch period. 'At last, they're coming, that was a long three hours Gill.'

'Louise, why did you get the guns from Paul, and how did you get them?'

The direct question following three hours of idle chatter surprised Louise, why wait till now to ask? She thought before answering. 'I went over yesterday afternoon to the practice to confront him about Grey. There was no one there so I got in through the fire door again, the gun cabinet was open, I knew we needed the tranquiliser gun so I just thought, now or never.'

'Guns, I asked Lou, stop the bullshit, why take the hunting rifle, I saw it in your boot.' Louise knew she could hide it no more, the deceit was eating her inside.

'Ok you're not going to like this Gill, I tracked Grey last night. The Price brothers and Paul used Grey for sport, you were right earlier when you guessed that. They were out hunting, before I could intervene with a dart they shot him.' As the lies left her lips a warm swell of blood rushed through her temples inducing a pumping headache. Please don't ask me anymore she thought.

Gill put a comforting arm around her and said. 'Bastards, I knew they were up to something, you need to stop doing all this on your own Lou, we're in this together. But why take the hunting rifle?'

'As I said Gill it was back up in case anything went wrong, there's something more though.'

'What Lou, tell me?'

'Grey isn't, or wasn't, a natural Panther, Paul is involved with a cloning company in Korea. They have taken DNA and produced Grey. I'm not sure how but they're using him for hunting.

Gill held her hand to her mouth and replied. 'But they would need a surrogate, which means they must have a female Panther or species related, wait I read something about this in our journal, there is a company in the far east that has developed a cloning technique to help endangered species.'

Louise picked up on Gills knowledge. ' That's who Paul was working with, when I left him. I didn't know what he was up to at the time, thought it was just research. We had a Panther in our care at the practice. It was brought in after a road traffic accident by a farmer in West Wales, anyway after treating its injuries Paul said he had taken it to the wildlife sanctuary in Bristol. It turns out he didn't though, I think that was the surrogate.'

'So why didn't you tell me all this from the start Louise? I feel like you're not telling me everything.' Gills head dropped then looked away from Louise towards where the boys would be arriving from. Louise took a moment to compose her thoughts and decided that honesty was the best policy.

'It's not good Gill and Im ashamed, promise not to judge me, you're the only true friend I have now.'

'Lou, tell me.'

'So when Paul came back from Bristol with the Panther I knew something was not right. It turns out he went to meet the Koreans at a research facility in Norfolk. They persuaded him to use the Panther in a programme they were developing. He asked me to assist, I was uncomfortable with it but I agreed. The animal captivated me Gill, just as they do now. I wanted to help but my idea of helping was to release the animal back into its environment and monitor its progress. Just like we are doing now, these animals have been forced to adapt to this environment and as we know have survived and overcome, they have improved their survival chances by embracing their environment, learning safe routes and habitats and adapting their prey requirements. When Paul explained the programme to me to produce cloned cubs I couldn't resist the thought of caring for those little bundles.' Gill held up her hand and objected.

'When we first started our monitoring and gathering information about the Panthers it was based on trust Louise, we had our first encounter if you remember finding the tracks and the boys had the footage. We didn't know the female from west wales, but you knew all along, and you never said a word Louise, so the past three years have all been lies, everything you said. That hurts Lou, I thought I knew you but clearly I don't.'

Louise felt the full force of losing trust it sickened her. 'Gill I'm sorry, I had no choice, and what I knew wouldn't have changed a thing, I just thought if I told you it would prejudice what we were trying to do.'

'No you're missing the point Louise, trust is about telling the truth and letting your friends decide. If I knew we were chasing surrogates and clones, well things would be different. I would have eliminated them straight away, it's not the natural order Louise, don't you see that. Look you need to understand something, when an animal is introduced to a food chain, albeit when there isn't an apex predator, it effects the whole balance of that food chain. Unfortunately or fortunately whichever way you look at it these Panthers entered a very delicate system back in the seventies, we are forty years on now so they are now part of that system. What we are doing is research and monitoring of that environment to educate ourselves and others so we can help where possible to maintain that system. That's it Louise, that is our duty and our desire, nothing else.'

'Im sorry Gill, what can I do to make it up to you?'

'Nothing Louise, I need time to think about this, I could be struck off, so is Tonmawr a clone?

'No definitely not, she has survived and flourished on her own, like I said I don't know what happened to the first female, I released her when I found out what Paul was up to and then we had that bust up, you know the rest I went into meltdown and had the injunction so he must have re-captured her and then started the programme.'

Look the boys are here, I'll do the next shift with Mike and I'll call you when we need to swap, Rhys can come back later and sit with you. I can't get involved with this illegal activity Louise, neither should you'

'Please Gill, let's not fall out over...' Louise couldn't finish her plea before Gill jumped up and strode to meet Rhys and Lewis, she help up a palm to Louise and stated.

'No, leave it there Louise.'

Louise dragged herself over to the group and offered her account of the first three hour shift. As she finished Gill got into Rhys' Landrover and sped off leaving Louise to travel home on her own.

Refreshed from their break Rhys and Lewis settled into the makeshift hide in the copse. The warm drink Rhys had prepared was served up in steel mugs. The boys were in their element at one with nature.

Movement to their left on the far edge of the copse alerted the boys. As Lewis arched his back and slewed his field glasses to the point of the movement he whispered to Rhys. 'Its Tonmawr, she carrying something large in her mouth, looks like a small deer and the cubs are following her.'

Tonmawr strained to keep moving , her hind legs were being tripped by the trailing legs of the Doe she had been carrying for over five miles of rough terrain. She made for the same group of trees that the boys were hiding in. They watched as Tonmawr settled, exhausted below the upturned roots of a fallen cherry tree. The cherry struggled to fight for space amongst the spruce and beech, it was strangled by vines and had succumbed to the thin loose soil and its heady weight.

The cubs could now feed and proceeded with vigour to devour the soft meet of the Doe. Tonmawr was satisfied with her catch and stood to view her surroundings. In the dead of night she had returned to her favoured den, fulfilled she strode into the open leaving the mauled carcass to the scavengers of the woodland. With her cubs in toe she scaled the escarpment with ease and without forgetting her instinctive routine she doubled back twice and criss-crossed the area searching out unfamiliar scents before making the final push up the rocks to her den.

Rhys watched her every move. ' There she goes Lew, now is the moment of truth, do you think she will kill the cub?'

Lewis refocused and as he looked at the tracker to confirm the cub hadn't moved he was disturbed by another movement to his left.

'Shit, its Grey, I thought he'd gone.'

Rhys followed his brothers angle to view the large form stalking the fringes of the copse. 'Fuck, look at the size of him compared to Tonmawr. She wouldn't stand a chance, it must be Grey, looks like him.'

'So those remains we found last night must be a Deer then?'

'I can see the collar as well so hes being tracked, what do we do?'

From her vantage point in a narrow indentation on the rock face Tonmawr surveyed the bog flat terrain below her position, she ushered her two cubs behind her. The scent grew strong, she sat and waited.

M8 sat too and waited for the unfamiliar scents to soak in, he sensed humans were close but the overwhelming female scent was now stronger than ever. At a quarter of a mile apart the pair could not see each other nor hear but there scents were entwined, reaching out ever closer.

'We've got a standoff here Lew, they must know each other is there, I guess Tonmawr is trying to break away from Grey, maybe they've lost trust or maybe Grey attacked the cubs, whichever way this goes the cub in the den is in danger, what shall we do?'

Lewis looked at his brother, returned his gaze to Tonmawr and replied with a calm voice, as if from his mother. ' We wait and observe, it's the natural order Rhys, they have to work this out for themselves we can't interfere, if the cub gets killed by Grey or Tonmawr then that's how it's meant to be. Once we start interfering we've lost it.'

'Alright Mam.' Conceded Rhys knowing it was how his mother would have replied.

The two predators with completely different desires dug into their respective positions, waiting for the other to make the first move. Tonmawr in the high position had the upper hand, plus she knew from previous encounters with Grey that he could be outwitted. M8 sat and soaked in the scent with fascination. The freedom that been afforded to him was overwhelming. He wanted to explore, track, stalk, all the things that had been eating away during his captivity were now available. In this instance he matured his thoughts and waited for Tonmawr to expose her position, to expose her size, he needed to know what he was up against.

Claire De Motta and Adrian Miles had trudged over the moor and were enjoying the soft undulations leading up to Horseshoe Ridge when they decided to rest. Their journey had followed M8 over difficult terrain, they were both still full of energy but Arian sensed another punishing bout of steep climbs and boggy ground.

'Here Claire, have some warming refreshment.' He offered Claire his leather bound flask.

Claire took a delicate sip, her nose close to the alligator skin covering oozed its heady scent of single malt and Adrian's aftershave, a wood and spice mixture.

'Thank you Adrian, so I can see from the tracker that M8 has settled next to a copse up ahead, probably about a mile from our position, as long as he doesn't move again we will catch up in about twenty minutes.'

'That's good, I think our guests will enjoy this type of night, but we must offer them a reward at the end of it. Tom and Alan should be further north, could you confirm?'

Claire called Alan to relay their position, sure enough they were north of Horshoe Ridge, they had followed the tracking signal and anticipated M8's destination.

'Alan suggested we head up to the copse, Tom has stalked from that position before and they know it's the territory of another Panther called Tonmawr, she is completely wild, but there may be an opportunity for another trophy tonight, maybe for you to take back to the club Adrian.'

'Your generosity never fails to amaze me Claire, now that would be a bonus.'

Louise was exhausted mentally and physically as her car drifted on the narrow mountain tracks towards her lodge. It was after midnight, the roads were wet but starting to crisp up from the onset of a dive in temperature. Outside in her warm clothing she had not noticed the chill whilst she lay with Gill waiting for Tonmawr. With not another vehicle encountered and with Gill taking her sons car back home Louise felt exposed to the night, alone and bitter about her argument with Gill. Her mind was recalling events and how or why she could have handled the situation differently. As she moved the pieces of the events around the desired pattern could not be found, her thoughts muddled again she slammed the steering wheel and screamed her frustrations out loud.

In the opposite direction Tom and Alan Price were heading to Horseshoe Ridge, they had veered off road and took a short cut across a forest track and were about to re-join the main road. Oblivious Louise cornered a sweeping right bend and as she straightened up, the angled lights of the red Landrover rose into her path dazzling her view. She had no option and reacted with an instinctive pull to her left which lurched her Passat onto the bunded edge. The Landrover skimmed her back wing but continued crabbing up the road until it took grip and sped away.

Louise screamed her anger at the inconsiderate motorist who pushed her off the road, the flash as its headlights and fleeting glimpse of its grill took a moment to register. 'That was TP50 , Tom Price, what the fuck is he up to and where the fuck is he going?' She thought. Louise dialled Gill, she had to warn the boys. The call lingered for signal but then offered only its answerphone. The signal afforded little hope of getting a message to Rhys from her position shrouded deep in the valley bottom. She had no choice but to turn around and head back up to Horseshoe Ridge.

Chapter 36

The cub had woken from its enforced sleep with a raging thirst. The darkness added to her confusion, the unfamiliar surroundings offered no comfort. She was unaware of the proximity of her estranged family but shifted her lying position to the dim light framing the den entrance. The scent was taken in and it sparked a memory of familiarity which encouraged her to stand and take small steps to find the boundaries of her refuge. She absorbed the constraints by sniffing out the corners of the den. A forward stretch and yawn transferred to a steady call from the ledge where she had been deposited earlier in the night.

Tonmawr recognised the call the second it registered in her alert senses. She looked up to the overhang expecting a sign, the cry reached her ears again confirming her maternal expectation. She motioned towards the den then stopped with a focus back to the predator below. She had to extinguish the threat before she could investigate the call further. Her siblings recognised the call also and returned their own cry without the caution of their mother.

M8 heard the calls but without previous memory could not determine the origin. It was enough though to confirm that the female scent had remained where he had thought it was. This confirmation sprung his decision to move closer to the ridge and confront the female. His urge overtook his patience.

Alan Price turned to his brother Tom and asked. 'Did you hit that car Tom? We should go back and check, I think it went off the road, they could be injured.'

Tom Price finished the dregs from his flask and realising that his bottle was empty and there would be no refill placed his flask in the centre console before replying to his brother.

'Fuck off Alan, I'd lose my license again if they called the police. Anyway we've got this Panther to tranquilise and take back for our guests tomorrow.'

Alan was becoming increasingly frustrated by his brothers drinking and the risks he was taking. He wanted out of this plan but knew they had to retrieve the Panther. The tracker revealed the current position of M8, south of Horseshoe Ridge moving north. Alan called Claire to discuss their next move. 'Claire we are parked north of Horseshoe Ridge, it looks like M8 is moving up the ridge, are you familiar with the area?'

Claire viewed the location of M8 and replied. 'Yes, I remember the area, it looks as if M8 stopped at the bottom but is moving now up the banking, how do you want to play this?'

Alan and Tom took in the information realising that they needed M8 to scale the ridge and join the flatland which fell down to their position at the quarry edge. 'We need him to scale the ridge, we have been up here before and have a decent arc for the dart gun. If he doesn't scale the ridge then we need to come down to the copse, you should be close to there now?'

'Coming up Alan, we should be there in five minutes, we'll wait just inside the wooded area and await your call.' Claire turned to Adrian and he nodded his approval as the pair, refreshed, strode out towards the copse.

Louise arrived at the layby on the road that passed Horseshoe Ridge, she thought about driving to the quarry where they started earlier that night but instead decided to get closer to the boys, she had to warn them about Tom Price. She dialled Rhys, 'come on, come on answer.' She pleaded.

'Hi Louise, you won't believe who we've just seen.'

'Tom Price I guess he just passed me on the road, well the fucker ran me off the road to be more accurate.'

'Tom Price? No, anyway, its Grey he's at the side of us, Tonmawr as well she is halfway up the ridge with her cubs.'

Louise was confused, how could it be Grey she killed him last night, then the realisation hit her hard. They have another male predator on the loose. 'Rhys, don't move, stay there Im coming over to you.' Louise scrambled to her boot and retrieved the hunting rifle, rounds and the dart gun. She ran down the short embankment and scaled the forest track gate. The copse trailed towards her and she headed for its cover. Out of breath she flopped next to the boys and held up her hand waiting for her breathing to ease.

'Not bad for an old woman Louise, you can move when you want to.' Lewis stared in disbelief as Louise retold the events from the previous night. Lewis was amazed that Louise had withheld the information. 'Why didn't you tell us earlier for fuck sake, so who is the male Panther over there, have a look he's identical to Grey?'

Louise rolled into position and scanned the dim light of the open ground to her left. It lead on a gentle slope towards the toe of the ridge before rising with a sharp crest. M8 came into view, he was sat upright with his nose high, surveying in the direction of the ridge. 'It is, you're right Lewis, identical to Grey, do you recall Saturday night when you picked up another signal from the tracker, it was marked M8 wasn't it?'

Lewis nodded and nodded before replying. 'You're right Louise, it was, but it didn't move and we traced it to Aber-llia house. So it must have been another Panther. Rhys have you still got the URL on the laptop?'

Rhys was one step ahead, he had re-booted and was waiting for the tracker to load. 'Here we go, M8 is showing up, wait, exactly where that Panther is sitting.'

Louise added. 'So it's true they have more than one Panther tagged and ready to go.'

Rhys called to Lewis. 'Look at this Lewis, there's another signal popped up as well, on the far side of the ridge, where we parked up on quarry road, stationary its showing M9!'

Louise felt an overwhelming panic creep through her body, her heart raced and her hands were shaking, as she refocused on M8 the male Panther darted out of view towards the ridge.

Tonmawr logged the movement, her prediction was right the male predator would attack. She had no choice but to ignore the calls from her lost cub and protect the two with her.

Her cubs were frantic, they had realised it was their missing sibling and longed to be re-united. Their mothers growl and movement quashed any intention of reunion. Their escape took them down the east ridge towards the forestry road. At a canter they covered the ground as one leaving M8 still climbing the ridge on the opposite side. The male predator focused now on the lone cub, realising that the female was long gone. On unfamiliar ground he had no knowledge of the area and was running blind, save for the cries from the stranded cub. M8's hind legs pulsed as he entered the vertical rock face. Claws extended he gripped the rock through its moss covering, straining his whole length to find the next foothold. The cubs curiosity pushed her to the ledge as she nosed below, waiting for what she thought was her mother. The male predator was now within sight, he sniffed the air and worked out the final few steps to the den. The cubs enthusiasm turned to panic when she realised it was not her estranged mother who was calling, but a predator.

'I've lost sight of M8 Lewis.' Louise scanned the heights but could not distinguish the shapes before her.

'The tracker doesn't give us much more on the vertical face, he's up there but the signal dips in and out. What about the cub Rhys?'

'She hasn't moved at all, though probably awake by now, what shall we do?' Rhys' answer was more of a plea for ideas as he looked to Louise for an answer.

Louise knew what she had to do, she prepared the hunting rifle unrolling it from its cover. The rounds were loaded and she stood viewing the ridge through its night scope.

'Wait a minute Louise.' Called Lewis. 'You can't just kill him, what about preservation, observation ?'

Louise continued her search of the heights and replied. 'All well and good for natural animals but these are far from that, they have been generated by some sick individuals, they have no place amongst us, I know it's hard Lewis, but your mother agrees, they have to be eliminated, it's not their place, they have been put here for sport.'

'Ok I get it, but you're never going to get a kill from here, we need to be closer, come on if we go up the east ridge about halfway there's a position which has the perfect view of the den, that must be where he's heading, for the cub.'

Claire De Motta put her left hand onto Adrian's forearm, stopping his advance and whispered. 'Wait, I heard something in the copse, it sounds like voices, I thought Alan and Tom were at the top of the ridge, unless its Peter, but they never said they were going there, shhhh, I heard it again did you?' The pair crouched low, they were no more than fifty yards from the copse, Adrian nodded and confirmed the voices coming from the copse.

'I'll text Alan.' They stayed low, they could not make out what was being said but the voices were definitely coming from the copse. Alan returned with a negative, Peter had returned to the quarry and was with Alan and Tom.

'Who the fucks in there then?' Said Claire to Adrian. Her question was answered as they viewed three figures, one of them armed with a hunting rifle silhouetted against the sky. ' I recognise that woman, its Paul Morris' ex-wife, Louise I think, what the fuck is she doing here?'

Adrian replied that he didn't know her, and asked. 'What do we do now? She's armed.' Alan texted back to Claire 'Abort, Abort return to vehicles at quarry.'

Louise and the boys found their position and viewed the rock face in search of the male predator. The den was almost level to their position but shrouded in darkness. The three searched the shadows, highlights and swaying outcrops of heather which bowed in the wind. Louise was desperate to end the life of M8 before he took the life of the cub. The view was not clear enough and her inexperience of shooting weighed her ability to take a clean shot. Lewis and Rhys did not offer any help, they sat dejected knowing the Panther would be eliminated. Louise sat too and rested, she looked at the forlorn pair and offered support. 'I can't get a clean shot, he's too well hidden, even against the rock face. I can't do this without your help boys, now come on we have to do this. This Panther is interfering with the natural order, he has to go. Once I have him in my sights I want you to shine your torches to the spot, the Panther will freeze for a moment before he darts away, that'll be my opportunity to shoot.'

Lewis and Rhys trained their night scopes onto the rockface just below the den and picked up the grains of tone outlining the Panthers shape. Rounded shoulders, thick set neck and blunt nose. Its triangulated ears twitched. Louise held firm with her aim, no shaking, her breathing relaxed. Her cross hairs fell to the darkened mass but still she could not see clearly enough. The Panther was no more than forty yards from her, slightly elevated. 'Ok boys on my call, it's our best chance, wait....wait....' As Louise was about to say now, the Panther exploded up and out of shot in a vast leap to the den entrance. 'Shit, shit, shit, he's gone.'

The large male predator landed without sound on the ledge of the den with ease. The startled cub walked backwards and arched its back as the large male closed in. A swipe from his oversized right paw with claws extended was enough to concuss the cub. She could offer no resistance and succumbed to the weight bearing on her throat.

Satisfied the cub was immobilised the male sprayed the den with his thick scent and stood triumphant on the ledge of the den, his nose high and chest pushed out. Louise could now focus on the male, she primed Rhys and Lewis again. With tears welling she blinked then wiped her eyes, her rifles' muzzle waved as she struggled to keep still.

'Come on Louise now, it's our last chance, now.' Encouragement from Lewis drew her breath in deep and she blew through closed lips to calm her nerve. Louise took up the slack of the trigger then squeezed. M8 dropped from the ledge as the crack echoed through the curve of Horseshoe Ridge.

Louise sat back dejected and unaware of the fate of the cub in the den. She, Rhys and Lewis walked in silence across the narrow levels towards the lower reaches of the den. As they reached the point where only a vertical climb would get them to the den they found the still warm body of M8. Motionless he lay, no sign of trauma. Lewis with a gloved hand lifted its head and illuminated the eyes with his Maglite. 'The bullet went straight through his upper chest, probably his heart, at least he felt nothing, what a beast.' Amazed at his size close up the trio sat in silence.

It was broken by the buzzing of Louise's phone deep in her pocket. She answered Gills call and explained the situation. 'Ok, ok we will, as soon as we know. That was your mother boys, she wants us to meet her at Paul Morris' surgery, but first one of you needs to climb up to the den and retrieve the cub.'

'Did you hear the shot Alan?' Claire panted as she reached the parked cars on the quarry road.

'Yes Claire and I think we know who took the shot last night as well, but how did she know where to find the Panthers?' Alan replied.

As one they realised and said together 'Paul Morris.'

Alan Price rounded the front of the Landrover and shouted to everyone. 'Come on, we need to get to Paul Morris' Practice on the back end of the industrial estate. Now.'

Gill arrived at the practice building, it was shrouded in darkness apart from a dim light at the back of the reception area. Her wait for Louise and her boys provided time for her to reflect on the last few hours. Despite Louise's involvement at the early stages Gill knew that Paul Morris was the driving force behind the controlled release of the cloned Panthers. She decided to confront Paul straight away and strode out towards the building. Paul Morris exploded through the front door as Gill arrived, their combined startled expressions stifled a greeting. Paul carried a large holdall, his briefcase and medical bags as he attempted to lock the door behind him. Gill gathered her thoughts and asked. 'Where are you going in such a hurry Paul?'

Paul half turned as he fumbled with the lock. ' Sorry Gill gotta go, it's an emergency call out.'

Gill did not believe him, she eyed the bags and deduced he was leaving for another reason. 'Well before you go we have to talk Paul.'

Paul carried on towards his Range Rover brushing passed her. 'Sorry Gill this will have to wait, and why are you here so late?'

'I know about the Panthers Paul, M8, Grey and the others you are planning to release. If you don't stop now and talk to me I'll be reporting this to the authorities.'

Paul Morris dropped his bags at the boot and leant onto the tailgate his head banged the rear window. 'You don't understand Gill, you have no idea what is going on and if I don't leave now…'

Gill did not wait for him to finish. ' Cut the bullshit Paul, it's over, the whole plan, the Panthers everything. Grey and M8 have been eliminated, we know where M9 is and he will be next. What you need to do is give up this game and tell me where the surrogate is.'

Paul turned, leaned then slumped to the floor, his head in his hands. I need to get away from here Gill before the Prices come, I can't go home they'll find me there.' He looked up through tear filled eyes for an answer from Gill.

'Ok leave your car here and come with me we can talk on the way.' Gill felt at ease with Paul, there was no threat from this broken man she thought. The pair sat in the warmth of Gills Landrover. 'Where are we going Gill?' Paul asked.

'Much against my better judgement we are going up to Louise's lodge. You need to tell us everything so we can end this.'

Louise eyed the text message from Gill. 'Scrap the Practice meet back at your lodge NOW.'

The capitals emphasised an urgency in Gills command which Louise took as serious. She waited with her rifle across her knee for the brothers to return from the den. Her hope being that the cub was still alive. She eyed the dark mass edging lower before the boys turned along the slender path towards her, they crouched low and held the upper face of the escarpment as they edged through the unstable walkway of stone and roots.

'Your Mam wants us back at the lodge now, it sounds urgent, what did you find?' Louise was hopeful but her monotone knew the outcome.

Lewis looked up and answered. 'Sorry Louise she's dead, the male killed her. Weve got her with us to take back, couldn't leave her there.'

The forlorn threesome trudged into the garage at Louise's lodge, Lewis placed his rucksack next to the cage and eased the dead cub out. Louise opened the cage and retrieved a blanket, she shrouded the cub, whispered sorry and eased the bundle into the cage.

As the three stood back Gill strode in followed by Paul Morris. Louise turned to him, tears overflowing, she could contain herself no longer lunging at Paul shouting and screaming.

Gill separated them and instructed. 'That's enough you two, come on into the house we need to sort this out like civilised human beings.'

The familiar surroundings calmed Louise down, she stood before her fireplace in the living area, looking down at Paul slumped on the sofa. Gill sat to his side with Lewis and Rhys behind the sofa as if guarding the situation. Louise opened up. ' Well come on from the start let's hear it.'

Paul stuttered his opening then rubbed his nose before composing himself.

'As I said to Gill I've been pushed into this by the Prices, I had a programme with Dr Kim and it was working well, we were just trying to establish a pattern of behaviour and demonstrate we could re-introduce a species, namely a predator. The model was working but I needed more cash. The Prices and Claire provided the cash to keep the Practice going, when they stumbled across the Panthers they wanted more, and before I knew it they blackmailed me into providing Panthers for a hunt. I didn't want to but I was in too deep, and the cocaine, well that just made it worse.'

Louise shook her head. 'No Paul, you made it worse by being greedy, the Panther programme was never meant to be introduced here in Wales, it was purely a lab project.'

'That's where your wrong Louise, I never told you at the time but Dr Kim needed to prove it in the field before he could sell the model, we were so close.'

Gill stood and sided with Louise. ' So what you are saying is that you introduced live predators to our countryside for the sake of an overseas programme, just for cash?' Gill shivered and continued. 'The surrogate, she must be Tonmawrs mother then.'

'Yes Gill.' Replied Paul before continuing. 'She has produced three males from her last litter who are fully grown, Grey, M8 and M9.'

Gill replied. 'So where is the surrogate now?'

'Dr Kim closed the programme yesterday, whilst I was running around trying to please the Prices, Ji-a, you've met her once I think Lou.' Louise nodded remembering a slight girl at a dinner party three or four years ago. ' Well she came over to assist me with the surrogate as her current pregnancy had issues, she must have seen how out of control I was and last night, well she had arranged to move her to a practice in Norfolk before shipping abroad to continue the programme elsewhere.'

Rhys viewed his phone and showed the image to Paul. ' M9 we have him on the tracker, hes at the quarry north of Horseshoe Ridge, been there for a few hours.'

Paul eyed the image. ' In the back of the Tom prices Landrover, they were planning to release him for a hunt tomorrow. M8 was the practice run tonight, that explains how you knew where M8 was then Louise.'

'Yes Paul we have been tracking Grey & M8, they are both eliminated.'

Paul continued. 'Good, then we just need to eliminate M9 and this whole thing is over.'

Gill shook her head. ' I don't get why though Paul, you're a vet, where are your morals?'

'Gone with the coke habit Gill Im sorry.'

'But how were the clones produced?'

Paul felt better and stood. 'We developed a new technique, it took three litters to get it right, but we managed to produce and gestate three identical males from Tonmawrs mother, but she's tired now, I doubt she will survive the journey to Norfolk let alone being shipped to South America. Don't you think Gill in principal it is a good thing? We are promoting the chance to protect and re-introduce endangered species.'

Gill was quick to reply. ' No Paul, your just meddling and doing it without the backing of the authorities, its illegal and you should be struck off. Don't kid yourself, it's dangerous in the wrong hands and this episode has proven that, you had enhanced male predators on the loose, God knows what could have happened. When you start interfering with the natural order the outcome is always wrong. Look at Tonmawr, she has survived naturally in this area, and she will continue to, ok she lost one cub, but that's natural. You have no right to interfere and you know it.'

Rhys had taken all this in and was keen to ask. ' What I don't get is why you thought you could run around the Brecon's with outsiders shooting Panthers for sport and get away with it, you're just a greedy stuck up twat.'

Louise smiled as she agreed with Rhys and added. 'Not once Paul back then did you have any intention of doing this properly, with our help the programme could have worked, but your fucking ego got in the way, well you've got what you deserved now and you're lucky you're not in prison.'

Gill held up her hands. 'Ok that's enough, we need a plan, M9 is still out there and needs to be eliminated, Paul you need to take us to him.'

Paul froze. ' Gill I can't, if the Prices catch up with me God knows what they will do, I owe Tom twenty grand and Claire about the same if not more.'

This information sparked Louise into another rage. 'You gave up everything for that bitch to make a fool out of you.'

'My only way out of this is to sell the practice, pay them off and start again.'

'That was my fathers practice you bastard.' Louise spouted.

Gills temper was fraying, she again held up her hands and quietened the room. ' M9. We need a plan, now come on, how are we going to get to him?'

Rhys looked at his phone and cast the image onto the flat screen. ' Ok so hes on the move, at that speed he must be in the Landrover, on the forest road towards the industrial estate.'

Paul Morris edged to the screen. ' That's the practice.' He pointed on the screen then traced a line back to the tracker. 'He's on his way to the practice, told you, hes after me.'

Rhys refreshed the screen, the tracker stopped at the forest gate track exit, just before the main road took a sharp right leading onto the industrial estate.

The flashing icon changed to a steady red then grey indicating it was off.

'They've removed the tracker.' Lewis announced.

In the Landrover the two brothers Alan and Tom sat in silence, Claire sat alone in the back gazing into the dark. She contemplated the parting words from Adrian Miles. ' With no prize the deal is off, I'll make my excuses but this will not go down well at all, and obviously the money must be transferred back immediately.' Claire's plan to make enough money from the Panthers to invest in her failing property portfolio had crashed. She rued the weakness of Paul and wondered why she believed he could pull this off. Claire blamed herself for her own poor judgement but also was furious at Louise for interfering. Why was she involved? What had she to gain? Claire mused. Tom gripped the wheel and leaned forward as he fixed his glare to the extents of the beam from the headlights. He twisted his grip in anger and turned to Alan. 'That's the end of Paul Morris, he owes me over twenty grand and this was his way of getting it back to me.' Claire added her outstanding money and the potential losses from the Panther.

'That fucker has pulled out of the deal and fucked this whole thing up, you said you would take care of it Claire, so what have you been doing?' Shouted Tom.

Claire was in no mood for Toms rant and let loose her anger, leaning forward between the front seats she replied. 'Let me remind your thick head it was you that introduced Paul as a sure-fire bet. What matters now is that we secure the final Panther and manage the next hunt ourselves, try and get something back from this, Ill speak to Adrian once he has calmed down.'

Alan brought his hand across the centre and instructed Tom to pull over. As the Landrover lurched to an abrupt stop outside the entrance to Pauls practice he turned to the squabbling pair. ' Don't you both realise this whole thing is over, finished, we have nothing to gain from chasing Paul, what can he give us? Nothing but trouble. The best thing we can do is kill M9, before this gets out into the public domain.'

Tom and Claire knew he was right but wanted revenge, and they knew their loss could not be recouped. Alan continued. 'Claire there is one more thing you need to do before Louise reports this to the authorities, you need to tell her that we know she is involved with Paul and the keeping of illegal animals, that way she won't try to report this.'

The Landrover back door opened, Tom Price took out his hunting rifle and fired one round through the cage directly into the heart of M9.

Claire did not expect Paul to answer, but with Louise and Gill insisting that he took the call Pauls shaking hands pressed call accept. Louise pulled the phone from his ear, set it down on the coffee table and pressed speaker phone.

'Paul, don't hang up but listen. Whatever you and that bitch of an ex wife of yours were planning, its finished. M9 is dead. Its all landed back on your doorstep, literally. We will give you one month to pay back the money to Tom and myself, I don't care how you do it. We have enough evidence to arrange your arrest and have you struck off, so take my advice Paul.'

The phone went dead. Louise wept into Gills arms. 'Sorry Gill, so sorry.'

'Gill looked over Louise's sobbing shoulders at Paul and said. 'There its done, leave, do what you have to do, but keep my friend out of it she suffered enough at your hands.'

Chapter 37

Tonmawr took in the scent of the early evening mist rising from the River Wye and looked down on the swollen mass of water before her. Three nights of relentless cantering had brought the trio to the deep deciduous woodland of the Wye Valley. The scents were familiar yet fresh and had none of the tension of the Brecon's. The cherry wood with its circular flaking bark deposited a sweet mulch in her pads as she clawed the trunk. Beech trunks provided a smooth muscular ribbon for fresh water to run down. The steep valley sides with fallen trees offered numerous options for a dry den, the scattered fallen logs supported prey from pheasant to fallow Deer. The male cub followed Tonmawrs every move, scanning front to back, alert, inquiring. The female had matured in stature, she now stood shoulder to shoulder with her mother. For two years, since their forced ejection from the barren expanse of land rich in prized red Deer but also wild with human hunters, the trio had settled unopposed on the Welsh English border.

The male, despite his early growth spurt and accelerated development stopped short of Tonmawrs full height at the shoulder, yet his mass was more dense, his reactions explosive and manner more aggressive. Proud Tonmawr revelled in his form and groomed him as if his minor. The cubs had both achieved an understanding of their surroundings and were ready to leave their mother. She eyed the expanse of water at the eastern fringe of her territory and headed north to the shallow rapids where salmon provided late spring temptation. Each night Tonmawr teased the distance between her cubs. She often crept from the den alone and observed from a distance her fully grown cubs late arrival at the nights start point for the hunt. Tonmawr ambushed her female cub in a final flurry of lessons before the summer set its deep heat into the soil below the thick canopy of wide bright leaves. The male cub had spent two nights alone, he was at ease with his surroundings, he searched out his mother before sunrise but cared not to follow her night hunt. He had yet to score big but regular small prey were becoming easy. The salmon were not so easy a prey, Tonmawr was still learning. She spent hours fixated at the same spot as the shallows of the river on the inside bend slowed in current. She could see and smell the activity before her as the water folded and peaked. The salmon would expose their mouths to the cold night air and thrash their return to the bed in a flurry of silted freshwater.

A new challenge, a succulent prize, what a predator needed was a new challenge, push her instincts to the limit, expose her own weaknesses, improve, surpass, survive.

The male cub had a vast area to cover to cement his own territory and was the first to leave, no long farewell, no final embrace just a look toward his mother and sister from a distance. As the females looked his way he darted down into view to show his intention then turned without noise disappearing into the half-light.

The female cub shadowed her mother for the full summer. Tonmawr was growing tired of her daughter and needed to force her out. The playful tumbling's turned ferocious one morning, overstepping the line the cub pushed too far leading Tonmawr to crush her rebellion with a clawed crash of paw. The cub knew she had to leave, no malice from Tonmawr but a timely reminder that she was boss and it was time for her daughter to go.

Tonmawr looked up on her first night alone for two years, scents of distant males filled her thoughts, time to find a mate. She travelled north with the river on her right shoulder. As towns and villages came into view she moved deeper into the hillside giving a wide birth to any sign of humans. As she dropped down into the dark a natural path lead her through a limestone gorge. In the dead of night with not a breath of wind she rested at water level. The river almost as still as a lake, the depth at its greatest Tonmawr picked up the scent of a male Panther across the divide. A bridge of steel rope wide enough for her to traverse the river lay open and empty. The scent of dogs at its base was strong amongst the fresh shoots.

Bounding up its incline the bridge rattled its joints as her weight induced a sway, keep going, faster, faster, she was past halfway and heading down to fresh ground away from her cubs, new ground, new challenges, fresh prey.

The End

Printed in Great Britain
by Amazon

73164606R00194